STATES OF GRACE

Mandy Miller

Literary Wanderlust | Denver, Colorado

PRAISE FOR *STATES OF GRACE*

"States of Grace is engrossing, unpredictable, and fast-paced. So grab yourself a drink, settle into your easy chair, open the book, and begin. You're home for the evening. You are about to be carried away to a world more vivid and, in this case, a hell of a lot scarier, than the one you're living in."

—John Dufresne, Author of New York Times Notable Books of the Year—*Louisiana Power and Light* and *Love Warps the Mind A Little; Storyville; The Lie That Tells the Truth: A Guide to Writing Fiction*

"The dialog zings, the plot races, the Florida setting is richly detailed, the characters are 3-D, intriguing and fresh, and the prose is muscular and witty. Oh, yes, then there's Grace, the star, a full-bodied, complicated and fascinating woman. The pages flew by in a happy blur. What more can one ask for in a legal thriller? Even more amazing is that this well-crafted story is a debut novel. Mandy Miller is the real thing, a writer of consequence who I'm certain will have a long and distinguished career."

—James W. Hall, Edgar and Shamus Award Winning Author of the Thorn series

"Miller's debut, States of Grace, about a weary war veteran and lawyer working her way back to redemption, is a twisting, dark and gritty mystery set in South Florida that takes you on a harrowing ride until its final, shocking ending. You'll love Grace Locke and you'll love this book."

—Jamie Freveletti, internationally bestselling and award winning author of the Emma Caldridge series and Robert Ludlum's *The Janus Reprisal* and *The Geneva Strategy*.

"Miller's States of Grace takes us on a tense and wholly entertaining romp across the Florida landscape of pain clinics, jail innards, and snooty posh schools populated with a mélange of edgy characters from Vinnie, her former mobster landlord to her aptly-named tripod dog Miranda. Watch out, Iraq vet lawyer Grace Locke, a woman beaten but not broken, will win your heart as fast as she wins her court cases."
—Christine Kling author of the Seychelle Sullivan series

A down on her luck former prosecutor, Grace Locke has been given a second chance—as a criminal defense attorney for a young woman who appears a slam dunk for a life sentence for murder. Mandy Miller's legal thriller, States of Grace, grabs you from the first page and doesn't let go until the last page. Full of twists and turns, this book sets a new bar for authors in the legal thriller genre. Well done!
—Chris Goff, award-winning author of *Red Sky and Dark Waters*

States of Grace

Published in the United States by Literary Wanderlust LLC, Denver, Colorado.

www.LiteraryWanderlust.com

ISBN Print: 978-1-942856-71-9
ISBN Digital: 978-1-942856-74-0

Cover design: Pozo Mitsuma

Printed in the United States of America

Dedication

To the defenders everywhere who keep the faith, and to the prosecutors who thwart the guilty.

Chapter 1

August 2009
Fort Lauderdale, Florida

Innocence isn't all it's cracked up to be. A truly innocent client, one who didn't do it, that's the rare, unfortunate soul that will keep you up nights and hijack your brain like a catchy song. And if lady luck forsakes him, that's the client who will haunt you forever. Innocence is funny that way. Seems like a good thing on the surface, but at its core, it's a burden.

I don't have to worry about innocence today, or almost any other day for that matter. Defendants are in the habit of being guilty of something, even if it's not what they're charged with—at least that's what I used to say. Winning's important but, thankfully, I'm going home a loser today for sure. And right now, that's all I want—to go home, assuming you can call The Hurricane Hotel a home.

The jury will be back in soon to announce the inevitable— "We find the defendant guilty." How do I know he's guilty? Because my client, the accused, the one slumped down in the chair to my right, his bony frame swamped by the funeral-director suit I bought for him at Goodwill, he did it, no questions asked. Told me so himself. Said he beat the crap out of his girlfriend because she smoked his last crack rock. Said the only thing she had the sense not to do was call the cops, at least until some do-gooder counselor convinced her to file a report. But, lucky for him, by that time, the bruises were gone.

"She had it coming, and that bitch counselor at the shelter will get it too, if I ever see her again," was what he told me in the holding cell this morning. Then, for good measure, as what I can only assume he saw as added incentive for me to do my job, he added, "Grace, you get me out of this hole, and I'll show you what a real man can do for your bad attitude."

Willing my face to be as devoid of emotion as his hollow eyes, I told him he wouldn't have to trouble himself with my happiness or lack thereof, because the moment the jury heard his story, the well-worn yarn about girlfriend falling in bathtub, the outcome was as predictable as another steamy day in Florida. And that's how it went, his lies echoing off the courtroom walls like prayers from a non-believer who's found his way into a church in a last-ditch effort to save himself.

For some ungodly reason, and in spite of my client's stomach-turning lack of remorse, I'm still a believer—not in innocence, maybe not in even in fairness anymore, but in the system. Making sure his rights are protected is my duty and I intend to fulfill it, even if he is an unrepentant wife beater. I learned the hard way that everyone deserves a defense and the right to look your accuser in the eye and question his version of the truth.

"Sit up straight," I say, poking him in the ribs as the jury files back into the courtroom, his response to which is to lean his head, bald and shiny like a cue ball, atop elbows resting on the defense table as if his neck can't support its weight. I poke him again, harder this time. Jurors deserve respect. Most folks dodge jury duty like a well-thrown punch.

Things aren't looking good for our side, however, and the

jaw-grinding grimace on my client's face tells me knows it too. The jury was only out for fifty-three minutes. Hardly enough time for me to guzzle a cup of putrid cafeteria coffee and pick up my court-appointed counsel's check, a pittance for my trouble.

I count off each member of the six pack as they enter—two men and four women. Even if every single eye weren't cast down, I'd still know what they decided back in the windowless jury room, sustained by stale bagels and the desire to get home by dinner time. It's all in the sound. A quick shuffle of feet, like a foxtrot—not guilty. A dragging sound, like a slow waltz performed by a drunk—guilty. And what I'm hearing is one hair stylist, one teacher, a mail carrier, two unemployed realtors, and a retired fisherman waltzing.

"I understand you have a verdict, Madame Foreperson," Judge Grant says, peering over his half-rim tortoise shell glasses at a world-weary forty-something woman. I knew she'd be the foreperson from the jump. With her slit-eyed scowl she'd scare the others into submission quickly so she could get home to reality TV to escape her own.

"Yes, Your Honor."

During jury selection, she said she was a hair stylist at a salon in Pompano Beach and she delivered her answers during voir dire with a certitude of one desirous of being seen as a good citizen, the type we can trust with momentous decisions like whether or not to lock someone up. Yet her bird's nest of fried blonde hair and too-short skirt revealing a tattoo of a thorny rose belie another truth, also known as a lie. She's no hair stylist.

If I have a superpower, it's the ability to spot a lie—from clients' excuses for their bad choices to cops' flimsy explanations for how an accused developed a raging shiner *after* the cuffs went on. I've even become good at telling myself a few lies, such as the one about how I can keep defending the types I used to lock up. What is true is that I'll keep doing this work, defending the guilty. I have no choice. I need to be gainfully employed throughout my probationary period. It's either serve as court-appointed counsel or forfeit my law license again when I go back in front of the Florida Bar Disciplinary Committee a few months from now.

What else can I do? Lawyering is all I've ever done, if you don't count my stint in the Army as a military police officer which, come to think of it, paid better than defending criminals who can't afford a "real lawyer." But that misadventure cost me a limb. Besides, it's not like I'm in any kind of position to attract the upper echelon of criminals at this point. It's the bottom feeders for me, for now—until I figure out a plan, a way out of this dead-end gig.

My client's pitiful victim is seated in the first row of the gallery. Tiny, like a malnourished bird, all sharp edges and jumpy. I wonder if he sensed she'd be an easy mark. Wife beaters tell me that. That they can smell which ones will put up a fight and which will bend to their will again and again, grateful to have something to rely on.

Madame Foreperson steps down from the jury box and hands the verdict form to the judge's clerk. On the way back to her seat, she glances in my direction and shrugs. I sigh in relief. She was his one hope. A woman who'd taken more than a few hard knocks and gotten up. But then, hope is not a substitute for an actual defense.

Truth is, it's an advantage knowing they're guilty. It simplifies things. It means I don't have to worry about screwing up. Prosecutors need to win over all six jurors. No room for error. All I need is to make one gullible soul believe in reasonable doubt. I find it an unnerving thought. Even so, there are no prosecutors with losing records, proof that *accused* and *guilty* are as good as synonymous. Although, odds are I put away the rare innocent back when I was Assistant State's Attorney Grace Kelly Locke, back when I considered that possibility a cost of doing the business of justice. Another unnerving thought.

Judge Grant scans the verdict form, stone-faced, and returns it to the clerk between thumb and forefinger like a smelly sock.

"The defendant shall rise."

I get to my feet but stay more than an arm's length away from my client. I notice I'm holding my breath, but why? Habit? Or maybe it's the haunting clank of the shackles as the accused stands. Will it be guilty or not guilty, actual innocence being out of the question? In my mind, there's no suspense.

The clerk holds the verdict form like a town crier and clears his throat before pronouncing, "We the jury in the above-entitled action, find the defendant not guilty."

"Hot damn! Yes!" my client yells, his fists pummeling the air as if he's hitting a heavy bag.

A refrigerator lands on my chest and I struggle to catch my breath. I pivot to the jury box. Maybe they filled in the form wrong? Maybe the clerk read it wrong? But not one of them flinches, every one of their faces marked with the satisfaction of one whose work is done.

Judge Grant stands, arms wide in benediction, face expressionless, in keeping with the black robe. "Ladies and gentlemen of the jury, thank you for your service. You are hereby excused." Before exiting through a door behind the bench, he stabs a finger at my client and says, "Sir, once you are booked out of the county jail, you are free to go. Good luck to you."

Sir? Who's he calling sir? This guy's not a sir.

"Thank you," my now-acquitted client mumbles. Before a sheriff's deputy leads him away, he faces his victim and winks. A chill slithers down my spine. A feeling that my mother, Faith, would attribute to someone walking across your grave, an odd analogy given she's still alive and kicking butt at bridge twice a week at the Palm Beach Country Club and pruning her beloved rose bushes herself despite a gaggle of gardeners at her beck and call.

I flop back into my chair, bile rising in my throat. An older woman I assume to be the victim's mother, ushers her sobbing daughter from the courtroom, an arm shielding the desperate waif from behind. As if anything other than the eradication of my client from the face of the earth could do anything to protect her now.

My adversary, a baby-faced Assistant State's Attorney, approaches, features twisted in confusion. "Aren't you supposed to be happy when you win?" he asks, eyebrows hunched over clear eyes, eyes that that will grow dark when he understands bearing witness to human suffering is his chosen profession.

I plaster on a smile. I wish I could blame him, tell him he didn't do his job, that it's his fault a guilty man's walking free. But I can't. He did what he had to do We both did. It's just that I, apparently, did it better. Without a doubt, the most unnerving thought I've had today.

"Have a good night," he says, shambling off, dragging a wheelie file cart identical to the one I used to pull back when I believed getting justice and winning were the same thing.

My phone vibrates, skittering across the table like a roach on the run.

A text from Manny. "Our Starbucks. 9 a.m. tomorrow. Don't be late."

"There is no more *our*," I mutter, sweeping a stack of files into my tattered briefcase, a gift from my parents for my law school graduation.

I double check to make sure I'm alone, then retake my position in front of the empty jury box. "Ladies and gentlemen, you would have no way of knowing this, but less than a year ago, I would have been physiologically unable to convince you of anything other than the guilt of the man that sat beside me today. But now..."

I avert my gaze to a bronze statue of blindfolded Lady Justice behind the bench. "But now, please, forgive me. I had no idea I'd be good at this."

Chapter 2

I get off the bus and walk across State Road A1A to The Hurricane Hotel, a two-story, L-shaped, 1950s structure, parking lot in front. The rusty catwalk fronting the upper floor looks to have been repurposed from a penitentiary. Some might call the architectural style mid-century modern. Others, no-tell motel. Me, I call it one storm away from condemned. But for now, I also call it home. It is what the broke and broken can afford within earshot of the ocean, my one true love.

No question about it, The Hurricane's a far cry from the mansion I used to share with my soon to be ex-husband Manny on Idlewyld Isle, a peninsula that juts into the Intracoastal Waterway like a big middle finger to the have-nots, the types I used to prosecute. That was back when I believed in lily-white innocence, that black hats cover black souls, and that we all get what we deserve.

Truth is, life's simple at The Hurricane and I like it that way. For now.

And then there is Vinnie, my landlord. Vinnie's good at

keeping secrets, and I've got plenty of those.

And there he is, Vinnie, manhandling two gigantic trash cans across the rutted asphalt, like a Greco-Roman wrestler fighting way above his weight class.

"You need some help?" I ask.

"Nah, I got it."

Cans lined up on the curb, he wipes his hands on a pair of dungarees that make him look like a farmer, albeit a swarthy one with a long rap sheet and a last name ending in a vowel to complete the stereotype.

"*Buonasera, signorina,*" he says, with a deep bow.

I curtsy. "Good evening to you, *Vincenzo.*"

I point at two blue plastic bins overflowing with newspapers, liquor bottles, soda cans, and all manner of recyclable detritus. "Sure you don't want help with those?"

"Them ones for recycling. Still gotta sort all that," he says with a tortured scowl, which makes the task seem less desirable than an enema. "Separate the whatevers I'm supposed to separate from the other whatevers." He raises his arms to the heavens. "*Per l'amor di Dio.* Don't you remember when garbage was just garbage?"

"I might think about wearing gloves to do that if I were you. Might not be safe. You never know what your clientele might think is recyclable."

"Yeah, yeah. Like you're one to talk about clientele."

"Girl's gotta make a living," I say, keeping my tone light, although his comment stings.

"Speaking of girls, the blonde on the news says a storm's comin' our way."

My throat constricts. "Hopefully, it's just another fire drill."

"Ain't that the truth," he says, his Ts sounding like Ds and the look on his face proof that we've been through this routine one too many times. "That last one, whatever that bi—" Vinnie pauses. "Whatever that old gal was called, she ripped off half my roof tiles. Place looked like a kid with a bad haircut."

It is amusing to watch the hurricane media circus on TV—supermarkets running out of bottled water and batteries; videos of chichi types, for whom canned food is usually an anathema, piling shopping carts full of the stuff; and my favorite, the "cone of opportunity," the megaphone-shaped impact zone with a mind of its own. But the truth is, storms—all loud noises for that matter—still petrify me, transport me straight back to that day in Fallujah, as if I never made it out of the Humvee.

"Ophelia's the name," he says.

"What?"

"The storm. They're calling it Tropical Storm Ophelia." He shakes his head hard from side to side. "Have you heard a word I said?"

I head for the recycle bins outside the office, anxious to distract myself, to do something with my hands, my head a riot of the incoming storm and questions about what I might have done to walk a guilty man.

I did everything I could to defend him, sure. But it's my role in the play. Right?

I just thought the jurors would do their part and see through his lies.

"Let's get these sorted," I say, slamming cans and bottles into bins. "They can call the storm whatever they want, just wake me when it's over. Who makes up these names anyway? Didn't Ophelia drown?"

Vinnie takes a step back. "What's got you all bent out of shape?"

"Nothing."

He rolls his eyes. "Right. Nothin'. That's what my second ex-wife used to say right before she smacked me upside the head." He kneels beside me. "What happened today, kid?"

"I won a case."

He claps me on the back. "Congratulations. Winning's supposed to be good, ain't it?"

"So I've been told. But winning's not always right,

remember?"

His eyes harden and we revert to sorting in silence.

Three wasted years are a lot to a man like Vinnie, on the back nine of his life, and I share his anger at the injustice, not to mention the guilt I carry for my part in it. In another lifetime, I prosecuted Vinnie for knifing a man to death in The Hell Hole, a biker bar on Second Street, back when Vinnie had enemies. The jury convicted him and sentenced him to death. A year later, as part of a police corruption probe, I discovered a trio of crooked cops had conspired to bury an eyewitness who would have testified Vinnie had been thirty miles away betting on the greyhounds at the Biscayne dog track when the hit went down. It took me two years to make things right, but I did. Fought all the way to the Florida Supreme Court and convinced the Court Vinnie had been railroaded. As a result, I became Enemy Number One of the local cops. The battle cost me my job, not to mention my freedom, for a time.

When Vinnie got off death row, he thought he owed me. Not long after, when I was unemployed, broke, and living out of a rust-bucket car parked in a different lot every night, he set about repaying me by giving me a place to stay. He'd bought The Hurricane with the settlement money he got from a lawsuit I brought against the Fort Lauderdale Police Department. Vinnie may be old school mob all the way—cops are crooked, rats deserve whacking, and only family can be trusted—but I appreciate his counting me as family, as well as his company. I keep telling him he better start taking my money for rent or I'll move out, but he won't hear of it. "Family don't pay."

The rhythm of working side by side frees my mind. Watching Vinnie sort each item into the proper bin, I am struck by how many lives one person can live, how many faces we have to show to the world. While Vinnie might wear his hard life on the streets and two long bits in prison in the tight set of his jaw and steely stare, his jailhouse tattoos have faded along with too many scars to count, and he's become a good man. He keeps the safety on his gun and the beat cops' cell phone numbers on speed dial. He goes to City Commission meetings and pays his taxes early. Like me, Vinnie doesn't want any more trouble, but he can still smell it a mile away.

Task complete, he extends a hand to help me stand, Oscar, my prosthetic leg, not being the most flexible of limbs. "How's about we have some chow, kid?"

"Thanks, but I'm tired."

"You sure?" he asks, as we haul the last of the recycle bins to the curb. He worries I don't eat enough. He's constantly plying me with his home-made manicotti or corned beef and cabbage, legacies from a Sicilian father and an Irish mother.

"I'll grab a snack upstairs."

"Promise?"

"I promise."

"Your loss, kid. But thanks _for the help, even if I said I didn't need it."

"Thanks for the company," I say, heading for the stairs.

I don't look back, but he'll watch over me until I'm safely inside.

***

Efficiency #7 is just that—an efficient use of very little space. One room for all purposes. Bedroom, kitchen, bathroom, closet, all in one. A waist-high wall hides the commode, an arrangement that would have appalled me only a year ago. The bedroom lacks an actual bed. Instead, I sleep on a futon which, by day, doubles as my desk. The shower stall is a tiny, rusty metal box adjacent to an equally rusted out metal basin which doubles as the kitchen sink. A microwave and coffee maker sit atop a mini-fridge, the type I had in my freshman dorm room at Yale— all three appliances beat up and scratched like the rest of the furniture I bought at the Salvation Army store with a loan from Vinnie.

"You couldn't swing a cat in here," is what Faith would say if I ever let her see the place. The thought of the grande dame of

Palm Beach slumming here makes me smile. When she and my late father, Percy Danforth Locke III, shipped me off to boarding school in the hinterlands of Massachusetts, Faith insisted on paying double for my housing so I could have my own suite. As an only child, I'd been looking forward to having a roommate, someone to stay up late with talking about boys and painting our nails, but Faith's phobia about my sharing a bathroom with a stranger put the kibosh on that.

I power up my laptop and, within a second or two, a screed of email messages appears. No question, the internet at The Hurricane's first-rate—it's the only thing that is—and, while grateful, I do question why, given almost everything else in the joint is either on its way to decrepitude or already non-functional. The only explanation I've ever come up with is that Vinnie likes internet porn a whole lot.

I change into one of Manny's old T-shirts, the only thing of his I have left, and flip on the news to combat the deafening silence.

Another murder in Liberty City, another drug bust in Overtown, another local politician arrested for taking bribes. Just another day in South Florida.

Unhitching Oscar from my stump, I glance over at a flashing Breaking News banner on the screen. Oscar drops to the floor with a thud and my entire universe pinholes until all I can see is the face of Gretchen Slim—statuesque blonde, former beauty queen, and the last straw that broke my marriage to Manny.

"Mrs. Slim! Mrs. Slim! Why did your daughter shoot Brandon Sinclair?"

I stab the remote at the TV to jack up the volume.

"My daughter Zoe is one-hundred-ten-percent innocent," Gretchen says, staring straight into the camera, doe-eyed, as a bevy of reporters jostle for real estate below her on the steps of the Broward County Jail. Microphones on long booms poke up at her, camera flashes illuminate the windowless fortress behind.

"Mrs. Slim, how is Zoe doing? Has bail been set? What was your daughter's relationship to the victim?" The questions come rapid-fire, but Gretchen doesn't respond. Just dabs at her eyes with a tissue. She's wearing a cream colored, boxy Chanel suit, no doubt a calculated choice to tone down her curves and add a dash of old money and propriety, although she has neither.

I grab the laptop and Google "Slim" and "murder."

"Oh. My. God."

More than one hundred search results. Story after story from local and national news outlets. Zoe Slim, the only child of Anton Slim, plastic surgeon to the stars, and his wife Gretchen, a former beauty queen and runner up in the Miss Florida pageant, has been arrested for the brutal killing of Brandon Sinclair, a beloved guidance counselor at St. Paul's Preparatory School.

My heart thuds as my husband's lover declares, "As I have already said, my daughter is innocent."

"My daughter had nothing to do with the murder of Mr. Sinclair," she says, her tone moving up the octave on its way to what, I assume, will be a full-blown crying fit.

Another question catapults out of the crowd. Gretchen cups her ear and points at a man in the front row. I recognize him as the reporter from the *Sun Sentinel* assigned to the courthouse beat.

"Do you keep a gun at home?"

"I wouldn't answer that if I were you," I warned TV Gretchen.

Gretchen recoils, a manicured hand pressed to her ample chest.

"A gun? Of course, I don't have a gun." she says, before dissolving into tears and wobbling off to a waiting limousine on a sky-high pair of Christian Louboutins, black patent leather with red soles, identical to the pair still sitting on the floor of my closet on Idlewyld Isle.

I turn off the TV and climb under the covers, my thoughts pinballing between, *This is just what I've been waiting for,* and *Only shameless hacks chase cases.*

Then again, Percy, a Navy man, named me Grace, a.k.a. "Amazing Grace" after Grace Hopper, the first female rear admiral in the U.S. Navy. Percy loved to quote her—"It's easier to ask for forgiveness than it is to get permission."

But, lying in the dark, I wonder how much forgiveness is left out there for me.

Chapter 3

I hesitate outside Starbucks, jaw tightening at the distasteful prospect of capitalizing on a mother's misfortune, even if it is the mother who stole my husband when I was in jail. But with few options and even fewer dollars to my name, not to mention a tenuous grip on my Florida Bar card, I remind myself career-making cases don't come along every day. And when they do, I'm in no position to let my feelings or law school ethics get in the way. As a prosecutor, the inventory of cases had been self-sustaining, but now I need to hustle which, today, means hustling my soon to be ex-husband and his lover.

The moment I heave open the door, a blast of arctic air hits me in the face, dousing what little fire was fueling my I-can-do-this pep talk, leaving me chilled to the bone and praying for Manny to be a no-show.

Inside, the caffeinating of the day is well underway, the ebony jet fuel required to turn the wheels of life spewing from spigots like gargoyles appended to the colossus of an espresso machine. A production line of baristas orchestrates every drink, adding each ingredient in order lest the caffeine gods strike the contraption dead. Heart in my throat, I pick my way through office workers nibbling on scones and talking into phones crooked between neck and ear. I catch a snippet from a gaggle of women in yoga pants about how it's better to get Botox than leave things be, unless, of course, you bite the bullet and go for the full face lift.

Not in this lifetime, no matter how much my face or my ass sags.

But I've been under the knife one too many times out of necessity, so maybe I'm not one to judge.

I look down and groan at the sight of my sweatpants and faded green Army T-shirt. Not a good choice for this land of Barbie mommies and the always stylish City Commissioner Armando Martinez, a.k.a. Manny. I should bolt while I have the chance, but my escape plan is derailed by a waving hand.

"Grace, over here." The familiar lilting *cubano* accent stops me in my tracks, its cadence reminiscent of the rhumba we used to dance and the mojitos we used to drink until the wee hours in Little Havana. The sound, once appealing, now a galling reminder of the man who called when I returned broken from war, and said, "Come on down to Miami, the weather's fine and there's lots of crime," and later, left me to rot in jail.

I follow the hand to Manny seated at a tiny round table in the back, a manila folder labeled Settlement Agreement in front of him.

"Good to see you," he says, pulling me in for a hug, the word "you" coming out as "chu," the Miami Spanglish accent of his youth as hard to get rid of as a vulture on roadkill. But the thing is, that's what I liked about him from the day we met in the student union at Columbia—the sharp edges of his less than privileged youth, his utter lack of artifice. With Manny you get what you see, not a curated version like the blue-blooded boys I grew up with in New England. Manny is nothing if not a product of his roots in Havana, the city ninety miles to the south, a paradise frozen in amber at midnight on January 1, 1959, its desiccated buildings and cars still lovingly preserved by those left behind. Like Manny, his parents are people of action, not the kind to await their fate, be it crushing poverty or Che Guevara's firing squads. They fled with nothing but the proverbial clothes on their backs and their will to make a better life. Like a good immigrant son, Manny took to the education his parents had been denied and coupled it with their work ethic and, later, me. And voilá, instant American Dream.

Until the dream turned to nightmare.

I slip into the chair opposite him.

He runs a hand through his wavy, dark hair dappled with gray now, a development that serves to soften his hawkish features. "Can I get you a coffee?"

"No."

He's wearing a custom-tailored suit in khaki with a pale blue tie in a double Windsor knot, the dimple perfectly centered. He stirs his usual two packets of sugar into a thimble-sized cup of steaming espresso, a gold Rolex peeking out from under his cuff. "Not quite the *café con leche* we used to get at Versailles."

"Not even close."

Spoon suspended mid-air, he says, "You look good, Gracie."

"You sound surprised."

"On the contrary, looking good was never your problem."

"But, *being* good was another issue, right?"

He gives me the type of tight smile intended to cover all manner of painful history. "For both of us," he says, sweeping a couple of crumbs off the table. "But that's all in the past. It's time for us both to get on with our lives." He pats the folder.

"Fine, but there's something I need to tell you first." I take a second to tamp down the anger percolating in my gut and try for a more conciliatory tone so as not to blow my chances. "Actually, something I need to ask you."

"I knew it. I knew you had some other reason for coming. I mean, you've been dodging me and my attorney for weeks. You didn't even text me back. I half expected you not to show. Out with it. What do you want?"

I brace my arms across my chest. "I'm going to defend Zoe Slim."

He leans back, tongue in his cheek. "And how do you figure that?"

"Because you are going to make it happen. You get me the case, and I'll sign whatever you want, no questions asked."

"Like you'll ever run out of questions."

As much as it pains me, I can't stifle a smile at how well he knows me. "Manny, I'm not kidding. Zoe Slim is big news. It's the kind of case that will get me back on the radar, the kind of case that can make a career."

His clears his throat. "Or, in your case, remake."

I slide my chair close to the table. "And it's the last favor you'll ever need to do for me."

"No offense, Grace. You may have your license back, but I'm not sure you're—"

I spring up, spilling his coffee. "I shouldn't have come. I should have known better than to think you'd help me."

"Hey, take it easy. Sit back down."

"Sorry," I say, wiping up the coffee with a napkin as I retake my seat. "All I need is a chance, Manny. I'm trying. I've been trying, but I need a break to get me out of the rut of having to take court-appointed cases for indigent clients which pays less than I could make waiting tables. I'm still a damn good lawyer."

He turns his palms out. "I'm not saying you're not a good lawyer, or that you're not trying, but you and I both know the mega-rich hire only the top echelon, especially when the life of their wrongly accused kid is on the line."

"You sure about that?"

"About what?"

"The wrongly accused part?"

"It's hard for you, isn't it?"

"What's hard for me?"

"Having to represent bad guys."

"And girls. And no, not really. I have to do it. For now. And, it turns out I'm pretty good at it."

"But what about right and wrong, truth and justice, all that stuff you were so fond of spouting back when you were a prosecutor? I mean it can't be easy to be on the other side now."

"Maybe not, but those ideals are luxuries I can no longer afford. You cut me off remember? For now, I'm doing what I have to, to survive." I take a deep breath to compose my thoughts. "That's why I'm here. I have a proposition for you."

He puffs out his cheeks. "Grace, I'm not in the deal-making mood. And you're in no position to bargain."

"I'm not?"

A flash of anger sparks in his eyes, no doubt as bright as the one he just ignited in mine. "No, you're not."

"I'd say that puts us both in the same position."

He presses his palms on the table, as if he's counting to ten to calm himself. "Anger in Armani" is what my friend Rita used to call him when his temper got the better of him.

"Hear me out. I'm not here to argue. The opposite, actually. You'd be doing us both a favor," I say, my tone purposefully breezy, unlike the weight of the fear rising in my chest that he's about to walk out.

"I'm not sure you've got any favors left in the favor bank at this point," he says, reaching for his briefcase.

"Wait. Maybe you need a little incentive."

He pinches the bridge of his nose. "Meaning?"

I dig my fingernails into my thighs and forge ahead. "Meaning how would it look if I happened to let it slip, let's say to some tabloid, that City Commissioner Martinez has been doing more than the mambo with the wife of one of the county's most prominent citizens?"

The color drains from his face.

"Wouldn't go over well with your conservative constituents, would it? The ones in those big houses on the water who contribute so generously to your campaigns and for whom you appear at Mass every Sunday, even though you don't believe in God?"

He juts his chin out, a ropy vein pulsing in his forehead. "Neither of us is without blame for what happened to our marriage, and you know it."

"True, but I don't have a reputation to protect."

"Anymore."

"Touché, but I do have one I need to rebuild, and that's where you can help, given your relationship with Mrs. Slim." I'd make air quotes with my fingers around the word "relationship," but my hands are shaking so hard I keep them anchored under my thighs.

I steel myself, determined to keep any hint of self-doubt out of my voice. "The way I see it, what I'm proposing is a win-win for everyone. Zoe Slim gets a good lawyer. I get a payday and some much-needed good publicity. And you? Well, I think I've already made myself clear on that."

Without taking his eyes off mine, he brushes some non-existent crumbs from his pants.

"And one last thing. I'd appreciate your returning my car," I say, referring to Percy's British racing green Jaguar E-Type roadster. The car I learned to drive in. The one he picked me up from boarding school in to go leaf peeping. The car we were in on September 12, 2001, when I told him I'd enlisted in the Army. "That was a mistake," he'd said. Maybe he was right. While my father believed in doing one's civic duty, his idea of service was more upscale, less hands on. Maybe the State Department and a nice posting to London. The Peace Corps, even. But enlist in the Army and in war time? A mistake, for sure.

He sighs. "You finished?"

"Maybe. Do we have a deal?"

A tug on the tie, his classic tell when he's on the ropes. "Whoever represents Zoe isn't up to me."

"Technically, you're correct. But, come on. Like I said, you can make it happen. Or at least, Gretchen can, and I think she will come to understand it's in her best interest to use her powers of persuasion on her husband."

"Soon-to-be ex-husband."

I glance at the folder. "There's a lot of that going around."

He fingers the bulbous University of Miami class ring I gave him to remind him of home when we were at Columbia together—me in law school, Manny in business school.

"And no, we are no longer involved, in case you were wondering, although I no longer owe you an explanation for anything."

"Did I ask?"

He ignores the question, staring off into the distance. "She's not a bad kid. No way she did what they're saying."

The wistful look in his eyes punches me in the gut. It's the same one he got every time we visited his seven brothers and sisters in Miami. How I'd relished his family's backyard barbecues, so different from my parents' stuffy soirées attended by politicians, business moguls, and famous artists. In Miami, with Manny, I'd felt hopeful for the first time since returning from Iraq. Racing around with his rambunctious nieces and nephews as the older generations watched with pride, it was easy to imagine that we would have a brood of our own, and that they would be watched over by grandparents saying, "*Sí, eso es. This is what life is all about. This is why we made the journey on a raft of sticks.*" But none of that was to be.

"She was adopted. From a Russian orphanage when she was six. Like lots of adopted kids, she's had some problems. But kid stuff. Not murder, for God's sake."

"Maybe she did it, maybe she didn't, but she is facing the death penalty, so she does need a lawyer. I think you'd agree, I fit the bill."

He's chewing his upper lip, the way he always does when weighing the pros and cons of a business deal. A picture of calm, but the flush rising up from his neck gives him away. He knows he has no choice.

"And it would be what's best for Gretchen too, don't you think? Dr. Slim seems like the kind of man who wouldn't think twice about leveraging your little entanglement against his wife. Rich people are like that. And, of course, there is an election in your future, isn't there?"

He raises his hands in surrender. "If I can convince her to hire you, you'll sign the divorce papers?"

"And I'll be out of your hair forever. Do we have a deal?"

He picks a strand of lint from his sleeve. "You're relentless, Grace, you know that? You drive a hard bargain."

I affect a coquettish smile. "I learned from the best."

"And, if it's not too much to ask, maybe you could suggest that Gretchen send over a retainer. Let's say...ten thousand? By noon tomorrow."

He drums the fingers of both hands on the table for what feels like forever, before saying, "Okay, you win. I'll talk to Gretchen. But as for the car—I'm holding on to that for the time being. Percy left that old rust bucket with me for a reason."

I scrape my chair back, anxious to leave before he changes his mind. "I can live with that."

At the door, I glance back at Manny, his head lowered. "Please forgive me."

I duck outside into the soul-sucking sauna that is August in South Florida, hoping that one day, not too far in the future, I won't have to apologize for my behavior. Or ask forgiveness.

Chapter 4

The screen door to the Star Bar and Grill flaps in the night breeze, playing "now you see it, now you don't" with the hulking, barbed-wire-topped walls of the Broward County Jail across the street—four concrete bunkers, spitting distance away from each other, built to house five thousand but always overbooked.

The Star, the community center for defense lawyers on the way to or from the jail has a sign on the door warning, "Cops and Prosecutors Enter at Your Own Risk." The Star is the only legitimate business in the neighborhood. At least if you don't count the Booty Call, the strip joint next door, and the St. Vincent Mission on the corner that offers free hot meals to all comers. Cheap booze, an espresso machine, and lax enforcement of the no-smoking ban. The lone food item on the menu is a *medianoche*, a Cuban ham and cheese sandwich with pickles, and the only entertainment a vintage jukebox that takes a kick or three to get the 45s to drop.

I shoulder open the door and head for my usual perch, the

barstool nearest the exit and tonight, the farthest from two bedraggled suits, ties askew, heads craned back, watching a fishing show on a circa 1975 TV mounted high in a corner.

"Grace!" Jake's hand waves at me from the kitchen pass-through. "Be right with you."

Besides owning the Star, Jake is an on-again, off-again investigator and all-around muscle for defense lawyers, or whoever can pay him enough. Jake knows the streets. He also makes a mean martini. Or so I've heard.

I climb onto the red leatherette stool and drop my backpack atop the sea of sunflower seed shells carpeting the cracked linoleum floor. *Pepitas*, as Manny calls them. Just the thought of him makes my blood boil. Still, he did come through in the form of Gretchen's driver delivering a cashier's check for ten grand this afternoon with the word "retainer" printed on the memo line. It's a start, I guess. But the thought of another guilty client, so close on the heels of the wife beater, is discouraging.

Jake slips behind the bar, dish towel slung over his shoulder. "Drop shot?"

"Roger that. And make it a double."

"Good Lord, how can you sleep with all that caffeine?"

"Clear conscience," I say with a wink. "And I'm not here to sleep."

"Yeah, well, why are you up here so late, Counselor?"

I motion with my head in the direction of the jail.

"Yeah, who's the scumbag?"

I shake a scolding finger at him. "Client, Jake, client."

He turns his back to ready my regular poison, yanking on the levers of a brass espresso machine as big as a garden shed. Honest Abe's Bail Bonds is emblazoned on the back of the tight, black T-shirt, which does little to hide his muscular physique. He's tall and far from clean cut. A blond, sun-bleached mop hangs to his shoulders. Not my type, not that I have a type. I make it my business to keep to myself these days, unlike Jake, who makes it his business to know everything that could be of value about anyone who comes through the door. And then there's the fact that Jake was once a cop. Talk is that he went bad. Maybe he did or maybe he didn't, but all cops, good or bad, have something to hide.

"Who be the client?"

I stare at the shiny parade of liquor bottles assembled on the back bar until Jake drops the shot glass filled with steaming espresso into a pint of Coca-Cola and sets it in front of me. The viscous liquid bubbles up as the tiny glass makes a tinkling sound when it hits bottom. I take a swig and exhale.

"Zoe Slim."

He takes a step back. "The one who killed the dude at that fancy school? You're her lawyer?"

"You seem surprised."

"La-di-da. Moving on up the food chain, are we? Not that you're not a good lawyer and all. With all that family money you'd have thought they'd get some shark."

"So, I've been told."

"You never know, maybe she didn't do it," he says, wiping down the bar. "I mean why would a kid like that kill someone? Rich. Pretty. A life of luxury. Only poor people kill people, right? What would be the point?"

"Thank you for your wisdom and humor, Mr. Philosopher Bartender. And that's exactly why reason isn't a defense, isn't it? One thing we both know for certain is that you can never really know what a person is capable of, no matter who they are."

I survey the den-like space, but I can't fool myself. I'm stalling going across the street to visit Zoe Slim. "Where are the storm troopers tonight? I assume your shindigs are still the best place to weather storms north of Key West."

"No doubt, but Ophelia's gonna be a bust. Not even a Cat 1 hurricane. Just some tropical shower. Spoiled what could've been a rockin' good time in here."

"No chance for violent death and mass destruction is always a downer, I suppose."

"Three months left in hurricane season, my friend. Plenty of time."

"Don't remind me."

He shrugs and jabs a remote to change the channel to the news. "Slim, your girl's father, owns a chain of plastic surgery clinics, right? Lots of ads on late-night TV."

"Yep, new boobs with interest-free financing." I wrinkle my nose. "Seems like there are two things in this world you shouldn't go cheap on."

"Yeah, what's that?"

"Plastic surgery and lawyers."

He snorts, poking at the bottles on the back bar with a thing that looks more like a dead squirrel than a feather duster.

"How'd you catch the Slim case?"

I bite my bottom lip.

"Come on, you can tell ol' Jakey. Consider it the bartender's version of the priest-penitent privilege. I'll never tell."

I hesitate, uncertain if it's because I'm embarrassed or angry. "Gretchen Slim, the defendant's mother, is, or maybe was, Manny's mistress."

"Ouch!" He leans against the back bar, arms crossed.

I hold up my hand. "Not the best idea."

"Maybe not, but it's a big case. And if the money's right—"

"Hey, turn that up, would you?" I say, pointing at a reporter standing outside the headquarters of the FLPD.

"Excuse me ladies and gentlemen," the reporter says, pressing an earpiece to into his ear. "We have some breaking news from the Fort Lauderdale Police Department. The prints on the gun recovered during the investigation of the brutal murder of Brandon Sinclair have been identified as those of the teen accused of his brutal murder, Zoe Slim, daughter of plastic surgeon to the stars, Anton Slim."

I tuck a twenty under the empty glass. "Of course they are."

"Hey, that's too much," Jake says, but I wave him off and slip out into the cloying darkness.

Chapter 5

I drop my yellow legal pad, Florida Bar card, and a blunt pencil pilfered from a convenience store last time I bought a lottery ticket onto the conveyor belt and proceed through the magnetometer, a gargantuan metal detector at the jail entrance.

Beep beep beep.

"Shoot." I step back.

The guard seated to the side of the contraption, an older man with a paunch from years of sitting, doesn't take his eyes off a dog-eared copy of *Sports Illustrated*. "Got anything in your pockets, Miss? Change? A ballpoint pen?"

I pull up my left pant leg and shake Oscar in his direction. "Nope, just this."

He leaps up, bug-eyed. "Holy Mother of God." He turns his head this way and that, examining what, to the untrained eye, is nothing more than a metal bar attached to a flesh-colored shoe tree. "Can't rightly say I've ever seen one of them things up close."

I drop my pant leg and proceed, ignoring the beeping. "Then

you're a lucky man."

He thrusts his shoulders back and salutes in the practiced way of muscle memory that will never fade.

"What branch?" I ask.

"Army. Spent some time in Nam. Damn near killed me. You?"

"Same. Army. Iraq. Damn near killed me too."

"I'd say we're both lucky," he says, eyes drifting away to somewhere he'd been a long time ago. Back when he was young and everything was possible.

"You're good to go," he says, rushing to retrieve my belongings and hand them to me.

"Thanks," I say, chin high, hand cocked in the first salute I've given since leaving Walter Reed.

"No, thank *you*."

The guard mumbles into his shoulder-mounted radio and a barred gate slides open. I proceed to the central command post for the women's wing, the clickety-clack of my steps echoing off the cinder block walls. At the end of the long corridor, another guard stands behind a smudged glass partition, a frail woman with mousey brown hair with a thin body, like a plumb line suspended within her green polyester uniform.

I slide my Bar card and driver's license into the metal drawer along with a scrap of paper on which I scrawled the cell block location for Zoe Slim I found online. The guard pulls the drawer toward her, but leaves the card and license sitting there. Instead, she scoops up a drippy sandwich from a paper wrapper and starts to eat. I take a seat opposite the window and wait. I wait some more. Waiting's not a skill taught in law school, but it is one which has to be perfected to survive, as either attorney or inmate.

I try not to dwell much these days on my service, but the guard's reaction reminds me some still consider military service the height of patriotism. For me, enlisting was the most impulsive thing I've ever done, and that's saying something. On

September 12, 2001, I walked into an Army recruitment office and signed up, much to the chagrin of my father, who'd gotten me my first law job—a job in the North Tower of the World Trade Center in lower Manhattan.

As luck would have it, I was running late for work on September 11, 2001. The moment I emerged from the subway the first plane hit the North Tower. In an instant, my law firm was no more, my colleagues were dead, and the world had changed forever. No longer could I justify arguing about rich people's money for a living. I knew in my heart I had to actually *do* something—not just talk about it—not recite hollow prayers for the fallen and their families, only to go back to business as usual. I felt compelled to act. The terrorists had left me no choice. What I vowed to do was not stand on the sidelines and officiate, but to fight back with my own two hands to avenge the countless victims leaping from the towers against the backdrop of the bluest of bluebird skies I've ever seen.

I shake my head to chase away the horrendous memories and motion to the guard in a "Hey, I'm just reminding you I'm here" kind of way. It's been more than an acceptable period of time, even by jail standards, but a more direct approach such as a "Hey, will you hurry things along," will only cause her to use what little authority she has to piss me off by making me wait even longer.

She palms her forehead and takes a slurp of a swimming-pool-sized soda, stands, wipes her hands on her pants, and croaks into a microphone. "Attorney visit for Slim, Women's North Unit B, bed twelve?" It sounds like more like question than a statement. I look around to see if maybe I'd dozed off and missed the arrival of some other visitor. But, no, I'm alone.

"Tower B. One floor up," she says, pointing at a ceiling-to-floor gate constructed of thick iron bars. It opens as I walk toward it. When it clangs shut behind me, I cringe.

Tower B is stenciled in red paint on a door at the top of the stairwell, behind which are two rows of visiting rooms on either side of a security post. A black-and-white photocopied sign hangs on the door of each room, ATTORNEYS ONLY, which strikes me as a statement of the obvious, given my ilk are the only people allowed up here. Friends and family are permitted to visit once a week in cubicles on the first floor where they communicate via filthy wall phones, no physical contact. Inmates, however, can meet face to face here with attorneys twenty-four seven. Cops too, any time of the day or night, up here or downstairs, lawyer or no lawyer present—the jail's frequent fliers know better than to say anything to law enforcement.

"Room three. Hit the panic box if there's a problem," the guard says, focus trained on a console of video monitors.

The panic box is an alarm rigged up under the table. One swift kick is supposed to alert the guard to trouble, but on my first visit to the jail as defense counsel, I booted a panic box just to be sure. Nothing happened. Just the hollow sound of shoe hitting wood, and a sneer from the man with a face covered in tattoos on the other side of the table. I'm not cowed, though. Way I see it, if you're sitting across from me in here, I'm the last friend you've got, which is exactly how I need Zoe Slim to feel about me.

I step into the cave-like space to find Zoe seated at a metal table, not one inch of which is free from graffiti, her scrawny body dwarfed by a baggy orange jumpsuit, feet restrained by leg chains bolted to an iron bail cemented into the floor. Rubber shower sandals peek out from beneath her pant legs, the type worn by old men who sit in ancient recliners when style is no longer of concern. Her long, dark brown hair is matted and draped around her pale face like a curtain—no hair ties allowed in jail.

Before I have the chance to say a word, she attempts to spring from the chair, which results in her being ratcheted back by the leg irons. "Who the hell are you?" She juts her chin out. "Hey! I asked you a question. Who the hell are you?"

Resisting the urge to flee, I pull a once-white plastic chair back from the table, but as soon as my rear hits the seat, the uneven legs tip me to the left, shifting my weight onto Oscar and sending me face down onto the filthy table top.

I right myself as she continues to yell at me, her top lip curled back to reveal a row of metal braces.

She emits a mocking grunt. "Hey, don't ignore me! Who—"

There's one thing war and the law have in common—the best defense is a strong offense. I bellow back, "Shut the hell up!"

Her head snaps back.

I count to ten. "Let's start again, shall we?"

I extend my right hand, but she continues glaring, hands locked under armpits.

"My name is Grace Locke. I am an attorney. Your mother asked me to come."

She sucks her neck into her shirt at the mention of Gretchen.

When I retract my hand, she launches another attack, the words rushing out in a manic torrent. "Why would I talk to you? Guard! Get me out of here!"

Through the observation window, I see the guard reclined in his chair, feet on the desk, smiling. He makes a circular motion with his index finger by his ear and mouths the word "crazy."

I lean back and wait her out.

"What you lookin' at?" she says in a tone I assume she thinks sounds fierce, but comes out whiny, her energy spent on the first two outbursts.

I point the pencil at her. "You are definitely not cut out for prison."

She grunts, "I'm not going to prison!"

I motion the guard to let me out, pretending I'm on the verge of leaving. "I'd agree if you were my client, but since you don't want my help—" I stop mid-sentence, but the reality of her situation hits her like a brick to the head, fear taking the place of rage in her eyes, which are now clouded by tears.

The guard cranes his neck around the door. "You ready to go, Miss Locke?"

"Please stay," she whispers. "I didn't—"

I clamp my hand onto her shoulder. "Not another word."

Her shoulders tense up under my grip.

I wave the guard off. "Sorry, false alarm. I'll be staying."

He shrugs and rebolts the door.

I slide back into the chair, making sure not to lose my balance again. "Zoe, right now, I don't want to know if you did or didn't do what they say you did." I say this, because if I know for a fact that she shot Brandon Sinclair, I won't be able to put her on the stand to say she didn't, if it comes to that. Suborning perjury is a big no-no, and I don't need any more problems with the Bar.

"But I didn't kill him! I wasn't there. You have to believe me!" she yells, spittle spraying.

"Calm down. We've got plenty of time. Today, I just want to—"

She grabs my hands with her cuffed hands and squeezes it so hard I can't pull away, her ragged fingernails digging in. "I need to tell you what happened. How can they do this to me? I don't belong in here!"

Her escalating rant is cut short when the guard rushes in. In a flash, he uncuffs her hands from in front and recuffs them behind her back and to the back of the chair .Without warning, the memory of Reilly floods in, his pinning my arms behind my back so hard I had no choice but to sink to my knees in the road, the taste of whiskey coming back up my throat.

I gasp for breath. "I...I can't..."

"Ms. Locke, Ms. Locke. Are you okay?" the guard asks, dipping his head to my level. "Maybe that's enough for now?"

I suck in a gulp of air and attempt to refocus. "Sorry. No. Yes. Fine. I'm fine."

The guard steps to the door. "Maybe I should call the psych unit, get something to calm Miss Slim."

The reminder that of how it feels when you no longer have, and may never again have, control over anything, what you wear, eat, hear, or inject into your veins, turns the blood in mine to ice. "No. Leave her be. I'll let you know when I'm ready to leave, okay?"

"Whatever you say. It's your funeral," he says, a comment which makes me want to tell him to mind his own damn business.

"Someone's out to get me. They want to kill me. I need to tell you what happened," she says before the door's completely closed.

"Look at me, Zoe," I say, ducking my head to her level. "Look at me! I need to tell you something. Something very important."

She wipes her nose on the shoulder of her jumpsuit, avoiding eye contact.

"Do not speak to anyone, and I mean anyone, about your case," I say, enunciating every word as if it were its own sentence.

Silence.

"Do you hear me?"

Screeching like a strangled cat. "I didn't do it! I wasn't there!"

"I said—*Do you understand*?" Finger under her chin, I angle her blotchy face up. "I mean it. Not to anyone in here, no matter how much you want to. Not to any guard or investigator. Not to any cell mate. Not to anyone, no matter what they promise you. And say nothing, not even hello, ever, to any cop. Do you hear me?"

The spark of recognition in her face at the word "cop" stops me cold. "You didn't speak to the police, did you?"

She closes her eyes. "They asked me a lot of questions."

"Who? When?"

"The cops. When they arrested me. At school. In the principal's office."

My hearts lurches. "Did you say anything?"

She gives me a lopsided grin. "No."

"You sure?"

A little light comes into her eyes, enough for me to see they're green, like malachite, with flecks of gold. "Yes, I'm sure. I watch TV. I'm not a total idiot."

"Good," I say, trying to laugh, but her self-professed clearheadedness is disturbing. "So, again, nothing to anyone, okay? Not even on the phone, not even your parents. Not one word."

Her eyes flit back and forth, as if she's looking for an escape hatch to return her to her real life, the one where she goes to movies and the beach, where she's what Manny said she is—a kid.

"I'll be back in a couple of days."

"A couple of days? You've got to get me out of here!"

I squeeze behind her to the door. "I'll set a bond hearing," I say, willing the guard to hurry.

"What? What's a bond hearing?"

"It's where a judge decides if you should get out or if you should stay locked up until your trial."

"Trial? But I didn't do anything!"

I let my tone soften. Even if she did do it, I need this case, need her to trust me. "I'll do my best to help you. That's why your folks hired me."

Her shoulders sag. "It's always about money. You're getting paid, so you have to act all like you care and shit."

I pull a business card from my jacket pocket and drop it on the table. "Call me collect if you need to talk. Any time, day or night."

"Why? Like you said, you don't want to hear the truth. You don't care about my story. Get out of here and leave me to die, why don't you?" she says, straining forward against the cuffs.

I pick up the card and drop it into her chest pocket and slip out into the corridor.

"Have a good night," the guard says. "At least what's left of it."

"Same to you," I say, but the sentiment is nothing more than automatic, my thoughts consumed by the hope that Zoe didn't notice how much my hands were shaking when I dropped the card into her pocket. A scared defense lawyer is no good to anyone, least of all a kid accused of murder. Least of all myself.

Chapter 6

"Hurry up, man! You're driving like my grandma. Don't give these Hajjis a chance to get a bead on us, dude." Corporal Garcia claps Sergeant Jones, the driver of the Humvee, on the back and they both laugh with the carefree ease of friends cruising Main Street on a Saturday night looking for girls.

Not one to miss a rare moment of levity in this hell hole, I ignore the racial slur and add my two cents from my post in the back. "Yeah, Jones, get a move on, soldier. You keep driving this slow, I'll be on Social Security by the time you get us back to base."

The remark might rankle some superiors, but months of driving around Iraq with Jones, hunting bad guys together, has made rank irrelevant and irreverent banter our only relief from war. Our shtick is I razz Jones about his by-the-book nature, and he keeps a close eye out for me, the only female MP in Muleskinner Squadron, 3rd Cavalry Regiment, United States Army. The entire 3rd left Fort Hood in January 2004 for Kuwait, then ended up here, Fallujah, after four private military contractors were killed and their corpses dragged through the streets then hung from a bridge over the Euphrates. Now we've got a front seat at the battle for Fallujah, an ancient city west of Baghdad, whose residents don't much care for Saddam Hussein and his secular ways, but like occupation by us infidels even less.

"Yeah, yeah," Jones says. "Garcia, got some hot hoochie mamma in a burqa waiting for your sorry ass back on base?"

"His standing appointment with the lovely, but equally untouchable, ladies of internet porn more like it," I say, a comment which causes Jones to swerve and almost hit a goat.

Like he does on every patrol, Corporal Allen, the gunner, is on the Humvee's roof, belting out "Gangsta's Paradise" and drumming on the M2 .50 caliber machine gun. Muleskinner Squadron's regular mission is reconnaissance, hunting bad actors and providing logistical support to the 3rd while trying not to get killed in the process, but today our mission's more festive—we're picking up crates of Easter decorations from the airstrip.

Garcia throws his arms up. "Man, this ain't no Sunday drive, okay? Faster, dammit!"

"If either of you two grunts wanna drive—"

A roar from under the Humvee.

Searing heat rising through the floorboards.

Everything goes black.

Clods of dirt fill my mouth and nostrils.

The putrid smell of rotten eggs mixed with the metallic scent of blood.

Something batting me in the face.

I rub my eyes.

"Shit!"

Allen's body, dangling upside down in front of me, a limp, bloody rag doll, suspended into the cabin by his ankles which are snagged in the morass of mangled metal that was the roof.

I dive forward. "You guys okay?"

Jones is slumped over the steering wheel, head twisted

sideways, a gaping maw where his mouth used to be.

"No! No!" It's as if my screams are someone else's in the silent vacuum.

Garcia's upright in the passenger seat. "Thank God!"

But his arms. Where are Garcia's arms?

Move legs, dammit! Move! Why can't I move?

Ringing in my ears so loud.

I clutch my head with both hands to stop the pain.

Flames licking through the air-conditioning vents.

Upright.

One leg buckles.

I collapse.

Red seeping through my left pant leg. Tacky to the touch.

The smell of blood.

Dragging the injured leg, I crawl to the side door and pull up on the latch. Nothing.

I remember bodies falling from windows, arms spiraling like windmills. Mushroom cloud of smoke.

I'm not supposed to die here! Not like they did!

I crawl forward on my belly and lever myself up enough to yank Jones's body back off the steering wheel. I hoist myself onto the center console between Jones and Garcia. Using my right leg, I kick at the driver's side door, the force sending me sprawling backward, into Garcia's body which folds forward like an abandoned marionette, a seething crimson divot where his ear used to be.

I draw my palm over Garcia's eyes, fixed and black like bullseyes, and shove his body into the footwell to make room to kick the passenger side door open.

It too, holds tight.

Keep your wits about you, Grace! Keep your wits about you!

I lose my balance again and topple into the back seat. Back where I started.

The pain in my leg's infernal, consuming me from the inside

out.

Up front, flames licking through the vents like tongues, ignite Jones's fatigues.

I drag myself to the far back, beside overflowing cartons of candy bunnies and eggs nestled in shredded paper grass the color of green food coloring. I curl into a ball. Silence so complete it hurts. Nothing moving, as if the bomb sucked out all the air, leaving only death in its wake.

The fire will devour us all.

I close my eyes and the scene replays in slow motion, the way it will play in perpetuity, whether I live or die.

Boom!

Rat-tat-tat, rat-tat-tat—machine gun fire hitting the metal plating Jones and Garcia had jerry-rigged on the Humvee.

The rending of metal.

Shattered glass floating like confetti.

I pull my sidearm from its holster.

I will not be taken alive.

I force my eyes open.

I will not die a coward.

I take one last look around at the smoking carnage, the demise of best intentions and even better men. The waste of it all drives me to rest my finger on the cold trigger.

I'm being dragged, powerful hands under armpits.

Unfamiliar voices.

Radios squawking.

"One extracted. Specialist Locke. Left leg's hamburger."

Gusts of super-heated air, a blast furnace.

Another voice. "Let's get her in the bird fast. She's alive. Hillbilly armor saved her. 'Bout time the brass up-armored these tin cans."

"Nothin' woulda saved the others. IED enema right up their asses."

"Tourniquet!"

"Tighter."

Thwump, thwump, thwump, thwump.

***

Complete darkness. My face compressed against glass. Fists banging, clawing. Brain on fire.

Where am I? Where are Jones and Garcia?

Metal banging.

A rush of damp air.

An old man, back-lit with something long and black pointed at me.

"Get away from me!"

"Jesus, you okay? Did you have another one of your dreams?"

I get on my belly and crawl.

"It's me, Gracie. Vinnie."

I freeze. The voice is familiar, soothing. Hand rubbing my arm.

"Vin?"

"Yeah, sweetheart. It's me."

Hand reaching. "You okay to stand? Looks like you're still wearing Oscar."

Oscar, hanging half-off like a doll's broken limb. "What happened?"

"You had one of your bad dreams. I heard you screaming, all the way down in my place."

"What?"

He points at the banging noise coming from the window. "I'm sorry, I need to get to fixing those rusted-out tracks. A couple of the shutters are loose, and the storm was blowing them against the window."

"The storm?"

"Ophelia, remember?" he says.

I fumble to reattach Oscar. Together we hobble outside to look at the ocean. To breathe in the salt air. I lean on the railing and stare out at wave after wave battering the shore. Palm fronds skittering across A1A. Torrential rain like liquid silver lashes.

"Jesus, kid, let's get you back inside, you're shivering." He lights a path with a flashlight. "Power's out. Probably will be 'til this thing passes. Too dangerous to send crews out in this."

I take his hand and shuffle to the futon.

"You don't look so good. Why don't you sit?" He drapes a blanket over my shoulders. "Them rickety old shutters clatter like a freight train, don't they?"

I pull the blanket tight around me. "Or a helicopter."

He sits beside me. "Ah, I see. War'll do that to ya."

I reach a hand under the blanket to stroke the tattoo on my left upper arm. I visualize the multi-colored clapboard houses on stilts surrounded by a shimmering sea, a gilded moon on the horizon, and the coordinates 25.6546 N, 80.1744 W. Stiltsville. My oasis of peace. I got the tattoo before I left for Iraq. Before I was blown up. Before I spent five months in Walter Reed trying to hold on to my leg and regain what was left of my sanity, the former a failure. The latter? The jury's out on the latter.

"But better days ahead, baby girl. Better days ahead," Vinnie says.

"How do you figure that? You got a crystal ball?"

He snaps his fingers. "Trust me, the great Vincenzo knows all. Just cos I'm old don't mean I don't got a plan."

I drop my head on his shoulder. "What plan?"

"All in good time. But for now, anything I can do for you?"

I wonder how Manny's faring. Did the Intracoastal come up over the seawall into the yard like it did during our last hurricane together? The one we spent huddled under the covers, like kids in a pretend fort, telling stupid jokes to keep my mind occupied until the most spectacular dawn broke pink above the horizon as if nothing had happened.

"Would you mind sitting with me for a bit? Until the storm passes."

"Whatever you need, sweetheart. No one should be alone in a storm."

Chapter 7

I get off the bus across the street from the headquarters of the Fort Lauderdale Police Department, a concrete bunker west of downtown, conveniently located in the backyard of the most drug-infested area in the city. Satellite dishes like praying mantises loom down from the roof, antennae angled in every direction to capture radio communications from forty square miles. Across the street sits the Dixie Court Homes, the city's largest public housing project. Next door, a fried chicken restaurant which shares space with a check cashing/payday loans store. Much like bank robbers rob banks because that's where the money is, the city put police HQ here because this is where the criminals are.

Immediately, the soles of my shoes adhere to the blacktop, tacky thanks to the relentless summer heat.

"Shit."

I high step toward the entrance like a majorette, a cumbersome task given Oscar's lack of responsiveness. I named the damn thing after Oscar Pistorius, the blade runner turned murderer, in a fit of dark humor. I'd hoped we'd become fast friends. But so far, we're only reluctant acquaintances, like college roommates with nothing in common, forced upon each other by circumstance. Still, it's only been six months since the amputation, although it feels longer given the countless hours I've spent in physical therapy and endless days and nights with phantom limb pain.

I hesitate outside the entrance. My last visit here was the night Detective Frank Reilly took the wheels off my party wagon for good. I'll never know for sure, but I'm convinced Reilly set me up as payback, given I was *persona non grata* for getting Vinnie exonerated. I don't have any hard evidence that Reilly and his crew were staking me out, waiting for me to get in my car outside the Ragin' Cajun on Mardi Gras last year. Hell, maybe my luck bucket just ran dry. Or maybe it was a coincidence that they were there. Then again, it's not coincidence when they're actually out to get you. Either way, at least I'm alive to carry a grudge.

I check my phone for messages. Maybe a potential new client or two? Would be nice. But no. The only message is from yesterday. The voicemail from Detective Sonny Sorenson that brings me here. I have to say, his message surprised the hell out of me. He said he wanted to talk to me about Zoe Slim's case, fill me in, whatever that means. We may have once been more than friends, but he's still a cop, not to mention Reilly's partner. Maybe he wants to hustle me into a plea deal. Bait me enough to convince me Zoe's case is a loser and that going to trial would be a career-ending mistake. As if I haven't already committed one of those. That's what ASA Locke would have done—"save us all the trouble of a trial." Maybe not in so many words, but that'll be Sonny's message. As if trials are not to be wasted on the guilty. A ludicrous irony, but one grounded in the fact that the criminal justice system would collapse if every defendant insisted on their constitutional right to a jury of their peers.

And then there is the fact that Zoe's looking mighty guilty

given the gun with her prints plastered all over it. So, maybe a plea's something I should think about.

Maybe the reason Sonny called me down here has nothing to do with the case. An excuse to see me again? That might not be so bad, would it? Shoot. Yes, it would. I can barely take care of myself. The last thing I need is romance.

"I'm here to see Detective Sorenson," I say into a speaker mounted in the bulletproof glass wall separating the desk officer from the waiting area.

"Got an appointment?" asks the young blonde officer, a twenty-something who, without the stiff navy-blue polyester uniform, would turn a head or two at Mickey's, the cop bar on Andrews Avenue.

"Yes, I do."

"Name?" she asks, with the put-upon sigh of someone who believes they deserve better than taking names. I can't blame her. If I were one of the few women who make it through the academy, I sure as hell wouldn't want to sit in a window playing receptionist while the boys get to have all the fun out on the streets.

"Locke. Attorney Grace Locke," I say, the "attorney" part awkward in my mouth.

"Take a seat."

There are only two other people in the waiting room who, by the pissed-off looks on their faces, seem to have been here a long time. One is a wizened old gal in fluffy pink bedroom slippers, the other a large Latino dude in a wife beater, arms crossed over a beer belly, a tattoo of a snake crawling up his neck. The gal is generating a shuffling sound by moving her slippers back and forth on the filthy linoleum floor. The man lets out a *coño* every few minutes.

I perch on a metal chair in a corner, one turned away from the entrance—just in case Reilly walks in. It's bolted to the floor. Why? To avoid it from being used as a projectile? Certainly no one in their right mind would want to steal the damn thing.

And again, I'm waiting. For what seems like hours, although I suspect it's my anxiety talking. Cops parade in and out through a security door with a shrill buzzer that jolts me out of my seat each time it sounds. I'm tempted to make a run for it. If they have a solid case against Zoe, I'll hear about it sooner rather than later. And if not, if they've got squat, they'll make it seem like they've got something, just to yank my chain.

Pink Slippers and Wife Beater give up and leave.

And still I wait.

As I'm about to leave, the security door buzzes open and Sonny Sorenson appears. He's dressed in standard detective attire—open-neck shirt and dress pants, gold shield on a lanyard around his neck, Glock on his hip.

He waves me over. "Grace, come on in."

"Sonny, yeah, hi," I say, trying to sound nonchalant. First rule for defense lawyers is the same as for jilted lovers. Never act needy. Be cool, but I blow that one right out of the box by spilling the contents of my purse onto the floor I'd wager last saw a mop during the Clinton administration—phone clattering out, lipstick rolling away, wallet, hairbrush, and Nicorette gum in a pile.

How I'd love a cigarette right about now. But I gave those up too, right along with everything else that used to make me happy.

Sonny holds the door, eyes crinkling up at the edges, seemingly amused at my scramble to retrieve my things.

"Good to see you again, Detective," I say, smoothing my hair.

"It's Sonny, remember?" His eyes lock onto mine. They're bluer than I remember.

And I do remember. We met when he was in narcotics and the arresting officer on several of my drug prosecutions. Later, he was partnered with Reilly in homicide division, the same cop who railroaded Vinnie, slapped the cuffs on my wrists and tossed me into the back of a patrol car like a sack of potatoes. A jury bought Reilly's good-cop routine and found him not guilty of falsifying evidence and witness tampering and sent him right him back to serving and protecting. His three co-conspirators, however, are still locked up in the same prison where Vinnie lost three years of his life, an injustice that enrages me still.

Sonny shepherds me through a rabbit warren of cubicles and along a hallway lined with interview rooms, the same corridor Reilly led me down in handcuffs, his beefy paws prodding me along in front of him like livestock.

Sonny stops at the last door on the left and stands back for me to enter.

The very same room.

"It's been too long."

Same padded walls, same two-way mirror. Same knot in my gut. "Yeah, how long is too long?"

He motions for me to take a seat. I choose the chair facing the door, the cop's usual position.

"Reilly's still your partner? At least that's what the arrest report for Zoe Slim says."

Sonny's reels back. "Whoa there. What, no time for small talk? Like hello, how've you been, Sonny?"

He drops into the seat opposite, reaching back over his shoulder to close the door. "And here I was, thinking we were friends."

"'Were' would be the operative word in that statement." I immediately regret the sarcasm. I should know better. Sonny's always been on the up-and-up. He has to be given his dubious pedigree. His father was Sal "Sideburns" Saladino, an old-time made guy in the Miami crew via the Bronx. Until he was executed by the Russians looking to take over his action. He took a bullet to the head and was found in the trunk of his Cadillac Seville on Sunny Isles Beach when Sonny was in high school. That left Sondra, Sonny's Swedish mother, to raise him. Sonny took his mother's maiden name to escape the stigma. He was first in his class at the police academy, and his stellar arrest and conviction record got him promoted to detective early. Sonny's intolerance for crime would make Eliot Ness seem like a slacker.

"To be clear, I had nothing to do with the Vicanti fiasco."

"I never said you did. But if I were you, I'd watch your back. I'm going to be watching mine this time around. The Slim case is big for me, and I'm not going to let him screw me or my client over."

He tips his chair up onto its hind legs. "If it makes you feel any better, Reilly's off today."

"Maybe that makes *you* feel better. Not likely he'd take kindly to your consorting with the enemy."

"I don't know what Frank did or didn't do, and I don't want to know. But he's a good partner."

"Whatever you say, Detective."

"Jesus, enough already. I always respected your work. The least you can do is give me the same courtesy. We made a good team. Put some real bad guys away, didn't we?"

"That's ancient history. Let's cut to the chase. Why'd you ask me here?"

He drops the chair back on all fours. "To give you a heads up on some preliminary information we've got on the Sinclair murder."

"Right. Because cops always want to help defense lawyers."

"None of us need to be wasting our time."

"And there it is, the inevitable efficiency argument."

"Please. I'm not your enemy here. I heard you caught this case, and I just wanted to bring you up to speed. You can do whatever you want with what I tell you, but you might find it interesting, helpful, whatever."

I raise my hands in mock surrender. "Okay, okay. Let's hear it."

He flips open a folder with the tip of a pen. "We found a gun at the school. A Glock 19, silencer attached. Covered in your client's prints."

"Old news. Saw it on TV. What else you got?"

"The Glock was found in your client's locker. It had been

fired recently."

I resist the urge to flinch.

"The ballistics on the slugs taken from the victim's body match the weapon."

I bite my upper lip.

"And the serial number on the weapon came back. The Glock is licensed to one Anton Slim."

Guilt is one thing, but no plausible defense is another. "Shit."

He laces his hands behind his head. "That's it. That's all I got for now."

He's right, even if he is trying to pressure me. This loser's going to plead out early and I'll walk away with nothing. No big payday, no media exposure.

"Yep. Your client's in deep shit. Didn't want you going out on a limb your first big case back without the actual facts."

"Your facts," I say, but with a grin.

"Shoe on the other foot now? How's it feel?" Sonny says, matching my grin with one of his own.

"Why is it everyone thinks it's so hard for me to do my job?"

"What?"

"Never mind," I say, pulling up my pant leg. "And a bad choice of metaphor, by the way."

His jaw drops. "I know we talked about it, but—"

"My only regret is that I didn't do it a long time ago. Before I took the first damn pain pill. The war didn't kill me, but that junk would have."

"And how is it?"

"What? Learning to walk again? Or not being whole?"

He presses his lips together, eyes full of pity, a common reaction and one I'm retraining my mind to interpret as an admission of an inability to comprehend the horror.

"It's coming along. Doc cleared me to run, if you can believe that. It's only been a few months."

"You always were one tough mother, Grace."

Another bad metaphor. This time he should know better,

but I let it pass.

He slaps the file shut. "I'm sure you'll get the rest in discovery from the ASA soon enough."

"That means there's more bad news?"

"One man's bad news, is—"

"Is another's ticket to walk a teenager to death row. Lucky me."

"I don't remember you as such a bleeding heart, Ms. Locke."

"You'll forgive me if I think you're dribbling out the key evidence, before I have the chance to see the whole picture, to get me to fold my tent and go home. Open and shut case. Nice and easy for you."

He clasps his hands in front of him. "Do whatever you want with the information. Ignore it, file it away, forget it, but whatever you do or think, this case is not going away. The chief's holding a press conference with the state attorney today. They are going to announce the State will be seeking the death penalty."

I blurt out the words, "She's a kid!"

"A kid who killed an innocent man."

I stifle a groan.

"One last thing, but you didn't hear it from me. You might want to ask your client about the text messages."

I resist the urge to curse. "What text messages? There was no mention of texts in the arrest report."

Digital nails in Zoe's coffin. Text messages and social media. No two things simplify cops' lives more.

"What you're saying without saying it is, I'm screwed."

"See you in court, Counselor."

"Yes, you will."

"And by the way, that leg looks good on you," he adds with a wide smile. "You'll be back out there running hard in no time."

At the bus stop, I shade my eyes, the squalor of the ghetto all around me incandescent in the bright-white light of morning. I reach into my purse for my sunglasses, but they're gone. They must still be on the floor of the waiting area. Or maybe Pink Slippers is wearing them, or maybe even Wife Beater.

Chapter 8

Bail hearings always were a circus, and nothing has changed. It's been more than a year, but as I look around the cramped, dank room buried in the bowels of the courthouse, it's evident life has gone on without me. I'm not sure why it wouldn't have. That the judge's robe would be anything other than black, and that the smell emanating from the jury box full of inmates anything other than putrid. It makes no logical sense, but the sameness, despite my absence, strikes a hard blow.

Maybe it's just that I used to believe I was indispensable to the mission of putting bad men and often worse women behind bars. ASA Grace Kelly Locke, rabid crime fighter, a top cog in the machinery of justice. All illusions. The legal juggernaut has lumbered along just fine, and I feel small, brought to heel not only by my own mistakes, but also because, as it turns out, mere mortals are inherently flawed custodians of justice. The best that we can do is pretend otherwise for as long as we can.

The moment I push through the gate separating the gallery and the well of the courtroom, a manic pen restricted to attorneys and staff, the stench hits me, forcing my breakfast egg sandwich and black coffee back up my gullet. Clearly, my nostalgia for all that I pissed away has overshadowed my memory of the aroma of the arena, which is as hideous as ever.

I survey the malodorous in-custody inmates, the majority of whom sport orange jumpsuits emblazoned with the acronym BCJ—Broward County Jail. The rest wear the rumpled street clothes in which they were arrested, a sleepless night curled up on the concrete floor of an overcrowded holding cell having taken its toll on whatever cleanliness they once had.

But I have to admit, I have missed all of this. The grit. The in-your-face harsh reality. As distasteful as the criminal law may be to many lawyers—especially ones like me from fancy law schools who tend to prefer clean hands and deep corporate pockets—a criminal lawyer is all I've ever wanted to be. Upon graduation from Columbia, intent on being a voice for the victims of crime, I accepted a position at the Manhattan District Attorney's office, but bowed to familial pressure and rescinded my acceptance, going to work at a Wall Street law firm instead. "Do you want to deal with that population every day? You'll do much more good doing pro bono work on the side for whatever cause you wish," was my father's pitch. It took 9-11 to scuttle his plan.

I pause for a moment on the periphery of the ruckus to take it all in. Two of the three rings of the circus are in action. In ring one, the ASA du jour marches back and forth in front of the prosecution's table trying to look like he knows what he's doing, his too-long pant legs mopping the floor. The second ring, the defense bar, a pulsing bevy of shiny suits and loud ties, a testament to their willingness, or perhaps, desire, to be classified as trouble-makers. Most are men, only a couple are women, dressed in pantsuits like the men, but their style more Brooks Brothers, less Italian flash. The presiding judge has yet to take the bench, yet the wheels of whatever justice he will dispense are being greased by the wheeling and dealing between State and defense like rug merchants in a bazaar, trading time for crimes.

The third ring, the bench, the elevated centerpiece, stands empty, except for the clerk to the judge's right hand, a squat woman barely visible behind a mountain of files. The files will be almost empty at this point. All the judge will have to go on today is the probable cause affidavit, a few illegible biased lines of scrawl to justify the arrest of the accused. Bottom line, do the charges have at least one rickety leg to stand on, just like me?

I stash my briefcase under the defense table because every inch of the surface is occupied by the assistant public defender's stuff, boxes and boxes of files for the majority of the cases that will be heard, those of defendants who can't afford a "real lawyer," indigent nomenclature for high-priced sharks. Rich defendants have already posted the standard bond and are back home, cocktails in hand, leaving their less well-heeled counterparts in shackles, hoping against common sense that they'll get released on their own recognizance, or that some long-suffering relative or friend will put up whatever little of value they own as collateral for a bond.

And then there are the ones like Zoe, rich, charged not with a garden variety crime, but with murder—one of the few no-bail offenses. Wealthy no-bail holds with high-priced sharks who donated to the judge's last reelection campaign will likely get bond. Given campaign donations are well beyond my current means, whether Zoe gets one last taste of freedom pending trial is a crap shoot and might depend on whether His Honor had a successful bowel movement this morning.

The polished brass plaque affixed to the front of the bench reads Hon. Michael C. Garrison.

Shoot. Not Garrison.

The docket pinned to the wall outside the courtroom lists Susan Childs as the presiding judge, a woman with a penchant for teary widow's and orphan's tales. "She must be sick or something, so Garrison's covering. Just my luck!"

Garrison's a bona fide hard-ass. All well and good when I

was an ASA. Not anymore. Once, at an event for his reelection, Garrison told me he takes no greater pleasure than "blowing up the world now and letting the bastards up in the appellate court sort it out later. In the meantime, I'd rather see an innocent man or two, or even a dozen, in jail than risk some violent thug walking out on my watch." After gulping what remained of his martini, he added, "Got to err on the side of public safety, don't we?"

How am I going to stay in the game with Garrison in charge? No way the Slims will pony up any more cash unless I get their little princess out. Somehow what seemed like a clever, albeit ethically dubious, plan to climb out of the gutter, might all be for naught unless I can persuade Garrison that Zoe deserves bail.

I prop myself up against the defense table to compose my thoughts, but a frantic wave from the back row of the jury box interrupts my train of thought. Zoe. She's even frailer and wilder looking than when I saw her in the jail. Hair more matted if that's even possible, skin so pale it's ghostly. A crazy-eyed waif who looks like she should call a psychiatric hospital home, not a waterfront mansion. Hardly the poster child for the upstanding member of the community I need her to appear to be today.

My path to the jury box is blocked by the bailiff, a burly, ruddy-faced man sporting a massive gun belt. The polished steel of a handgun, Taser, and handcuffs, glint under the lights, portending nothing good for the uncooperative.

The bailiff steps back and gives me a once over. "Ms. Locke, I didn't recognize you. I mean, it's been some time since you've been down here," he stutters, searching his lexicon for the appropriate thing to say, given the circumstances of my departure from the premises.

I recognize his face. He's one of the old-timers. He's been around this place as long as the right to counsel, but I can't remember his name. Shields? Shaw? Just another piece of the judicial jigsaw lost to time.

"Yes, it has. And why haven't you moved on upstairs to a

trial court? Haven't you been in this dungeon long enough?"

He gives me a knowing half-smile. "It's Shelton. And are you kidding?" he says, a bit too loudly. Whispering behind his hand, he adds "I like it this way. Seven in the morning 'til three in the afternoon. I tell 'em where to sit, when to stand, and when and where they can take a leak. Three o' clock on the nose it's off for eighteen holes and two cold ones before the sun sets. How sweet it is." With finger and thumb, he rolls an imaginary cigar, his impression of Jackie Gleason right on the money.

"Go on over and talk to your client, Ms. Locke," he says, standing aside. "And, Ms. Locke, it's good to have you back." He motions to the still empty bench. "And best to keep your voice down, way down. The judge is about to come out and he can be a real prick, if you know what I mean?" He gives me an exaggerated wink, turns on his heel and proclaims, "All rise. The Honorable Michael C. Garrison, presiding."

The restless, scared, hopeful, and hopeless seeded throughout the crowd and the jury box stand in unison, although none knows which word will describe them by the end of the day.

Judge Garrison bursts through a door behind the bench, black robe flapping. "Please be seated," he says as the door sucks shut behind him, sealing us in for the duration.

During his explanation of the morning's proceedings, I take note of his use of the word "individual" as opposed to "inmate," a rare concession of respect to the accused I must have heard a thousand times from him, but which strikes me now as more patronizing than sincere, given how few of them are anything other than guilty.

I tune Garrison out, silently rehearsing my arguments about how Zoe's a kid and hasn't been in trouble before, has parents and a home, and is not a flight risk—oh, and just forget that she's madder than a bag of cats. A voice keeps overwriting my thoughts, however, the voice of a prosecutor holding forth on the vicious nature of Sinclair's execution.

I suck in a deep breath and tiptoe over to the jury box. Shoulder to shoulder, shackled hands and feet, the defendants are packed in like rats on what looks more and more like a sinking ship with every "Bail denied" pronouncement from Garrison. A couple of the defendants are asleep, others are as agitated as bed bugs, their eyes shifting back and forth from the bench to their counsel to the ASA like spectators at a tennis match.

I squeeze into Zoe's row. She's between two women, one skinny as a reed, the other obese with several chins and a shaved head. Both look uninterested, as if whatever is going to happen is a foregone conclusion. Zoe is one of only three whites. The rest are African American or Hispanic, evidence of the racial inequity in the system alleged by defense counsel I used to dismiss as specious.

Wrists cuffed together, Zoe yanks on my sleeve. "You gotta get me out of here!"

"I'll do everything I can," I say, glancing over my shoulder at Garrison to make sure he can't hear us.

Her wrists strain against the cuffs. "I can't take it. I'm all alone in there, except for meals and showers, but that's even worse. Everyone stares at me like I'm some kind of freak."

"Shh, Zoe, lower your voice."

She yanks on my sleeve yet again. "I need to tell you what happened, Ms. Locke."

I shush her again.

She blinks hard to stem the torrent of tears threatening to breach their banks. "I'm afraid in there, Ms. Locke. It's really scary."

I squeeze her bony forearm. "I know. And please call me Grace."

I scan the gallery for the Slims, my ace in the hole to persuade Garrison that Zoe comes from a stable home, but, more importantly, to make it clear she's from a wealthy family, one that might be inclined to dig far into its deep pockets when reelection time rolls around.

Floating above the mass of unremarkable faces, I spot Gretchen's corona of blonde hair. But no Anton.

"Shoot. The least he could do is show up for his only kid."

"What?" Zoe says.

Garrison's head pops up from behind a file. I thought I was saying the words to myself. Apparently not. He lowers his reading glasses and pins me with the same hollow stare with which he's sent many a hard man away to prison, never to return, other than in a pine box. Garrison's small and wiry, but his hyper-kinetic presence galvanizes everyone to look at me, the object of his irritation.

I hold my breath. After a seemingly endless pause, Garrison pushes his glasses back up his nose, and resumes asking a defense attorney why he thinks his client, who has skipped bail on three separate occasions, deserves another chance at the "freedom enjoyed by the good citizens of Broward County."

Garrison gallops through the docket in alphabetical order, announcing a defendant's name and charge, his words ricocheting off the walls. Defendants pop up like jack-in-the-boxes, and sit down just as fast, heads bowed by the realization that they won't be seeing the sky without the benefit of chicken wire for a long time. He cautions those who have the ill-advised notion of saying anything in their own defense that everything is being recorded and, he narrows an eye, he can guarantee that it *will* be used against them. Ignorance of his warning merits a banged gavel and a hard shove from the bailiff.

Garrison had presided over bond court back when I took the ASA job Manny helped me get after I moved to Florida from New York. Garrison scared the bejesus out of me the first time I appeared in front of him. His rapid-fire dispensation of his version of justice is legendary, earning him the title, King of the Rocket Docket. As a rookie, I once watched him rule on two hundred and fifteen motions for bail in three hours. It was as if the State, the defense, and the accused weren't even in the room. Rapists, murderers, drunks, and thieves, they all got the same fifteen seconds of His Honor's time.

After an hour, Garrison reaches surnames starting with the letter S.

"State versus Zoya AKA "Zoe" Slim.""

"Yes, Your Honor," I say, feeling as if my shoes are on the wrong feet as I step up to the lectern on the left side facing the bench. The State's lectern is always on the right.

Garrison leans back in his throne of a chair, chewing on the leg of his glasses, peering at me like a lab specimen. "Ah, Ms. Locke. We've missed you." His obsequious tone might sound sincere to the ill-informed, but it makes me wish the ground would open up and swallow me whole, a reaction only magnified by a chorus of titters from the attorneys waiting in line behind me.

"Excuse me, Judge," the young ASA says, riffling through a stack of arrest reports to locate Zoe's.

I hold my breath. Unlike my colleague, I know what's coming. Garrison's going to crush the poor sod.

"May I have a moment?" the ASA asks.

And I'm not wrong.

"No, you may not, sir. Ms. Locke, please proceed. Mr. State's Attorney, you must be fully prepared when you come into my courtroom."

The ASA bends to pick up a pen from the floor, revealing one black and one brown sock. Whether the move is to stall, or simply to retrieve the pen, who knows, but it serves to draw even more ire from Garrison.

"Mr. McNeil, you will not delay my docket. Ms. Locke, proceed. Let's hear why Ms. Slim merits bail, why don't we?"

"May it please the court. My name is Grace Locke and I represent Zoe Slim."

Chapter 9

Only eighteen. No criminal history, has ties to community, etc. The basic dog-and-pony show a first-year law student could put on. It's all so predictable I've almost lulled myself into a stupor by the end of my presentation.

Garrison listens, tapping his pen every time I pause to indicate I should hurry up.

As much as it galls me, I'm forced to call Gretchen to corroborate everything I've argued, which sends the troupe of photographers, as rare to bond court as innocent defendants, into paroxysms, snapping shots of her gazing up at Garrison through librarian glasses I'd wager are clear glass. She's chosen another demure beige suit, and repeatedly raises her left hand to wipe a tear from her smooth cheek, the huge rock on her wedding finger catching not only the light, but also Garrison's attention. A little bling and a little blah, a nice touch, enough to show respect, but not enough to seem common.

When she's finished answering my questions, Garrison removes his glasses and gazes down at her, smitten. Exactly the effect I was hoping for. For my purposes. For now. Although I am somewhat appalled that I have seemingly been able to pull this off.

Just as she's about to step down from the stand, she gives Garrison the most angelic of looks, eyes ingenue wide, and says with a sweet Southern twang, "I assure you, Your Honor, that I will do whatever else you ask of me if you would, please, please, let my baby come home."

Garrison gives her the sweetest smile I've ever seen from a judge. "Thank you, Mrs. Slim, that will be all. You can step down, unless Mr. McNeil has any questions for you."

The words, "Go on, I dare you," are on the tip of my tongue, but I bite my lip and pray that McNeil decides to have a whack at the dutiful, not to mention stunningly gorgeous, mother of the accused, which will do nothing more than irritate the gobsmacked Garrison.

But no such luck.

"No, sir," McNeil says, with his own adoring smile angled in Gretchen's direction.

"You may step down, Mrs. Slim. And, again, thank you for being here today."

Every eyeball in the gallery is on her as she sashays back to her seat. I have to give it to her. Gretchen knows how to work a room.

"Mr. McNeil, does the State have any witnesses or any evidence it wishes to present?"

"Um, yeah. I mean— Yes we, I— I do," McNeil says, adding, "Your Honor," in an attempt to rectify his bungled response. "First, let me say that the defendant is charged with the most serious of offenses, that of first-degree murder."

I can't resist rolling my eyes. Still, I was once in his shoes. A zealous new convert to the cause of justice. And it does feel good to believe you're on the side of the angels. Even if it is an illusion.

"And—" McNeil continues, but Garrison waves him off.

"Yes, yes. Thank you for the statement of the obvious, Counsel. I am aware of how serious a crime first-degree murder is, and it was a very serious crime, even way back in the dark ages when I went to law school."

A collective chuckle from the gallery.

McNeil straightens his tie. "The State calls Detective Frank Reilly of the Fort Lauderdale Police Department."

It's no surprise as Reilly's the lead detective on the case, but the mention of his name still sends a jolt of fear through me.

On his way to the witness stand, Reilly passes so close I can smell the odor of cigarette smoke wafting off his shirt, the buttons of which gape, an unfortunate situation which would have been camouflaged if he'd worn a tie. His arms hang ape-like away from his sides, as if he's still wearing the gun belt he had to check at the entrance to the courthouse. His square, stocky build suggests he may have had a muscular physique once upon a time, but he's flabby now, wide-assed from years of sitting in a cruiser eating junk food.

Reilly settles his girth into the witness chair and pulls the microphone close to his brushy orange mustache. He swears to tell the whole truth, and nothing but the truth, all the while glaring at me. I refuse to look away, however. He got the better of me before, but I won't let that happen again.

Preliminaries complete—name, title, length of service with the FLPD, and his assignment to the Sinclair case—McNeil turns to the day of the murder.

"Detective Reilly, did you go to St. Paul's on the morning of Monday, August 24th of this year?"

"Yes. We answered the 9-1-1 call from the principal."

"And what did you find when you arrived?"

"Mr. Sinclair in his office."

"What condition was Mr. Sinclair in?"

"He was dead. So, not very good."

A burst of laughter from the gallery.

Garrison bangs the gavel twice. "Order. There will be silence in this court."

"Please go on, Detective."

"Mr. Sinclair was behind his desk. He had suffered two gunshot wounds. One to the head, the other to the groin."

McNeil checks the shopping list of handwritten questions on his legal pad. "Detective, have you brought any photographs of the crime scene with you?

Reilly holds up a manila envelope. "I have."

"Your Honor, may I approach the bench?"

Garrison nods and McNeil steps forward to hand the photos up to the judge.

I leap to my feet. "Objection, Your Honor. I have not had the chance to review the photographs, nor has counsel laid the proper foundation for their admission into evidence."

Likely, a baseless objection. Usually crime scene photos are for the jurors, to shock and horrify them into a conviction. These ones must be hideous if McNeil wants the judge to see them at this point. To seal his argument against Zoe's bail. Still, I have to say something. I can't sit here like a potted plant doing nothing. I have to make it look like I'm doing something to get Zoe out of jail. So, lack of foundation it is.

McNeil gets out a "Your Honor," before Garrison cautions him with a raised hand.

Garrison glances at the motley assortment of inmates still in the jury box. "Ms. Locke, there's no jury here. Save whatever objections you have for trial."

I lower my eyes in a contrived show of humility.

"Nice try, however, Ms. Locke. I see you haven't lost your flair for the dramatic."

Garrison wrinkles his nose at the stack of photos in McNeil's outstretched hand. "If the top one is anything to go by, those are, indeed, quite stunning. Counsel, please hand the photographs to Ms. Locke to review."

Shocking is an understatement. In one shot, Sinclair's lanky frame is sprawled back in a high-backed chair, pants at his ankles, black high tops poking out, arms hanging over the arms of the chair. A hole in his forehead the size of a golf ball crusted with dried blood. Another, a close-up, shows his head leaning against a bookshelf, its final resting place next to Merriam-Webster's Dictionary. I gag at another, this one of his groin, a gaping crater where his dick used to be, a fact not shared with the media. Not yet, anyway. When this gets out, it'll be open season on Zoe.

I return the photographs to McNeil, who hands them to Garrison. Halfway through the stack the judge's jaw starts to drop, but he catches himself and clenches it shut. His eyes flick to Zoe, resting on her emotionless face for a beat, and back to the photos with a shake of his head.

"Detective, was there anyone else in the office when you arrived?"

"Yes. Mrs. Bannister, the headmistress at St. Paul's, and a student, Serena Price. Mrs. Bannister said she heard screaming coming from the victim's office, and went in. She said she found Sinclair dead and Ms. Price screaming."

"Who called 9-1-1?"

"Mrs. Bannister. She stayed on the line with dispatch until the first uniformed officers arrived."

"Were there any other people in the vicinity?"

"No. The victim's office was in a small out-building away from the main building so, fortunately, no one else entered the crime scene."

"What did you do next?"

"At that point, Detective Sorenson arrived. He had been here, at the courthouse. At a hearing on another case."

"Go on."

"The scene was secured, and the school was locked down until it could be swept by SWAT and the bomb squad. They found nothing. Next, we got a warrant to search the premises."

The warrant must have been Sonny's doing. Reilly wouldn't recognize the Fourth Amendment if it slapped him in the face.

"So, you did get a warrant?"

"Actually, my partner, Detective Sorenson was the one to get the warrant. He left the crime scene and got Judge Rodriguez to sign the warrant."

Of course, he did.

"Why did you need a warrant, Detective?"

I stifle a yawn. Courtroom drama may play well on TV, but in the real world it can be mind-numbingly boring. A litany of procedural details parroted by trained witnesses who know exactly what they're supposed to say to get what they want—a win for their side.

"We had the school locked down and had verified that we were not dealing with an active shooter situation. Also, the bomb squad came through with sniffer dogs, just in case. We wanted to get a warrant to make sure, if we found any evidence related to the crime, that it would be admissible in court. We needed to search each individual student's locker, and we weren't sure who or what we were dealing with."

Hearing Reilly kissing up to the Court, making out that he's by the book, makes me sick.

"And what, if anything, did you find?"

"Detective Sorenson found a handgun, a Glock 19 with a silencer attached, hidden in a gym bag in a locker."

"And in whose locker did you locate the weapon?"

"It was in the defendant's locker. And it had been fired recently."

A few onlookers gasp, causing Garrison to bang the gavel again. "Order!"

"Please go on."

"We located Ms. Slim in her English class, and we put her under arrest."

"Did you run ballistics on the weapon you found?"

"Yes. The bullets taken from Mr. Sinclair's body by the medical examiner matched the gun we found in Ms. Slim's locker. The murder weapon was registered to an Anton Slim, the defendant's father."

All eyes are locked on Reilly, as if the litany of damning evidence is totally unrelated to the kid sitting in the box, as if her conviction is a fait accompli. As if she's not even in the room—at least, until Zoe starts banging her head against the back of the chair in front of hers, slamming her handcuffed wrists on her thighs, screaming, "No, that's not true! It's all lies!"

Garrison levels his gavel at Zoe. "Ms. Slim, restrain yourself. You would be well advised to say nothing at this point."

"But I want to tell you—"

Out of options, I resort to shouting over her words to avoid whatever she's saying from being captured on the record by the court reporter. "Zoe, please don't say anything. Please, do not say another word," I repeat again and again until she wilts like a dying plant, doubled over on herself, rocking back and forth in her seat, hands gripping her head as if it's about to explode.

"Proceed, Detective," Garrison says.

Reilly leans into the microphone. "As I said, we found the murder weapon in Ms. Slim's locker."

"Did Ms. Slim make any statements to you or Detective Sorenson about Mr. Sinclair's murder?"

I throw my hands in the air. "Objection, Your Honor. Objection. This may not be a trial, but my client does still have a few constitutional rights."

Garrison smirks. Perhaps he's amused by my voicing the argument I used to dismiss as the last-ditch protestation of the guilty—the Constitution. Valid objection or not, I have to stop this runaway train. And there's no doubt in my mind Reilly would lie about what Zoe did or didn't say. She told me she said nothing, but who knows?

Garrison points at me. "Grounds?"

I freeze, my mind running down the list of possible grounds for my objection. Relevance? Leading? Assumes facts not in evidence?

"Statement against penal interest," I say, conscious that it sounds a little too reminiscent of the graphic groin photograph.

McNeil's eyes bulge like a frog's. "No way! A statement against penal interest—"

"Mr. McNeil, please restrain yourself and allow the Court to rule on Ms. Locke's objection." Garrison sniffs. "And rest assured, I am well aware what a statement against penal interest is. I won't be needing your help on that one. I too, went to law school."

McNeil's shoulders sag. My objection may be a Hail Mary, but it is amusing to see McNeil shoved off his self-righteous perch.

"Objection overruled. Ms. Locke, I think you know better than that."

I look away, chastened by Garrison's statement of the obvious and praying that Zoe told me the truth about not saying a word.

"Answer the State's question, Detective. Did Ms. Slim make any statements to the police?" Garrison says.

My unblinking stare at Reilly screams, *Go on, I dare you.*

"Detective, did she?"

Reilly's mustache twitches. "No, she did not. She was quite uncooperative."

I exhale.

"I have no more questions for Detective Reilly."

"Ms. Locke, do you have any questions for Detective Reilly?" Garrison asks, his tone more solicitous than before, which I take as evidence of his pity for my loser of a case.

Zoe is sniffling behind me.

"Please answer the question, Ms. Locke. Would you like to cross examine Detective Reilly?"

Reilly's eyes narrow into dark slashes. We both know that any misstep I make will send Zoe back to jail to wait and wait, until either justice is done, or...or what?

McNeil expels an exaggerated sigh, as if I'm taking up his precious time. I know the sound, having made it myself when I was holding all aces. Prosecution poker. The defense has zilch. No need to show your hand early.

But I'm not about to take the bait, as satisfying as it might be to rake Reilly over the coals. "No, Your Honor, I don't. Defense rests."

Before Garrison has a chance to say another word, McNeil pulls what I recognize as an NCIC from his inside jacket pocket. "If I may. One last thing before you rule, Judge," he says, waving the background check from the National Crime Information Center, a resource available only to criminal justice agencies.

I wait for the bomb to detonate.

"It appears that my esteemed colleague has been misled. The Court should be aware that Ms. Locke's client, the defendant, does have a criminal history. She was arrested and charged with grand theft last year. Right here in Broward County. I'd say she's proven that she poses a public safety risk."

I snatch the report from his hand.

"Manners, Ms. Locke, manners. This is not a playground," Garrison says, wagging a finger at me.

McNeil clasps his hands behind his back and rocks back on his heels.

I scan the NCIC.

Grand theft. And two juvenile misdemeanor arrests for possession of marijuana. At least McNeil let those slide.

"Ms. Locke, do you have anything else to add?" Garrison says.

Before I can reconstitute my thoughts, pull whatever last ditch argument I can out of thin air, Garrison rules. "Bail is set in the amount of one million dollars. Cash or bond."

"But Judge, she's only—" I say too close to the microphone, causing a screeching sound.

Garrison puts his hands over his ears. "Please step away from the microphone, Ms. Locke."

"But Judge," McNeil says, "she killed the victim in cold blood."

"Perfect," Garrison says, waggling his fingers in the air like a magician. "Since you are both outraged, I must be doing something right. And yes, Ms. Locke, I am aware of Ms. Slim's youth, which is why I'm giving her this opportunity to go home until her trial. And, Mr. McNeil, my advice to you is to make better use of the word 'accused' when referring to a defendant charged, but not convicted, of a crime."

I follow Garrison's gaze to the back of the courtroom, to Gretchen. A tripod-mounted TV camera buzzes to life to capture Gretchen dabbing at her eyes with a pink handkerchief.

"Thank you for paying us a visit, Mrs. Slim. We infrequently get such infamous visitors at these get-togethers," Garrison says, before slipping out.

"I'll come to see you at home when you get out," I whisper in Zoe's ear, as she is shuffled out of the courtroom in a conga line of shackled inmates, behind a haggard peroxide blonde with a missing front tooth, whose case was decided before Zoe's. No bail for the blonde.

***

I drag Gretchen by the handle of her Louis Vuitton purse, away from the swarm of reporters and into the women's bathroom.

I check the stalls to make sure we are alone.

"Pay the bail as soon as you get out of the building."

"What the hell happened in there? A million bucks?"

"Get her out, today. Her type doesn't last long in jail."

"Her type?" Gretchen asks, furrowing her wrinkle-less brow.

"The kid type. The mentally-disturbed type. The kid-in-an-adult-jail type. Get her out and get her some help."

"Help?"

"Yeah, help. You know, a shrink? Your kid's got some problems, and I don't need them being used against her down the line."

She looks away for an instant, long enough to tell me Zoe's no stranger to psychiatric care.

"Post cash or find a bondsman and pay him ten percent if

you want your baby, as you called Zoe, home."

"But I don't have a million bucks."

"Maybe you do, maybe you don't. But I sure as hell know you know someone who has. And where is your soon to be ex-husband, by the way?"

She tucks an errant strand of hair behind her ear. "He's in surgery this morning." She admires her well-manicured nails. "And for your information, we're staying together." She lifts her chin. "For now. For the sake of appearances."

"Who's staying together? You and your husband? Or you and my husband?"

She grabs my arm. "You don't understand."

I yank my arm back. "Oh, I do."

She's fidgeting unconsciously with a tissue, ripping it to shreds. She must believe my bluff, that I'd actually expose her and Manny.

"It was hard enough to persuade *my* husband to hire *you*, of all people," she says, a quaver in her voice.

"So Anton does know about you and my husband. And that's why he wasn't in court."

She opens her eyes wide to stem the tears.

"Taking out your indiscretions on his kid. What a guy." I cross my arms across my chest. "I'm sure you can find a way to make him see the light on this. I think you're well aware what's at stake for everyone involved."

She leans into the mirror to fix a smudge of mascara. "For what we're paying you, you could have at least asked that cop Reilly a few questions." Her lips curls into a contemptuous smile. "Truth is, you seemed a little scared when he was up on the stand. But you have a history with Detective Reilly, don't you?"

I resist the urge to run, to leave Reilly and Gretchen where they belong—in the past.

Instead, I square my shoulders and take a step forward. "Thanks, by the way."

In an apparent effort to convey confusion, her Botoxed frozen visage ends up looking like she's stuck a finger in a live socket. "Thanks? For what?"

I take another step. "For the heads-up about Zoe's criminal record. Grand theft and pot? Didn't you think I might have wanted to know? Nice job hanging me out to dry in there."

She pulls herself up to her full height, at least a couple of inches taller than my five foot nine, her face full of the righteous entitlement of privilege, a look I've seen on my mother's face more than a few times when confronted with bureaucratic trifles. "For God's sake, it was just a pair of sunglasses. They charged her with grand theft because Gucci isn't cheap." She shakes her head. "It's all kid stuff. And pot? Who cares about pot? Anyway, it was in juvy court and juvy stuff doesn't count."

"That's where you've got it wrong. 'Juvy stuff,' as you call it, which in Zoe's case includes a felony, matters. It matters a lot. I'm not sure where you got your law degree, but in my universe, every last thing, juvy or not, counts once you're facing a first-degree murder charge."

"But she's just—" her voice falters.

"A kid? Yes, she is just a kid. So, find a way to get her out. Jail's no place for kids. Especially not one like Zoe. It could take up to three years to get a trial."

"What? Can't you make it go faster? Doesn't she have a right to a speedy trial, or something like that?"

"Lady, you've been watching too many episodes of *Law & Order*. In the real world, the one Zoe's in now, nothing happens fast. And we don't want it to. Delay is your daughter's new best friend."

"Why? We need to get this over with. I mean our family—we need to get on with the rest of our lives."

"We? Who's we? There's no 'we' here. Zoe's the one facing the death penalty. Not you. Not your husband."

She knuckles a tear away from the corner of her eye.

"Look, delays mean witnesses forget. Even die sometimes.

Cases get old and the State loses interest once the media storm dies down. Time is all we have on our side."

"But I thought the sooner the better for a trial."

"You're assuming she's innocent."

"And you're not?"

"All I'm saying is get her out of jail," I say, before I pull open the door to a frenzy of camera flashes. "And keep your head down. Don't say a word to the press. Not one goddamned word."

I link my arm through hers and ferry her through the mob of paparazzi and into the elevator, feeling very much the ugly duckling I believed I was in high school, when I would gladly have traded my brains for a skinny body and pencil-straight blonde hair.

As we descend in silence, Gretchen wipes a tear from her cheek, the unconscious motion causing the sleeve of her silk blouse to shift, revealing a bracelet of angry bruises on her rose-colored skin.

Chapter 10

The bottle's cool to the touch, the divots in the glass as familiar as my own skin. I rub my thumbs over the raised script on the neck. Jack Daniel's.

I peel away the crinkly, black cellophane top and let it flutter to the floor. I unscrew the cap. Notes of honey and spice laced with an acerbic edge. A sense of well-being rises up inside me. The movement of the liquid is hypnotic, the details of this shabby efficiency, myself and my life recede and the room is bathed in its golden hue. I circle the bottle under my nose, indulging in the syrupy aroma, the same scent that used to permeate my father's study in Greenwich.

I pour the contents into the sink, wash the empty bottle out with dish soap, and toss it into a plastic shopping bag bearing the name XYZ Fine Wines and Spirits.

I walk two blocks from The Hurricane to St. Anthony's Catholic Church. A lapsed Presbyterian, I was drawn to St. Anthony's not by doctrine, but by obligation. While couples dine downtown in trendy bistros, and suburbanites help their kids with homework every night, I am on my way to announce, for the umpteenth time, "My name is Grace, and I am alcoholic and an addict."

St. Anthony's opens the doors of its fellowship hall every night to those in need of support to kick habits borne of biology or circumstance. Some come because they have to by court order, others to repair tattered lives, relationships, or simply because they have nowhere else to go. Maybe I fall into every category. Or none, perhaps. I've never been certain. Except for the IED crushing my leg, who knows? Maybe I would never have taken a pain pill. And the booze? Well, I drank before the war, but the real drinking only started after I came home as empty as a spent shell but plagued with memories like live grenades.

The actual truth as to what I am has become irrelevant. An alcoholic? Addict? Both? Neither? No matter. The meetings control the unknown, control my fear of what could have been last year. How I could have killed someone driving two times over the legal limit. And this weekly booze test? This is my insurance that I'm on the right track, that I'll never want a drink so badly again that I'll be willing to risk my life and others'. One of many variables. A waitress on her way home from work. A father driving his kid home from soccer practice. Myself. "But for the grace of God" was what I would think if I believed in God. But I don't. At least not anymore.

I do find humor, however, in the fact that the so-called Bar mandates I attend a meeting of Alcoholics or Narcotics Anonymous twice a week until a committee of lawyers, a morality star chamber of sorts, says I can stop. That the Florida Bar has undertaken to keep me out of bars so I can rejoin the Bar, might be the only amusing thing about my situation.

When I appeared in front of the buttoned-up Department of Lawyer Regulation over a year ago, they suspended my law license and issued a public reprimand via an announcement in the Florida Bar Journal saying I'd been a bad girl. As if that could have been any more humiliating than my mugshot on the front of the *Sun Sentinel* the morning after my arrest. When I made my mea culpa to save whatever might remain of my career, I wondered how many of the earnest panel, each one a blue-suited carbon copy of the next, would end the day with a stiff drink.

At first, I resisted going to meetings, secure in my belief that it all comes down to willpower and I've got plenty of that. I told Vinnie I wasn't "like those people," that I didn't need the goddamned meetings, or the Twelve Steps, or whatever other hocus pocus The Program has to offer. Vinnie held his tongue. Instead, he took me by the hand and led me down the street to my first meeting at St. Anthony's. After a while, coming became a habit, one I'm now afraid to give up.

Tonight, the place is packed. Father O'Donnell would never admit as much, but St. Anthony's is better attended by NA members than parishioners, although the zeal of the former group for showing up may be somewhat less enthusiastic. While the end game of religious faith is to attain eternal life, the goal of NA and AA is to prolong our earthly existence, those of us for whom drugs or alcohol, or in my case, both plus a daily meeting, have become religion. Apparently, in my universe, anything worth doing is worth doing to excess.

I take a seat in the back row as the crowd filters in. Men, women, old, young, all shades and sizes. Some wear suits, others shorts and flip-flops. Some with hundred-dollar haircuts, others look like their last haircut was perpetrated by a blind man wielding blunt garden shears.

Seated between a young man wearing a faded Nirvana T-shirt, and a middle-aged man in a pinstriped suit who looks to belong more at the University Club than a church hall with a bunch of junkies, I survey tonight's crowd. Who among us has robbed their grandmother of her Social Security money? Who has sold their body for a fix? Who has excused themselves from a business meeting to do a line of cocaine from a toilet seat lid with a hundred-dollar bill? Who has killed? Who will die soon?

On any given night, there are more than fifty AA or NA meetings in Fort Lauderdale. They happen in churches like St. Anthony's, but also in back rooms of car dealerships, the library, high school gyms, and even one on the beach conveniently located in front of the Elbo Room, the oldest dive bar on The Strip. I come to St. Anthony's because of its proximity to The Hurricane, but also because I like the anonymity of the large crowd. Absolute equality in mutual affliction. From time to time, I recognize an attendee and nod, but mostly I keep to myself. Here, I'm nobody. Not the one who took her life well-lived as a conscientious student, soldier, lawyer, wife, and threw it in the trash like junk mail. At St. Anthony's I'm just like everyone else—trying to get by, one day at a time.

Every now and again, I go to an AA meeting at the community college downtown, but I mostly stick to NA and at St. A's. I prefer NA over AA. The NA crowd's harder core, more authentic, although the idea that someone who jams needles into her arm, foot, groin, is more authentic than someone who drinks a fifth of firewater every night, does seem perverted. Maybe I just enjoy NA's no-holds-barred gallows humor about how it takes much longer to drink oneself to death than it does to OD and thus, drunks think they've got more time to cheat.

Not long after I started coming to St. A's, Hachi, my soon-to-be sponsor, tried to lighten my mood with a well-worn NA joke. "You know the difference between drunks and junkies? The drunk steals your stuff, but the junkie steals your stuff then helps you look for it."

So here I am. Still coming. Still sober. Scared shitless of losing it again. Of losing what's left of my life.

A hand cups my ear. "Traffic sucks. Sorry I'm late."

The hand belongs to Hachi. She's a diminutive Seminole woman with cinnamon skin and a ready smile which belies the trouble she and her people have seen. She's from Sugar Bay, a one-stoplight town on the banks of Lake Okeechobee, where addiction is as common as undocumented pickers. Hachi drives sixty miles east across Alligator Alley to attend meetings because there are no meetings in Sugar Bay. She says her people prefer stay loaded than get sober because all that would mean is they'd have to face what little's been left to the descendants of the great Chief Osceola. She may be exaggerating a little, but if that's what gets her here, I'll let it slide.

A skinny woman shuffles up front to face the crowd. Even from the back row, I can see she's short on teeth and long on nerves, body and voice trembling, a barely breathing live wire.

"My name is Beth, and I am an addict."

"Hi, Beth," the crowd replies.

Beth tells the story of how she used to be a second-grade teacher with a husband, two kids, and a home. Now she lives under the Third Avenue bridge, because she was raped at a homeless shelter—it's safer to sleep on the streets. Beth describes having had back surgery two years ago, after which her doctor prescribed painkillers. When the prescription ran out, she asked for more, and then more again, and again after that. Eventually, the doctor refused, and Beth moved on to another doctor at a pain clinic, a place she'd seen advertised on the back of a free local rag. And then on to another clinic, and another, each one giving Beth what she thought she wanted. "They were prescription drugs, so I thought it was okay," she says. But as with all things that seem too good to be true, she was wrong.

Hachi grasps my hand and squeezes tight.

"It was easy," Beth says. "I kept showing them my old MRI from before the surgery. I said my back still hurt. I'd get three hundred and sixty blues, you know, Oxy, and a hundred and twenty Xanax every monthly visit at every clinic. Nobody checks how much you're getting. But the more I took, the more I wanted. I started to sell half my stash to buy the next. Before I knew it, I was shooting up heroin in the public bathroom at the bus station. And then I got arrested. When I got out of jail, my husband was tired of believing my promises to quit, so he moved the kids out of state, and I moved in under the bridge."

From my days prosecuting drug crimes, I know all about pill mills. So-called pain clinics are one-stop shops for junkies like Beth. Like me. For a couple of hundred dollars, a "patient" can see a doctor and spin tales about the pain she's in that would make a soap-opera writer proud. A few chart notes later, the doctor hands over a prescription for 240 thirty-milligram tablets of OxyContin, and throws in prescriptions for Xanax and Adderall for good measure. The unholy trinity—one painkiller, one tranquilizer, and one stimulant—the addict's version of heaven on earth, courtesy of Big Pharma. One hundred percent legal. Often one hundred percent lethal.

After Beth's brutal testimonial, the moderator suggests a break which, in NA speak means "time for a cigarette." I'm no longer a smoker, but a time-out from the despair seems like a good idea, so Hachi and I troop out to the parking lot with the band of not so merry-makers.

"Grace, sooner or later you're going to have to get up there," Hachi says.

I pretend I haven't heard her, routing around in my bag for a piece of Nicorette.

"I know you said they could make you come here, but they couldn't make you say the words. But haven't you been stubborn long enough?"

I start to walk away, but she grabs my shoulder.

"Come on, you've come a long way on the Twelve Steps. It would do you good to share."

"I can't," I say. "I've never missed a meeting since I got out of jail. But it's not my way to wear my heart on my sleeve."

"That's not what sharing is, and you know it. It's about facing up."

I stare up the inky night sky perforated by thousands of stars.

"Not that I think it's a great idea, but if you can buy a bottle of booze every week, look at it for the entire seven days, and never take a sip, I'd say you're strong enough to stand up there and share your story."

"H, please, not tonight."

"What was your poison this week?" She points at the plastic bag.

I feel my nostrils flare.

"Okay, okay, I'll shut up," she says, and leans against the wall beside me to watch the crowd milling around the parking lot, a captive audience for drug dealers. I'm glad to see a police cruiser across the street, its blue lights a reminder of the high cost of failure for all of us, no matter our vice.

She puts an arm around my shoulder. "How are you doing?"

"One day at a time, as they say. And I hope you're keeping track of those days."

Hachi keeps a log of the meetings I attend, which she sends monthly to the Bar on my behalf. She doesn't much like the assignment, doesn't much like authority at all for that matter, but, like me, she's committed to my staying clean, so she puts up with reporting to the Man, as she calls any authority. Ten years of sobriety has done little to tone down Hachi's rebellious nature, an instinct rooted deep in her Seminole history. Although staying sober has allowed her to rebuild her life and relationships with her family and friends who had written her off as a lost cause back when she was mainlining smack, she admits the urge has never gone away. Never will, she says, and it's that concession, that inability to bullshit, that makes her the perfect sponsor for me. I'm not one for happy talk or false promises.

She turns to go back inside to make her own allocution. "You coming?"

I shake my head, anxious to check on whether Zoe's out of jail yet.

"Maybe we can grab a coffee soon?" she asks.

"You know where to find me."

Once she's gone, I pull out my phone and scroll through emails, one from Faith asking if I'm coming up to Palm Beach for her annual Labor Day clambake. Another from Marcus Jackson, one of the few people from my ASA life I still keep up with, asking me if I want to go to a preseason Dolphins game.

"I heard whoever did him gave him a blow job before he got capped."

I look around for the source of the comment and spot a man and a woman leaning on the hood of a car a few feet away, smoking.

Pretending to be engrossed in my phone, I inch toward them.

"Yeah man, it's so random," says the cadaverous man. "Bet the parents are all pissy. Pay a fortune to send your kids to a school like that and..." He pantomimes shooting a gun.

The man's companion, a woman with mushy features and yellow teeth, snorts, "Dude didn't deserve it right where he got it, though," she says, moving a curled hand up and down by her crotch.

They both dissolve into laughter, but, as if a switch has been flipped, the woman's face hardens into a grimace. "Maybe the asshole got what he had coming."

They take a few last drags on their cigarettes and disappear back inside.

I could follow them or wait for them until the meeting is over. But no. The powers that be may be able to make me go to meetings every night, but they cannot make me listen to every last tale of sorrow and loss. And the thought of waiting out here with the cops and the dealers hanging in the shadows, both waiting to take advantage of the ones that fall off the wagon tonight, is nothing I need to be part of.

I drop the plastic bag in the dumpster behind the church and head for home.

Chapter 11

The dog is as black as night, icy blue eyes like stars. The dog doesn't bark, doesn't move an inch. The dog just sits at attention, as if the dog has been waiting for me to come home.

I step through the gate.

"Vin, who you got there?" I say, approaching, but tentatively, given the size of the wolf-like beast. Some kind of behemoth mix. Shepherd? Husky?

The dog's plume of a tail starts swishing back and forth.

The dog's wearing a camouflage vest.

"Remember that last bad dream? When you asked me to keep you company until the storm passed?"

"Same damn nightmare every time."

"And I told you I had a plan?" He holds out the leash. "Well, this here is my plan."

I find myself stepping forward and taking the leash.

"Sweetheart, you shouldn't be alone so much. So I thought—"

"You got me a dog?"

"Sure did," Vinnie says, a look of childlike pride on his face.

I run my hand through the dog's thick, bristly fur.

"Way I see it, you got bad dreams, and you're alone too much, and you always had dogs as a kid, and—"

"And you didn't ask me first?"

"Nope. Just got her."

"Her?"

"Yep. A her. Like you."

Vinnie commands the dog to stand, which the dog does. On three legs. The back left leg is missing.

"You got me a dog with three legs?"

"Yep. Like I said, just like you."

"I have one leg and a fake."

"True, but you get the idea. She's a tripod, at least that's what Dogs of War call her."

The dog licks my hand and sets about sniffing my pant legs.

"Dogs of War?"

"That's the rescue where I got her. They bring retired military dogs back from war zones and adopt them out to help veterans. Like you."

I zero in on the embroidered words on the dog's vest— Working Dog. Do Not Pet.

"You think I need help?"

"Sweetheart, we all need help sometimes, right?"

I ruffle the dog's ridiculously large teepee-shaped ears. "You are a pretty girl."

The dog's tail wags double time.

"Look, she likes you. I knew she would," Vinnie says.

"Likable, right. That's the first word people use to describe me." I hold out a hand for her to sniff. "What service?"

Vinnie's face darkens. "She was assigned to a Marine handler in Afghanistan. They got ambushed when they were out on patrol. Handler was killed and she was shot in the leg. Had to amputate it to save her, so she was no good as a military dog no more. Dogs of War paid for her to be brought back and to find her a home."

I point at myself.

"Yep, you. Your casa is her casa now. You have some training to do together, but other than that she's good to go."

"Wait a minute. I'm the vet here. How'd *you* get her?"

Vinnie bites his lip, as clear a confession of guilt as I've ever seen.

I raise a hand. "I don't want to know."

Vinnie pulls several pages from his back pocket. "Your discharge papers."

"I can't believe you took those!" I reach out and snatch them back.

He pulls a dog biscuit from his pocket. "Sit, Miranda, sit," he says, and she does, long pink tongue lolling to one side.

"Her name's Miranda?"

"Yep, Miranda. That's always been her name. They said it wasn't good to change it."

I cover my face with my free hand, keeping the dog I now know to be Miranda, on a tight leash with the other.

"Wha...What's wrong? You don't like her?"

I pull my hand away from my face and laugh so hard Vinnie starts laughing too.

After a few seconds he stops. "Why are we laughing?"

"Miranda? Really?

"So?"

"You have the right to remain silent, etc. etc. You remember that, don't you?"

His eyes widen. "Like the Miranda warnings the cops read you to get you to tell them all the shit you'd rather not talk about?"

I extend my hand. "That's ten bucks for you this time."

Vinnie's hand goes to his mouth. "Oops."

"And yes, Miranda from Miranda versus Arizona, the most famous criminal case ever."

"She's perfect for you, right?" he says, a slight note of worry in his voice.

"Come on, black hair, blue eyes, missing a leg, what dog could be more perfect for me?" I lever myself onto my knees, not the most elegant of moves given the lack of flexibility in Oscar's ankle area, and Miranda hops up and gives me a kiss on the nose. "She's got a little hitch in her giddy-up, but she gets around pretty good for an old war dog."

Vinnie stands back like a proud father. "I'd say you both do," he says, but his words are muffled due to the fact that I have my face buried in my dog's warm, furry neck.

***

My phone rings.

Vinnie levels a BBQ spatula the size of a shovel at me. "Let it go, why don't you? Nothing good happens after the sun goes down," he says, flipping a burger high in the air. "Unless it's happens between the sheets. If you know what I mean."

"Men, all the damn same. Right, girl?" I say to Miranda, her eyes fixed on the flying patty.

I pull the phone from my pocket. I can't take the chance of missing a paying client. Criminals get arrested during their workday, which is night. "Hel-lo," I say between bites.

"And she wasn't breathing and there was blood, and..." It's as if I've walked in on a conversation, each word merging into the next in a manic flood.

It's a woman. Can't quite place the voice.

"Oh my God! Oh my God!"

I hold the phone away from my ear, the screams like nails on a blackboard. Miranda's ears prick up and she sits at attention, as if she's waiting for a command.

"Who is this?"

Silence for a second. "It's me, Gretchen. Zoe's mother, for Christ's sake."

"She hit her head when she fell. There was blood all over."

"Who? Zoe?"

"Yes, Zoe!"

"Fell where? How?"

"In her—" her voice cracks.

"Slow down, Gretchen. Take a deep breath and start at the beginning."

She's gasping, trying to get out the words.

"Anton and I were at a function at the Ritz."

"Wait, what? First tell me, did you bail Zoe out?"

"Yes, but they didn't let her out until 4 a.m. Can you believe that? Who's running that place?"

"Gretchen, what about Zoe? Is she okay?"

"You asked me to start at the beginning, so stop cutting me off!"

I bite my tongue.

"We had committed to the gala months ago. We're major donors, you know."

I focus on the rhythm of the electric-blue pool water eddying around the filter to stop myself from saying, "Of course you are." Instead, I say, "Go on."

"And Anton goes to Guatemala to perform cleft-palate surgeries for free every year. And so we went. To the gala, I mean. We thought it best to keep up appearances."

"Gretchen, dammit! Tell me, what happened to Zoe?"

"We shouldn't have left her alone."

"Jesus. What happened?"

"Okay, okay." A few deep breaths. "My husband ordered in her favorite meal, spaghetti and meatballs. When we left, she was on the computer in her room. She said she'd be fine."

"Go on."

"We didn't stay long at the gala. Well, I didn't. I left about nine o'clock. Anton stayed."

"And?"

"And when I got home, I knocked on Zoe's bedroom door, but she didn't answer. She has a hard time sleeping, she's never asleep early. But I thought maybe she had headphones on or something. I went to my room to get ready for bed."

"You didn't go into Zoe's room? Was it locked?"

"No, we don't have a lock on Zoe's door. After the last time, and..." Sobs swamp her words.

After a few seconds of trying to calm herself, she squeaks, "Before I went to bed, I stuck my head in to say goodnight, and— Oh God, oh God!"

"What?" I say so loud Vinnie peeks around the grill to check on me.

"She was lying on the floor, not moving. Her head was twisted to the side. There was a huge gash on her forehead. And the blood. It was everywhere!"

"Had someone attacked her?"

"No. She fell off her chair."

"What?"

"There was an empty pill bottle in the counter in her bathroom. Her Xanax. She'd taken it all. Every last pill!"

I flinch at the mention of Xanax, the same anti-anxiety medication my shrink keeps trying to make me take and I keep refusing.

"Zoe was taking Xanax?"

"Yes, not all the time, only when she gets stressed out."

"Does that happen often? Her getting stressed out?" I say, which sounds stupid given what she's accused of doing.

"Lately, yes," says, her voice rising as if she's got something else to say, so I wait.

"A few months back she started cutting herself, and her doctor thought she needed medication."

"I see," is all I say, but what I'm thinking about is an empty house and a bottle full of pills—the perfect opportunity.

"She looked like...like a broken doll. Grace, it was awful."

"Is Zoe...?" I pause long enough to substitute the word "okay" for "dead."

"She was unconscious when they took her to the hospital. They said they would pump her stomach."

"They took her to the hospital?"

"Yes, but the police came too. I called for an ambulance and they sent the police!"

"They Baker Acted her?" I ask, my mind flashing back to six miserable months spent in mental health court, the place perfectly good prosecutions go to die.

"They said something about that. What does that mean?"

"It means they think she is a danger to herself." Or others, but I keep that thought to myself. "They'll keep her at the hospital until they decide it's safe to release her."

"No, they can't do that! My husband will be so angry when he hears she's been taken away again."

"Again?"

"You're her lawyer, do something! I told them I would get her to a doctor, but they took her away anyway. And not even to a private hospital. To that place downtown where they let drunks dry out."

The image of Zoe being carted away from Hibiscus Isle, a street on which Rolls Royces and Armani are more common than squad cars and cops in cheap suits, flashes in my head. Gretchen's utter horror at the prospect of being treated like riffraff might be amusing under other circumstances, but my mind has snapped into action, consumed by how this turn of events might be useful to help Zoe.

"What did you mean when you said 'again'?"

A sharp intake of breath. "She cut herself before. Last time was so bad she had to be hospitalized."

"Which hospital did they take her to?"

"Lauderdale something."

"Lauderdale West?"

"Yes."

"You okay to drive?"

"Drive? No, we have a driver." she says, as if I've asked her to do her own laundry or paint her own nails, or whatever else rich people don't do for themselves.

"Meet me there in thirty minutes."

"We'll be there," she says, and hangs up.

I note the "we." I thought Anton wasn't home, but the royal "we" might come as easily to someone like Gretchen as spray tans and personal chefs.

I hang up and windmill my arms like a cop directing traffic. "Hey, Vin. Road trip."

"Huh?" he grunts, burger suspended an inch from his mouth, bits and pieces of which are oozing out all sides of a flying-saucer-sized bun.

"I need a ride. Zoe's in the hospital."

"I thought you said you got her out on bail?"

"I did. But after she got home, her parents found her in her room, out cold and bloody. She tried to kill herself. I need a ride."

"What? You think I'm your chauffeur now?" he says, smiling wide like a kid going out for ice cream. "At your service, my lady. I'll see you out front."

I point at Miranda. "What are we going to do with her?"

"She's coming with. Her vest is her license to go everywhere with you. And when she doesn't, I'm the designated dog sitter."

Miranda yips.

"I think I'm beginning to understand why you're the newest resident of The Hurricane Hotel, pretty girl."

***

Miranda hops in between us on the front bench seat of Vinnie's 1995 Crown Victoria. She lets loose with a couple of deep-throated barks at the death rattle erupting from the engine.

"Good God. Is this thing gonna get us there without blowing up? Maybe Miranda should sniff around for explosives."

We have a similar exchange every time I get in the car. Vinnie only keeps the clunker because once upon a time it was a police cruiser. He bought it at an auction after he got out of prison. He can afford something better. He's got money squirreled away. Add to it the cash from the settlement, and he's got enough for anything he might need from now until the finish line, unless he outlives the actuarial predictions for aging mobsters. But Vinnie loves a good joke, and the car's just that, a thumb of his thrice-broken nose at authority. Besides, he drives it about as much as he goes to Mass, which is almost never.

He pats the dashboard. "Fear not. She's solid, a battle ax, like Carmela."

"Who the hell's Carmela? Don't tell me, you've found some young thing who mistook you for the most interesting man in the world?"

He bumps over the curb onto A1A, and I grab the sides of the sticky vinyl seat and Miranda's collar to keep from listing into him. "Take it easy there, cowboy."

"Carmela was my second wife. Solid as a rock, more a diesel truck than sports car. Reliable as they come."

I know better than to go down the rat hole of Vinnie's private life, so I slink down, arm on Miranda's back, and watch the deserted beach slide by, the only evidence of life are the deep divots in the sand which will be wiped away by the sand rake late tonight, making everything new again for tomorrow. I can make out the silhouette of a homeless man propped up on the seawall, a phantom unseen by the passersby. His feet are swollen and bloody from diabetes, bursting out of his battered canvas shoes like toxic souffles. He's there every night, tips his cap when I walk by, the walker by his side his only companion.

To calm my nerves, I crank open the window and stick my head out to locate the dog star. "That one, that's Sirius."

"Serious? What's serious?"

"The Dog Star. The brightest star in the night sky."

"Hear that, pup? The Dog Star. It must be fate." He strokes Miranda's fur. "How'd you know about this Dog Star?"

"My dad showed me. We used to look at the stars through his telescope every night before I went to bed."

"My father showed me the back of his hand most nights," he says, hands tightening around the steering wheel, tanned knuckles turning white.

We cross the bridge from the beach to the mainland, multimillion-dollar yachts docked in the sprawling marina below, swaying in the breeze like gigantic egrets.

"Pretty fancy street for a mental hospital," he says as we descend onto Las Olas, a boulevard lined with royal palms laced with twinkling fairy lights as if every day were Christmas.

We cruise by the entrance to Idlewyld Isle. "Appearances can be deceiving."

Chapter 12

"This thing's got the turning radius of a cruise ship," I say, as Vinnie manhandles the Crown Vic into the space nearest the entrance of Lauderdale West, his sinewy arms muscling the steering wheel as if he were at the helm of a sailboat in a storm.

Once we've jolted to a stop, the engine idles with a symphony of clanking and screeching that causes my teeth to hurt and Miranda to bark.

I point at a blue sign of a stick figure in a wheelchair. "This space is handicapped and neither of us is."

He pulls back and eyes me.

"Well, I am, but then I don't have my car back yet, so I don't need a handicapped tag."

Vinnie reaches under the seat, extracts a handicapped tag, and slaps it onto the rearview mirror.

"Shit! Where'd you get that?" I roll my eyes. "Forget it. Don't tell me. Another thing about you I don't care to know."

He leans around Miranda who's sitting tall between us like a hirsute hood ornament and slaps my arm. "I thought you were trying to clean up your language?"

"I'm trying, I swear."

He holds out his hand. "Funny one. But that'll still be ten bucks."

"Like hell!"

"That makes it twenty. We had a deal. You curse, you pay." His lips pull into an innocent smile. "It's for a good cause. The sisters at St. A's thank you and your potty mouth."

"Okay, okay," I say slapping the cash into his hand. "You wanna come inside?"

He pokes a finger in his chest. "*Moi?*"

"Yeah, you. Who else would I be talking to?"

He turns to Miranda. "What are you, chopped liver?"

"She's coming," I say, attaching the leash to her collar. "Are you?"

"What you need me for?"

"I don't need you for anything, but I think your finely tuned people-reading skills may come in useful. We can say you're my investigator."

Vinnie throws his head back. "That's classic. Me doing the investigatin'."

I get out and rearrange Oscar, followed by Miranda who hops down with the grace and confidence of a four-legged dog, as if the missing leg was something she had no need for all along.

After checking our identification and taking a close look at the service dog license attached to Miranda's vest, the front desk attendant hands over two visitor passes and directs us to the seventh floor.

"That license worked like a charm," Vinnie says. "Like I said, she's street legal."

I give him a one-eyed stare. "More than I can say for the pretenses under which you got her."

"Geez, I think I forgot to tell you, when you finish the training together, they'll give you her real license," Vinnie says.

"Real license? Don't tell me you—"

"Hurry up would you," he says, holding the elevator door.

"I can't believe you."

He chuckles. "You're not the first, sweetheart."

When the elevator opens onto a waiting room, Gretchen rushes me. I pass off Miranda's leash to Vinnie.

"Thanks so much for coming," she says, hands flapping. Except for the bloodshot eyes, she's still every bit the beauty queen, all decked out in a pink velour track suit emblazoned with a designer logo of a crown in rhinestones. Skin-tight pants hang over rhinestone-sequined sneakers made without any athletic purpose in mind. Over her shoulder stands a squat man in a tuxedo. Anton Slim, I presume, although slim he is not. He's as big around as he is tall. Balding. Puffy face. Bow tie undone, a limp ribbon around his bull neck. What I assume to be a red wine stain mars the front of his pin tuck shirt. Arms braced across his barrel chest, he's rocking back and forth on his heels, the high polish of his shoes reflecting the fluorescent light from the ceiling strips.

"I trust you got the check we sent over?" he asks.

"I did. Thank you."

"You'll receive the rest when you get my daughter out of this mess," he says, looking me up and down, which leaves me feeling grossly under-dressed in my Pink Floyd *Dark Side of the Moon* T-shirt and board shorts.

Out of the corner of my eye, I catch Vinnie examining the fronds of a potted palm, Miranda at his side.

"We apologize for being this casual. Mrs. Slim's call was unexpected."

"For some, maybe," Anton says, scowling at Gretchen.

Gretchen glances at Vinnie. "And this is?"

I rest my hand on Vinnie's shoulder. "This is Vincent Vicanti, my investigator. He'll be working with me on Zoe's case."

Vinnie takes Gretchen's hand with a slight bow. "It's a pleasure." He smiles and pets Miranda. "And this here is Miranda."

Gretchen withdraws her hand as if she's touched a hot burner. "She's big."

"And fierce," I say.

Vinnie turns away, pretending to fuss with Miranda's lead to hide an evil little smile.

I slide a single sheet of paper out of my purse and hand it to Gretchen along with a pen. "If we could get a little preliminary business out of the way, I'd appreciate it. If you would please sign this release so I can have access to Zoe and her records."

Anton snatches the form. "Ms. Locke, my wife and I are private people. We're not in the habit of letting strangers nose around in our business or our family. In your line of work, you understand the importance of discretion."

"Of course, Dr. Slim. And believe me, no one wants to keep Zoe's presence here from becoming public more than I do. It's my job to make sure she gets a fair trial, but to do that, I need access."

Anton hikes his pants up over his belly. "We can share any information about Zoe on an as-needed basis. I'm sure Dr. Kesey, the attending psychiatrist for Zoe, will help you with that."

I cut my eyes to Vinnie, one leg bent up, foot against the wall, gnawing on a toothpick.

Gretchen blinks fast to stem the tears bubbling up in the corners of her eyes, threatening to cause her mascara-laden eyelashes to wilt. "Please, honey," she says, stroking Anton's arm.

Anton pulls a pair of wire half-frame reading glasses from his inside pocket, scans the single-spaced text, and shoves the release at his wife. "Sign it if you want, my love."

Using her thigh as a table, Gretchen scrawls her name on the signature line. "You have to get Zoe out of this place, Grace."

"I'll try, but understand this. The doctors think she's a danger to herself, she'll be here for at least seventy-two hours. After that, they can ask a judge to keep her for longer, if they think she's still a danger to herself or others."

"Zoe is not a danger, Ms. Locke!" Anton says, so emphatically that his protruding belly bounces in time with his words. "And I think you would be well-advised to remember you were hired for only one reason."

"Is that so?" I ask.

Anton shoots me a cautionary glare. "Let's just say we all have a lot on the line here,"

His face turns puce, the black enamel studs on his white shirt straining against his heaving chest. Placating the entitled few has never been my strong suit, although I have learned that practiced passivity in the face of power is often the best way to get what you want. For a man like Anton, however, being told what to do, even in polite tones, is not an experience to which he takes kindly.

Gretchen flashes me a wide-eyed look as if to say, *Back off, why don't you?* then turns to Anton and says, "Honey, let's let Grace do her job."

Anton lowers his bulk into a chair and lights up a cigar.

"Have you been in to visit with Zoe?" I ask.

"No, they wouldn't let us talk to her," Gretchen says. "Dr. Kesey says it might upset her even more. When she woke up in here, she wouldn't stop punching and kicking the staff, so they sedated her."

"One thing, though. I don't want any of this to get out to the media or the state attorney before we figure out what it means for her case. Please, don't breathe a word of any of this to anyone."

"You don't have to worry about that, Ms. Locke," Anton says.

Roger that, fat man. As if I didn't get the message the first time.

"Of course, sir," I say, nodding in agreement, until it hits me—I haven't said "sir" since the Army.

But it seems to have done the trick. Anton extends his hand. "Please save our little girl, Ms. Locke."

"Let's go home," Gretchen says, helping Anton to his feet. "We'll come back tomorrow."

As the elevator door closes, I hear Anton's voice. "I told you this would happen again."

"What a lovely couple. Nothing like it. Boobs and a bully, a love match for the ages," Vinnie says, tossing the toothpick in the trash.

"More like one of mutual convenience."

"One man's convenience is another man's trophy wife."

I spot a phone on the wall beside a door with a safety glass window embedded with chicken wire. A sign, Locked Facility. No Unauthorized Visitors, is duct taped to the door. Behind which are people who are not free to leave. No matter what you call them—crazies, criminals, traumatized, evil, or plain scared out of their wits—they're all prisoners in here. But exactly which type Zoe is I need to figure out before they lock her up and throw away the key, or worse.

I grab the phone from its cradle, scroll down the list of extensions taped beside it, and dial Dr. Kesey's number.

"Doctor, this is Grace Locke."

Silence.

"Zoe Slim's attorney. I'd like to see Zoe."

"Not possible."

"Why not? I'm her attorney. I have the right as well as a release signed by her parents."

"Actually, you don't have any such right. Not here. This is a psychiatric hospital, not a jail. I get to say who sees a patient. And for now, Zoe is in no condition to see anyone, release or no release."

"Also, I'd like a copy of her chart."

"All medical records requests have to be made through the Administrative Office on the first floor between 9 a.m. and 5 p.m., Monday through Friday. Have a good night," she says in a monotone and hangs up.

Anger rises up in my chest at the thought of Zoe's chart

sitting on Dr. Kesey's desk. The girl must be under constant monitoring on a suicide watch. There's no way the chart has been filed away already. But fighting bureaucracy is futile.

"Maybe if I had listened to her, she wouldn't have—" I say, pacing around, Miranda Velcroed to my side.

"Let's go, kid. None of this is your fault," Vinnie says, shepherding Miranda and me to the elevator. "Don't go taking the blame for something you didn't do. It's enough that we have to take the blame for what we did do."

Chapter 13

I can't sleep. Again. And on the rare night when sleep does come, the nightmares return.

I dangle my arm over the side of the futon and stroke Miranda's fur until the first rays of sunrise worm their way between the missing slats in the blinds, another thing Vinnie keeps forgetting to fix. Unlike me, Miranda's snoring with the innocent contentment reserved for babies and rescued mutts. Me? I'm resigned to the fact that it's hopeless to even attempt to sleep at this point.

One minute, I'm a pathetic, bleeding-hearted fool for being taken in by Zoe's histrionics, the next, it's my fault for not hearing her out.

Out of habit, I dig my phone out from under the pillow. A new email. At this hour? It's from someone at sao.gov, the State Attorney's Office, with an attachment labeled Motion to Revoke Bail.

"What the hell?"

Under Miranda's Zen-like gaze, I grab a suit off the

handlebars of the stationary bike/clothes rack, splashing my face with cold water before attempting to brush my teeth with a hairbrush.

"That jackass Steiner or Steinman or whatever his name is," I mutter, trying to make out the Assistant State Attorney's scrawl at the bottom of the motion. "Freakin' cheap shot, filing a motion to revoke Zoe's bond exactly four hours before the time of a hearing he must have set up online in the middle of the goddamned night."

I strap on Oscar. "Technically she's in violation of Garrison's house arrest order, but holy mother of God, she left on a stretcher. It's not as if she sneaked out to drink beer with her friends in a park like I used to do."

Miranda sits stock still.

"Mental health care in the jail is bullshit. But ASA what's-his-face will argue it's just fine for Zoe. I've seen the psych pod" I say, pulling on a blouse that could do with an ironing. "It's a hell hole where the staff have been known to derive morbid pleasure from strategically pairing cellmates with conflicting psychiatric diagnoses. They once bunked a catatonic schizophrenic in with a bipolar man who talked twenty-four seven. After several days of getting no response from his catatonic cellmate, the bipolar man resorted to beating him to get him to talk, hitting him so hard he broke eight ribs and punctured a lung. Pathologically mute, the catatonic man suffered in silence for hours until a psychiatrist found him in curled in the fetal position on the concrete floor covered in his own feces. Nice, huh?"

A head tilt to the left from the dog.

"What? I'm going soft?"

Head tilt to the right.

"Stop that!"

The judge's name on the upper right-hand corner of the motion catches my eye. Not Garrison, but a trial judge, the result of random computer selection, a game of judicial bingo. And the winner is? The Honorable Josiah Twietmeyer. Back to square one ingratiating myself and Zoe with a new judge.

When I fling open the door, the humidity slaps me in the face like a wet rag, but the grandeur of the rising red-velvet sun, a fiery bridge between the horizon and the cotton-ball sky, makes the sticky discomfort worthwhile. For a brief second, I stand and marvel at Mother Nature.

"Well, well. Look who's up bright and early," Vinnie says from downstairs, broom in hand.

"Don't say another word. Not one thing about me not being an early bird. And nothing about why I'm wearing this itchy straight-jacket of a suit in the middle of July." I struggle downstairs, Oscar swinging wide each time I try to speed up, but Miranda hippity-hopping behind me as if it's the most natural thing in the world to be a canine tripod.

"It might be within the rules and everything to let the other side know about a hearing with only four hours to spare, but I am sure the legislature of the great State of Florida did not mean hearings should be set in the middle of the f'ing night."

Vinnie holds his hand out.

"No, not this time, old man. I'm not giving you ten damn bucks for saying f'ing, I mean, shit, it's not even a—"

Vinnie doubles over in laughter.

"Not like he couldn't have filed the damn thing yesterday. Maybe as a professional courtesy?" I jut my chin out at him. "Am I right? Or am I right?"

"Calm down, will ya? And just what motion are we talking about here, sweetheart?"

"To haul Zoe back to jail. Take away her bail."

"Isn't she locked up in the loony bin?"

"That's the point. She's supposed to be home, but she's not. Why? Because she tried to kill herself. Where? At home. Not exactly the best argument for persuading the judge to let her go back home. What I don't get is how the State knew? The hospital can't even say she's there. It's protected health info. Maybe the cops who took her in...I don't know." Out of the corner of my eye I spy Miranda squatting on her back leg, poised to water Vinnie's tomato plants.

"Hey, hey, no you don't!" he screams, shooing her away from the plants with his ball cap. "Hey, Gracie, she's a girl, right?"

"What? Zoe?"

"No, Miranda. Your dog. Ain't girl dogs supposed to, you know, squat?"

"She may be nuts, but it's not like she broke the rules to sneak out to a party."

"Who? Miranda?"

"No, for God's sake. Zoe."

He throws his arms up. "*Per l'amor di Dio!* Start at the beginning of whatever it is that's got you all pissed off."

I point at him. "You owe me ten now. So let's call us even."

He shakes his head hard. "Not a chance. You're into me for twenty. I only owe you ten."

"Okay. Since you asked, the State is trying to revoke Zoe's bail because she violated the judge's order."

Vinnie puffs out his cheeks. "I'm no lawyer, but the kid did try to off herself. Seems like she needs to be in a hospital, not a jail."

"Maybe, or maybe it's all an act. Maybe she wants to *look* crazy."

"You sayin' she's crazy like a fox?"

"It's a possibility. I mean she wouldn't be the first murderer I've seen put on a show."

"I remember this wise guy back in New York who went around in his bath robe and slippers to dodge a murder beef."

"Did it work?"

"Nah, they got him in the end. Just like they always do," he says, unlocking the office. "One thing I know for sure is that the government don't give a plugged nickel about following rules, so long as they get what they need to screw with you."

I look away, ashamed I was once a tool of the system that took away years of his life based on a lie, something I swore

I'd never let happen again. And I won. But the way the State is pushing full-speed ahead on this, I'm getting the creeping sense of inevitability I used to get when I had a defendant dead to rights and there wasn't anything the defense, no matter how good, could do about it.

As quickly as Vinnie's face hardened a few seconds ago, it brightens. "You're a smart cookie. You'll find a way. From what you're saying about that bozo making a sneak attack, I'd guess you know more than a little about how the game is played. That motion trick. The four-hour-rule thing you said. I'm thinking you've done this kinda thing in the past?" He wags a finger at me and steps into the street to hail a passing taxi. "Your chariot awaits."

Miranda's stares up at me, her bearing so trusting, despite what she's been through. "I'm sorry, girl. I have to go to work. We'll go to the beach when I get home, okay?"

She lets out two high-pitched yips.

I hold out the leash. "Would you mind? I need to get to the courthouse."

"Don't worry about your little girl," Vinnie says, fishing a treat from his pocket. "I'll take care of her. Now you go grab that bozo by the balls."

***

I text Gretchen to tell her to get over to the courthouse.

A few seconds later, she responds, "We'll be there."

"Any chance you could go a little faster?" I ask the taxi driver.

The driver is non-responsive. He's ignoring me or, more likely, he doesn't speak English. For some reason, the Yellow Cab company considers it brilliant marketing to hire drivers who speak no English and have no idea where they're going. Whatever this one's problem is, he's driving like he's visually impaired, all hunched forward on the steering wheel.

I stick my head through the smudged glass partition like an irate ostrich. "Hey, buddy. Can you help me out here? I'm gonna be late for court." I say, jabbing my finger at the clock on the dashboard which has only one hand, stuck on three.

He tunes the radio to a station playing some kind of chanting, which sounds more like cats being strangled than music.

"Court. You know, the place where you go to pay speeding tickets? Not that you've ever gotten one of those," to which the driver mutters a few words in a foreign language I don't recognize.

I slump back onto the stained cloth back seat. Better not to think too hard about what might have gone on back here.

"Please go south by the beach and across Las Olas. Don't take Sunrise, too much traffic during rush hour," I say. Both my possible theories for the driver's non-responsiveness, ignorance, and/or linguistic incapacity are invalidated by his continuing straight on the beach road, as requested.

"At least that's something," I say, and he flashes me a dirty look in the rear-view mirror.

To contain the knot of anxiety in my stomach, I belly breathe, the one suggestion made by my shrink, Dr. Fleming, that calms me, helps to bring my stress levels below those of a long-tailed cat in a room full of rocking chairs, an expression used by my mother to describe her jangled nerves before hosting one of her society lady events with finger sandwiches and tea.

Breathe in. Hold. Breathe out. Repeat.

Outside, a tropical diorama drifts by. A hazy mirage. Rich abutting ramshackle. Beach kitsch next door to the Ritz. Gone are the crazy spring break days with wasted college students falling off motel balconies, replaced by luxury hotels where twenty-dollar watered-down drinks are as common as wet T-shirt contests used to be. The innocence of Connie Francis and George Hamilton in *Where the Boys Are*, all unceremoniously replaced by gold-chain-draped rappers and silicone-enhanced hotties.

I'm not against change, it's inevitable, healthy even, but the wholesale substitution of the city's character with ersatz class in the name of progress does make me sad. There's something to be said for a cold Bud and a Philly cheesesteak at The Parrot, an iconic dive bar, the kind of joint where the old timers have occupied the same bar stools since the Nixon administration. The kind of place where the checks are accurate only for tourists and barkeeps charge the locals what they can afford. Or maybe I'm just getting old and nostalgic for a time that never was. I rub my stump, which is swollen from the heat.

As the taxi pokes along, I survey the morning parade along the beach. Guy dressed as a sailor with a squawking macaw on his shoulder, check. Geezer with skin like elephant's hide walking with bronzed blonde in bikini that looks to have been constructed from dental floss, check—boy or girl? I've never been sure. European tourists wearing socks and sandals, check. And the tide still rolls in and out. Just another day in paradise.

At the summit of the drawbridge over the Intracoastal Waterway, a siren booms from the bridge-tender's cabin and a steel arm descends silently in front of the taxi. The clenching jaws of the span rise and split apart to allow passage for a tall-masted sailboat. Below, a fleet of luxury motor yachts litters the marina like discarded origami, huddled together under the baking sun, most only used once in a blue moon, and otherwise left to bob in placid waters until their owners decide it's time to come back and play with their toys.

Inching toward downtown on Las Olas Boulevard, we pass The Isles, fingers of land separated by waterways. Palatial homes rise from the coral-rock isthmuses with names like Lido Isle, Solar Isle, and the Isle of Capri. The Italianate nomenclature is responsible for the city's moniker, the Venice of America, yet the canals are man-made and the architecture is more Mediterranean than Medicean, illusions of permanence built for show.

I ignore a stab of regret as we pass the entrance to Idlewyld Isle and switch my mind into tactical mode, much like I did when I was an MP. Enemy identified. Mission planned. Time to execute. Emotions are for sissies.

The driver rolls to a stop at the courthouse beside the concrete barricades erected after 9-11 to counter a terrorist attack, a laughable precaution given what they are protecting is a pressure cooker filled with vengeful, violent miscreants, many with nothing to lose, much like those the barricades are trying to keep out.

I go in through the main entrance in the old wing. Three doors to channel the masses: Attorneys, Jurors, and Visitors. As usual, there's a jackass who thinks his hoodie and saggy pants will allow him to pass incognito through the Attorneys line. The deputy on duty is not having it, however, and the interloper is escorted to the back of the Visitors line.

I place my briefcase and purse on the belt of the metal detector and walk through the body scanner.

Beep, beep, beep.

The deputy points at my feet, meaning, do my shoes have a metal shank in them? I shake my head and raise my pant leg to show him Oscar. He hesitates for a second before waving me through. Soon enough, folks here will catch on. It's just that they still remember me in my old incarnation. Sky high heels. Ego to match. Neither applicable now.

"Hello there, stranger," the deputy says, a tall man with a gray buzz cut and a warm smile.

"Deputy, deputy..." I say, as he hands me my possessions, racking my brain for his name.

"Tanner's still the name. And I assume Locke's still yours?"

I feel a blush blooming on my cheeks. Tanner's been a fixture at the main entrance for almost as long as I've been alive. "Deputy Tanner, of course."

Despite being on in years, Tanner still has the tight muscled physique that announces *mess with me at your own risk*. Never once did I see his polite manner fail him, not even when things got heated with people pushing and shoving to get to court on time, but he had no qualms about extracting the nightstick from his gun belt, although he never used it.

As I'm about to step away, Tanner puts an arm in front of me, stopping my forward progress. I brace myself, primed as I am to read trouble into even the most innocent of acts, but he stoops to my height and whispers in my ear. "Don't let the turkeys get you down. If I had a dollar for every lawyer and judge in this building that's been popped on a DUI, I'd already be living *la vida* up in Panama City Beach, if you know what I mean." He stands back. "Glad you're back, Counselor."

A sense of well-being washes over me. I give Tanner a thumbs up, struck as I always am, that so many of the people who work in this place, a cauldron of misery and loss, can be so kind, so civil, as if exaggerated humanity is the antidote to all the evil and hopelessness on display within its walls. I hope one day, I too will be forgiven, able to see the bigger picture again, be part of the collective effort to rise above the grimness. But for now, I feel like a spotlight is trained on me, and only me, even though I'm just one of hundreds trying to get to court on time to do her job.

Chapter 14

The ancient elevator lurches its way up to the third floor, the transit point to the new wing of the courthouse. The old wing has nine floors, the penthouse having been the county jail years ago, back before incarceration became an industry. The old wing has a musty smell due to the fact that there's mold in every nook and cranny, which has led to a slew of lawsuits. One was brought by a judge who claimed the mold caused her to develop an autoimmune disorder, although those who endured her tirades speculate it was her noxious soul that made her sick. Whatever it was, she died soon after she filed the suit, and the mold continues to grow unabated.

I cross the bridge to the new wing, a modern glass-and-steel structure housing the criminal divisions. The courtrooms in this part of the complex were designed to be large enough to keep the judges at more than striking distance from the defendants, and decorated in neutral tones, a doomed attempt to project a sense of calm, a mood not often on display in an environment where freedom is currency and life is cheap.

I squeeze through the morning crush, staring down a few double takes from former colleagues and adversaries. No way they expected to see me back in this building today, or any other day for that matter.

The thought tickles me a little and I feel, what? A little bold? Perhaps a little badass? Maybe I *can* come back?

As a child, the admonition, "No you can't," always baited my inner devil. Like the time my mother insisted, "No, you can't play on the boys' hockey team, dear. Perhaps, you should consider ballet." Ballet my ass. I strapped on the goalie's pads for what ended up being three winning seasons and two missing front teeth. Or the time my father said, "No, you can't enlist in the Army, Grace, dear. Ivy League graduates don't enlist in the Army. They run the Army." I signed up anyway. Two tours of duty and one accurate IED later, and I still deny foolhardiness had anything to do with my decision.

On automatic pilot, I find myself in front of Room 5800, Judge Twietmeyer's courtroom, and barrel through the two sets of doors designed to keep the hallway noise out and the court's business in. I head into the well, taking in the veritable cornucopia of humanity. Not one empty seat in the gallery. Worried family members, friends, and maybe even enemies, sit side by side. A rabbi in the front row hunches beside a guy in a leather biker vest who, apparently, finds it difficult to say no to tattoo artists. The back row is lined with cops. There are the obligatory girlfriends in stripper heels and tube tops, court being the only place they can see their men without a glass partition in between. An old woman fingers worry beads as the crackhead next to her picks at track marks like a nautical chart on his forearm.

A chain gang of inmates shuffles in from the holding cells, the singular scent of fear wafting off their soiled jumpsuits.

Oh, how I've missed the smell of crime in the morning.

I drop my briefcase on the only empty seat behind the defense table around which State and defense lawyers are going at it hammer and tongs, horse-trading the futures of the accused. The clerk, chewing gum in a way that says, *Been there, done that, nothing new under the sun,* is perched next to the empty bench. The court reporter is seated on a stool below the bench, fingers poised over the spindly three-legged device into which she will type every word uttered today in an alien language that looks more like chicken scratches than words. That chicken scratch will be used to condemn or exonerate.

I spot Zoe, slumped over, the lone inmate in the back row of the jury box, and the lone female. Disheveled, swamped by a jumpsuit for someone twice her size. Two burly sheriff's deputies, one on each side, stand guard as if she's some kind of serial killer. If she's got enough life left in her to kill a fly, I'd be surprised, given how doped up she looks. They're likely the pair who dragged her here from Lauderdale East like a rag doll under the dubious auspices of the violation of bail warrant attached to the motion to revoke bond. True, Garrison was explicit. Bail was granted conditional upon Zoe being confined to her home. But then she had to go and try to kill herself, giving the State the technicality it needed to throw her back in jail until her trial and, if they get their way, forever.

"All rise. The Honorable John J. Twietmeyer presiding," the bailiff announces at the exact same moment the doors at the back of the courtroom part, and Gretchen and Anton Slim enter like the guests of honor at a state dinner. Heads on swivels, everyone turns to face the fashionably late couple whose designer clothes and confident bearing set them apart from the little people.

The bailiff hustles over and manufactures space for them to sit where none had been before, by ordering an old man in a yarmulke and a small boy wearing a Sponge Bob T-shirt to squeeze up nearer to the others in their row.

Judge Twietmeyer, a middle-aged, portly man with Harry Potter glasses and a dubious comb-over, stays standing for a second, observing the Slims, before sinking into his black leather throne. I've appeared in front of Twietmeyer many times. He's fiercer than his appearance suggests. A former prosecutor, Twietmeyer's sympathies tend to lie with the State, cold comfort to me now.

"Good morning all, and it is a fine one, isn't it?" he asks rhetorically.

A few mumbles of "Yes" and "Uh-huh" from the group.

I stay silent. I dislike obsequious judicial pleasantries. A simple "Good morning" would reflect better on the black robe worn by every judge to convey impartiality. But some judges can't help themselves from reveling in their authority only to wind up sounding like imperious asses.

"I shall be calling the docket this morning in random order. Please do not get up and wander off if you have an interest in any case in particular. And especially if you are an out-of-custody defendant. Be warned, your absence will necessitate my issuing a bench warrant for your arrest, which would be unpleasant, indeed. For you, that is."

Preliminaries complete, Twietmeyer gets to work, calling case after case. Some are pleas of not guilty, others of guilty or no contest. Motion hearings and trial dates get set. Finally, he gets to "State versus Zoya AKA "Zoe" Slim."

The ASA stays seated until I'm at the lectern, affecting the nonchalance of one accustomed to high-profile cases. With a prefatory sigh, he announces his appearance for the record in a tone flatter than the topography of his employer. "Assistant State Attorney Robert Hightower for the great State of Florida."

I can't help but smile at the addition of "great" to the state's name, a direct lift from Florida's official seal, a grandiose flourish I wasn't above using when I was in his shoes.

Hightower is tall and reed thin, but he's not Stein what's-his-name, the signatory on the wee-hours ambush motion. Likely he had one of his more junior minions burning the midnight oil.

"Grace Locke, counsel for Ms. Slim, who is seated in the back of the box, Your Honor." I point at Zoe. Head bandaged. Wearing a red-and-black striped jumpsuit—not an orange one like the other inmates—with Maximum Security Risk stamped on the back.

When I turn to check the clock above the door, conscious of the short time the judge will give me to be heard, I spot Reilly propped up against the back wall, file folder clutched in his right hand, no doubt filled with evidence to convince the judge to lock Zoe up again.

It's odd. The State rarely goes to the trouble of dragging lead detectives in to testify about the details of an investigation for hearings to revoke bail. The affidavit of arrest usually suffices. Hearsay for sure, but the hearsay rule is for trials and, even then, is as shot through with holes as Swiss cheese. "Save your arguments for the jury," is what Twietmeyer will say if I make a hearsay objection.

Judge Twietmeyer removes his glasses. "Ah, you're Zoe Slim?" he says, his tone more question than statement. Perhaps his confusion is a product of her obvious youth, but chances are it's the jumpsuit, the uniform reserved for the worst of the worst which is at odds with the fact that she looks incapable of hurting a flea.

Head buried in her chest, Zoe doesn't answer.

"Judge, if I may," I say.

"Counsel, what is it? As you can see, we are busy here today."

I give a quick nod in concession. "Yes, but before we begin, may I ask why my client is dressed in that jumpsuit?" I'm asking, not because I am concerned about the hellacious conditions in maximum security, but to bait Hightower into overreacting.

And it works.

"Your Honor, Ms. Slim is a dangerous felon. Not only did she savagely kill—"

"Objection. Objection!"

Twietmeyer raises both hands to forestall either of us from saying another word. "Ms. Locke, would you like to be heard on why you think what the Assistant State's Attorney is saying is objectionable?"

My mind's racing from one thought to the next. Painting the ASA as a hothead to generate sympathy for the sad creature in the box is a long shot, but Zoe's age and condition are the only things I have going for me. I'm rusty. Or maybe it's that I have no idea what I'm doing over here on this side of the courtroom. After all, I am a rookie at this game. As a prosecutor, I had a script. Now I have to make everything up from whole cloth, and make the fabrication ring true.

"Respectfully, may we approach the bench?" I ask, trying not to sound overly solicitous, a dead giveaway for weakness.

"Judge, I don't think—"

"Mr. Hightower, you can tell me whatever is on your mind right up here in front of the bench. I don't bite."

The judge's remark elicits a nervous chuckle from the gallery, but his mordant stare shuts the hilarity down just as fast.

Tight-lipped, we march up to the bench, and wait in silence until the court reporter has shimmied herself and her contraption over to record our sidebar. A few spectators crane their necks to watch the impending brouhaha. Others use the interruption in the proceedings to take a cat nap.

"Ms. Locke, please proceed. We don't have all day."

"Your Honor, my client was detained in a locked psychiatric ward on a Baker Act hold because she was found to be a danger to herself. And that's what the State is asserting violates her bail."

"And others," Hightower says.

"Excuse me, Mr. Hightower?"

"She's a danger to others too, Your Honor."

"That's enough, Mr. Hightower, you'll have your turn." Twietmeyer flips to me. "Ms. Locke?"

"The very fact that Ms. Slim was Baker Acted is protected health information and, as such, is subject to the confidentiality protections of HIPAA, the Health Insurance—"

Twietmeyer groans. "Yes, counsel, I know what HIPAA is. Please do us all the favor of getting to the point, if you have one."

"Judge, I am objecting to any of this hearing being held in open court. My esteemed colleague here," I say, staring daggers at Hightower before continuing. "My colleague, ASA Hightower, served me with a motion to revoke my client's bail in the early hours of this morning. Or, his lackey did. A Mr. Stein-something. I'm sorry, the signature on the motion was illegible."

"Ms. Locke, I can do without the witty sarcasm. It'll do your client no good in my courtroom. I find it disrespectful which, I assume, is not the tone you are going for, correct?"

I attempt to look chastened. "I apologize, Your Honor. Anyway, had I been given the opportunity, I would have made a written motion to seal this hearing, but given the eleventh-hour tactics, that was not possible. Therefore, I am making my motion *ore tenus*," I say, pleased with myself for remembering the Latin for "orally."

Twietmeyer stirs the air with his index finger to tell me to get a move on.

"The fact that my client is hospitalized must be kept private, unless she agrees to its disclosure. And she does not. Furthermore, I have not made any motion that would place my client's health or mental health at issue, so I submit to you that this court is obligated to close this proceeding to the public as a matter of law."

Twietmeyer purses his lips, processing what I just said which, I have to admit, was somewhat coherent, although I still feel like I'm way out of my depth.

I've known since the moment I met her that I'd have to have Zoe evaluated both for competency to stand trial and, perhaps, for an insanity defense, but that would mean putting all the sorry details of her suicide attempt and entire psychological history at issue, meaning that all related proceedings would be heard in open court. Not good. At least not before I'm prepared to use it to my advantage. All I want now is a confidential evaluation from a private psychiatrist for leverage to keep her out of the death chamber. Thing is, she did go and try kill herself. So, here we are, with what I want to avoid happening right in front of me—a broadcast to the potential jury pool that Zoe is a danger not only herself, but to others, like Sinclair.

"I cannot surmise what evidence the State might bring before the court today that wouldn't breach my client's privacy rights under Florida law. And not only Florida law, Judge, but Federal law," I say, letting the word "Federal" ring in Twietmeyer's state court ears.

Twietmeyer tents an eyebrow. "Mr. Hightower, is that correct?"

"Is what correct?"

"Don't play coy with me, Mr. Hightower. What is the nature of the evidence that you intend to bring before the Court, and does it relate to Ms. Slim's medical or psychiatric condition? From where I sit, Ms. Locke has not put her client's mental state into issue." He casts a doubtful look in Zoe's direction. "Not yet, anyway."

Hightower rushes back to the lectern and pulls a stapled report from his file like a rabbit out of a hat.

"Judge, I have a psychological evaluation confirming the defendant as mentally ill, and that she is a danger to herself."

"Again, objection. On the same grounds. Judge, all of this is a bold-faced attempt to prejudice the jury pool with information that is not only protected by Federal law, a body of law over which, with all due respect, this Court has no jurisdiction. His evidence," I say, using my fingers to put the word "evidence" in air quotes, "is not only private and protected, but also hearsay, because the author of the report is not here in this courtroom to be cross-examined."

I'm way beyond winging it now. I have no earthly idea if the last statement is even true, but there's no one in the courtroom who looks like a shrink, although some of the ones I've seen look as unhinged as their patients.

Twietmeyer presses both palms down in front of him as if he's trying to keep the bench from flying away. "Mr. Hightower, this is, indeed, a highly unusual situation. Most motions to revoke a defendant's bail do not involve such sensitive information. But Ms. Locke is, in fact, correct. The nature of the information you wish to present is protected from unauthorized publication by Federal law. And the last time I checked, I'm a state court judge. Decisions that could potentially violate such lofty dictates are not what"—he pauses for a nanosecond—"the great State of Florida pays me to do."

I lower my head to hide the fact that I'm smiling.

"Accordingly, I am going to order this hearing sealed. When the courtroom has been vacated by the public and all other non-concerned parties, you two can have at each other with whatever evidence you have. I will give such evidence whatever weight I deem appropriate in deciding if Ms. Slim stays in custody."

Twietmeyer claps his hands. "Counsel, stand back. And Bailiff, please clear the public and the other defendants from the courtroom. The only people remaining should be Ms. Slim, her parents, and whatever witnesses either side wishes to testify. And of course, the attorneys can stay. We couldn't do without them now, could we?"

Chapter 15

Here comes Hightower. Smug grin, report flapping.

I sneak a peek at the report.

Dr. Kesey's evaluation from Lauderdale East. How'd he get that?

The Slims would rather drink box wine in public than have it known their only child is anything less than the perfect specimen of orphandom, the poor soul rescued from a life of gruel and hard labor in Russia by the most magnanimous couple on the planet.

Fine, it's not them. But who gave Hightower the damn report?

Hightower leans in and dangles the report in front of my face. "I think you might want to take a look at this, Counsel."

I snatch the report out of his hand.

"It's not exactly much of a mystery is it, Ms. Locke? From what I hear, you used to work for the good guys. Surely you know all the tricks? Or maybe you've forgotten how things work around here."

I'd like nothing better than to put him in his place, but his galling remark flips a switch in my head.

Under a weird quirk of the Baker Act, a civil statute, the State Attorney represents the psychiatric facility where the patient is taken by the cops, meaning Hightower got Kesey's report from the ASA that was at Zoe's initial hearing at Lauderdale West when she was admitted.

I skim the ten-page, single-spaced evaluation—Generalized Anxiety Disorder, Oppositional Defiant Disorder, rule out Bipolar Disorder. To make things worse, the report details Zoe's history of drug and alcohol abuse, as well as her aggressive behavior at school. A prior suicide attempt. Her self-mutilation. The last line reads "Zoe's condition can be managed with medication and appropriate therapies."

I resist the urge to bang my fist on the table. Twietmeyer can't set eyes on this thing. He'll say Zoe can get treatment in jail and, if he ends up sentencing her in the future, it'll color his view of her as violent and volatile, no matter how impartial he's supposed to be.

I turn around, burst through the gate, and corner Reilly in the back row of the gallery.

"What are you here for, Detective?"

Reilly holds up his hands. "Back off, Counselor. The ASA subpoenaed me."

"It's the gun, right? You figured there's no time like the present to make a good first impression on His Honor? An indelible, incriminating one?"

Reilly stretches his arms along the back of the bench. "Calm down, why don't you, Grace? Your pal Sonny told you about all of this, didn't he?"

I clench my fists at my sides. "It's Ms. Locke to you, Detective."

"Oh, dear. I think you haven't quite got used to losing yet, but you'd better do so and quick. And I'd advise you not to be like every other defense hack in this building and stop yourself from going down the road of actually feeling sorry for your clients. It's not a good look. Especially not on a former hard-ass such as yourself, Ms. Used-to-be-ASA Locke."

"Speaking of asses, I've got your number. What I did tell your partner was that if you even dare to try screwing with me on this case, I'll make sure you go down for good this time." Reilly's whiskers twitch.

I take a step closer. "And, by the way, you're the last ass I'd ever ask for advice. You wouldn't know the law if it smacked you in the ass."

I stride over to the jury box and drop into a seat beside Zoe, who is rocking back and forth, eyes closed. "Okay, here's the plan."

No response. More rocking.

I bump her arm with my elbow. "Earth to Zoe. I need you here and now. Zoe, pay attention."

Her eyes spring open, wild and searching, like an animal in a leg trap deciding whether to chew off the limb or wait to die.

"See that guy over there?"

"The asswipe who arrested me?"

"On that we can agree. Well, that asswipe is going to tell the judge that the gun that killed Sinclair was found in your locker, had your fingerprints on it, and belonged to your dad."

"That's all old news," she says, in the bratty way teenagers have of implying anything uttered by anyone over twenty is crap.

"When the ASA says it had your fingerprints on it, I need you to freak out."

She scrunches up her face.

"You know how to freak out, don't you?"

"What?"

"Come on, I know you know how. Dr. Kesey's report confirms you've freaked out a time or two."

Zoe wets her lips.

"We need to buy time, Zoe. You don't want to go back to jail, do you?"

A slight nod of the head.

"You know what crazy looks like, don't you?"

A more decisive nod this time.

"Do it, Zoe. Make them believe you're totally off the chain."

Twietmeyer reappears. "Counsel, let's proceed. I don't have all day."

"Let the show begin."

***

"The State calls Detective Reilly to the stand," Hightower says.

Reilly heaves his girth onto the stand, pulling the microphone towards his mouth, eyes fixed on me.

Since it's the State's motion, it's up to Hightower to justify his request to revoke Zoe's bail with evidence. Enough to convince the judge she is a risk to public safety or a flight risk, and that the State has at least some evidence of her guilt, hardly a stretch here.

I find myself repeating the anachronistic legal standard from the Florida Code of Criminal Procedure in my head, like a mantra. Proof is evident and presumption of guilt is great. Proof evident and presumption great. The same standard I brandished like a sword to keep many a bad guy locked up. But what the heck does that even mean?

Reilly lowers his eyes to where his notes would be. If he had notes. What he needs to say requires no preparation. It's simple. It's all about the gun.

And what other incriminating tidbits might they have unearthed during the investigation I don't know about? The deadline for the State to turn over all of the evidence against Zoe is more than a week away, so I'm flying blind. I need an Academy-Award-winning performance of bat-shit crazy from Zoe. A bed in a psych ward isn't ideal, but it beats three hots and a cot in the jail when you're a little rich girl with an attitude problem.

After swearing him in, Hightower gets straight to the business.

"Detective, did you find the weapon used to murder Mr. Sinclair?" Hightower's hands are clasped like a choirboy. No notes on the lectern. He thinks he's got this in the bag.

"Yes, we did. After we found Mr. Sinclair's body in his office, we obtained a search warrant, and initiated a search of the premises. We located the murder weapon, a Glock 19, stuffed in a gym bag inside the defendant's locker."

"And were there any fingerprints on the gun?"

I hold my breath in anticipation of the evidentiary depth charge, the one upon which this case rests. The one which could put the murder weapon in Zoe's hand and a needle in her arm.

"Yes, the defendant's fingerprints were on the gun, and the ballistics revealed the bullets extracted from the victim's body matched that same weapon."

"Liar! Liar!" Zoe screams, stabbing her finger at Reilly.

"You will contain yourself, Ms. Slim, or I will have you removed." Twietmeyer's eyes flick to Zoe and back to Hightower, who is pacing back and forth in front of Reilly like a TV lawyer.

"And did the weapon have a serial number?"

"Yes. It was registered to Anton Slim, the defendant's father."

In the front row of the gallery, Anton buries his face in his hands.

I shoot a wide-eyed glance over my shoulder at Zoe and nod.

On cue, Zoe follows her initial salvo with, "Screw you, you screwball!" A pause, followed by, "You're a lying bastard! You're all lying bastards! Kangaroo court. Kangaroo, kanga-roo-roo. Kangaroo. Bastard kangaroos," all of which she accompanies with the repeated slamming of her cuffed hands on the back of the seat in front of her.

Twietmeyer, who had slipped low in his seat during Reilly's testimony, to the point his glasses are barely visible above the bench, bounces up and bellows into the microphone. "If you cannot control yourself Ms. Slim, I will have you removed!"

"You don't care, Judge. Nobody cares. Care bear. Don't care.

Screw the bears."

Zoe flings herself back in her chair, curls into a ball, and launches into an off-key rendition of "The Star-Spangled Banner."

"Ms. Slim, that's enough. Ms. Locke, please control your client."

Before I have the chance to do or say anything, Zoe throws herself on the ground and bangs her head on the floor several times.

Apparently, the judge pressed the panic button under the bench, because four deputies, weapons drawn, wearing bulletproof vests, burst through the courtroom door.

"Detective, you may step down. And deputies, please escort Ms. Slim from the courtroom," Twietmeyer says, smoothing back what little hair he has with a shaky hand.

"I was with—" she says, as two deputies, one on each arm, drag her past me at the defense table, her shackled feet dragging behind.

Unable to hear what she said and anxious no one else does, I jump up and follow, but a third deputy orders me back to my seat.

A stunned silence freezes the scene. The Slims are clutching each other. Twietmeyer's chest is heaving. Hightower's cowering behind the clerk, who is making a show of filing her nails.

I seize the moment. "Judge, may I be heard?"

"Yes, yes, you may proceed, Ms. Locke."

"As the Court can see, my client is mentally unstable. I would ask the indulgence of the Court that this hearing be suspended for now, given her extreme condition, and that she be taken to the state psychiatric hospital. It's a locked facility. There will be no risk of her going anywhere, or of her further hurting herself."

All that's visible of Hightower is the crown of his head. Seated back at his post, he's searching for the legal equivalent of a lifeboat in a dog-eared volume of the Florida Criminal Statutes.

"I am ordering Ms. Slim be transferred to Everglades State Hospital. And, not to waste this Court's time coming back here for a third hearing for Ms. Slim, I am ordering the initial bond of one million dollars be reinstated when, and if, the good doctors decide Ms. Slim is no longer a danger to herself or others."

"But, Judge—" Hightower's whiny words echo off the walls in the almost empty chamber.

The judge flees the bench before Hightower can finish his comment. Soon enough, he'll realize he should have asked the Court to appoint a psychologist to examine Zoe for competency, a motion typically made by the defense to stall for time, but also an option for the State. That way he would be able to get all the damning details of her mental state back on the record.

The clerk shoots me a toothy grin and points a pen at Hightower, who is flopped back in his chair, hands over his face. It's easy to believe you're always on the side of the angels as a prosecutor. I don't envy him one bit. He's going back to his moldy closet of an office to report defeat to his supervisor who will make him feel like a turd for losing with a stacked deck.

On my way out, Anton grabs my arm. "What the hell happened?"

I spy a pack of reporters gathered by the elevators like a kettle of vultures. "What happened is I saved your little darling a trip back to jail, at least for now. Now you have to do something for me." I motion for the Slims to follow. "Come on. Not here."

We crowd into the stairwell, my back against the heavy steel door to keep the jackals at bay. "I bought us a little time to figure out who might have wanted Sinclair dead, someone that's not named Zoe. I need all her medical and psychiatric records now, and by now, I mean yesterday."

"Ms. Locke, I—" Anton starts.

"Stop," I say, waving him off. "Copies of everything, and I mean now."

"This is hard for my wife," he says, pulling a handkerchief from his pocket and gently wiping Gretchen's tears away as if she were a child. "We'll get her doctors to email you everything right away. Sadly, it's not a happy tale, but she's our only child, and—"

"I'm doing everything I can for your daughter. That's why you hired me, correct?"

"Of course, it is."

Chapter 16

I stare out the window and groan. "A monsoon. Perfect."

Miranda hops up beside me by balancing on her one back leg and placing her catcher's-mitt-sized paws beside my hands on the window sill, her huge head cocked to the side as if to say, "Speak dog, why don't you?"

Side by side, we stare into the rain blowing on shore in hypnotic waves, the wind whipping the ocean over the sea wall like a relentless taskmaster.

Miranda trails me to my munchkin-sized closet and settles herself on the dog bed Vinnie bought for her, a pseudo couch upholstered in red velvet.

I hold up a black Prada suit.

A low growl.

"You're right. Too fancy. It'll look like I don't need a cent at the mediation."

Then jeans. "Too casual?"

She looks away, one eye narrowed. "Bad idea. Too scorned, angry wife with no respect for the legal process, only one of which is true."

Trying to strike a balance, I hang up the suit along with the I-don't-give-a-damn jeans and opt instead for black pants and a blue button-down. I hold the outfit up in front of me. "What do you think? Faith would say it looks too manly, wouldn't she?"

She barks once.

"I agree. The perfect choice."

I slip into the clothes and check myself in the mirror. "Apart from you, Oscar," I say, patting him, "suburban housewife all the way. Not a trace of Racy Gracie."

"Give me that!" I grab a high-heeled shoe from Miranda's slobbery jaws. "Gotta be tall, even if I have to limp a little."

Experience has taught me that tall, good-looking people get more respect and get more of what they want than short, ugly ones. Fat ones are doomed no matter their height. True? Yes. Unfair? Also, yes. And I do love my heels, one-legged or not. It took some work, but I've trained myself to walk on them again since acquiring Oscar.

Miranda settles her head on her paws. "Easy for you to look so calm. You're not the one who has to air her dirty laundry in front of a complete stranger." I sit on the futon to put on my shoes. "Not that it matters any more. I'm tired of fighting."

I stroke her coat. "No more fighting for either of us, okay? Even warriors have to give up the fight some time. The key is knowing when to call it. Manny kept his end of the bargain and I intend to keep mine."

The Timex I won in a poker game in Iraq says tells me it's two minutes until the bus arrives. "Gotta run. Well, hobble," I say. "You stay here. I can't risk sicking you on Manny if he acts like a douche." She nuzzles my leg. "See, I knew you didn't know what I was saying. If you did, you'd be game to ride shotgun."

I grab a rain jacket and umbrella from the hook behind the door and step outside. The parking lot's swamped, cars in water halfway up their wheel wells, but Vinnie's parked at the bottom of the stairs, hand flapping out the driver's side window.

I fling myself onto the passenger seat. "There's a special place in heaven for you, Vin. I can't believe this rain. It's worse than Ophelia. There's no way the buses will be running on time."

"If you believe the weather girl, it's time to bust out the ark."

"Thank God we have this old boat then."

"Hey, lay off my trusty chariot. Beggars can't be choosers."

I pat the cracked vinyl dashboard. "Your ride is my knight in shining Detroit armor. I thank you, from the bottom of my heart."

As Vinnie steers into the flooded street, I sink into the seat and smile. Even in the worst of times, he's here for me. He may insist he owes me, but in my book, we're all even or, more likely, I owe him now.

"Thanks, Vin. The drowned rat look isn't in fashion for divorce mediations these days."

"How you feeling, kid?"

"Trying not to feel much at all."

"Probably a good idea."

"Would you mind looking in on the mutt while I'm out?"

"Would I mind?" The look on his face flips from serious to joyful in one beat. "What do you think?"

"I suspect there was more to getting Miranda than making a beat-up war dog feel better."

"You calling yourself an old war dog?"

I rub his shoulder. "Thanks."

Driving in a tropical storm is more akin to navigation. Reservoir-sized puddles. Jagged pieces of sea wall broken off and deposited in the road. Blinding rain and the occasional gust of wind so fierce it rocks your vehicle, even a four-thousand-pound hunk of steel like Carmela.

We sail on, Vinnie laser-focused on the road, me under the metronomic spell of the windshield wipers, escaping into a final dreamy montage of what life was like with Manny. Leafy afternoon walks through Riverside Park in New York, oblivious to the cold, warmed by the growing fire between us. How miserable I was when he went home to Miami after graduation and I stayed behind. How he cried when I told him I'd enlisted. His sweet missives when I was deployed—how he yearned for us to be together again, to have a family of our own. The care packages of M&Ms and foot powder which he cautioned in the accompanying note should be stored and consumed separately. How he did his best to keep my demons and leg pain at bay after he coaxed me south and found me my job as an ASA. South Florida was my home too, he assured me. The long hours we both worked were difficult, but we were building something, weren't we? His work as a real estate developer took him away to Tallahassee, some at first, and later, a lot, but he always called to say goodnight. At least until I wasn't there to answer the phone. The all-American success story on the outside. But on the inside, trouble was brewing.

I shake myself. "I just want to get on with it. With my life, or whatever's left of it. Or, maybe I'm done for and there's nothing left."

Eyes glued to the road, Vinnie says, "There's plenty left. Trust me. I know what done for looks like. And you ain't that." He slams on the brakes, shaking a fist. "Goddamn it! Use a turn signal why don't ya! And besides, now you've got someone else to be responsible for."

"You, my friend, are more than responsible for yourself. And that'll be ten bucks."

"Jesus, woman. I meant Miranda," he says and we both laugh hard. "You're gonna be fine, Gracie. Better than fine. Great. See, you and me and Miranda, we're survivors from way back."

***

The mediation is being held in a broom closet-sized room in the old wing. I know the location well. It's the place where summer interns went to do the dirty, at least until courthouse space was at a premium and it was converted into a hearing room. But "converted" is a gargantuan overstatement. The room is scarcely big enough for a scarred wooden table and five rickety chairs, one for each party and their counsel, and one for the mediator. Windowless, the space is lit by one flickering strip which chirps like a cricket.

I'm the first to arrive and choose the seat nearest the door, putting my briefcase on the adjacent chair which would be for my attorney, if I had one. I'm going it alone. Divorce lawyers make me sick, what with their shiny suits and vicious, underhanded tactics, like the mean girls in high school. Poke, poke, poke away until you expose a weakness, and then poke even harder until it bleeds. Not in service of freedom or justice, not even to win—they get paid no matter who comes out on top—but for the almighty dollar.

A couple of minutes after I arrive, a doughy, bespectacled woman enters, trailed by Manny and a tall brunette in a sleek suit and sexy librarian horn-rimmed glasses.

"Janice Bucknell. I'm your mediator," the doughy woman says, extending a hand.

The brunette chimes in. "Candace Knight, counsel for Mr. Martinez." Candace doesn't offer to shake my hand and sits beside Manny, crossing her long legs into pretzel knots.

"Ms. Locke, is it? Or is it Martinez?" Bucknell asks.

"Locke. I kept my maiden name."

"At least that's one less piece of paper you'll have to file when this is all said and done," Bucknell says.

"Sorry?"

"To change your name back, I mean."

No one laughs.

"And do you have counsel, Ms. Locke?"

"No, ma'am. I'm representing myself."

To avoid eye contact with anyone, I occupy myself with reading the divorce petition, even though I can recite chapter and verse on every last allegation Manny leveled against me.

Bucknell explains the ground rules like a school marm who doesn't want any trouble from her students. Each party will share a written settlement offer with the other, and then retire to separate rooms and she will engage in shuttle diplomacy to identify areas of agreement and define those in dispute. If a compromise results, the settlement agreement will be entered as a court order by a judge and its contents will not become part of the public record, an outcome Manny wants more than anything—wayward wives are hardly good for political careers. Abracadabra, no more "us." My only play would be to pressure him with the threat of a trial in open court. That is, if I wanted to. But I don't. A deal's a deal.

Settlement offers exchanged, I follow Bucknell to an adjacent room.

I flip through the document, looking for the time bomb. It has to be here, given I said I'd sign anything.

"Bottom line, there's $40,000 in cash, give or take, to split between you," Bucknell says.

It sounds like a fortune to me now, but it's a small fraction of what we once had, what we squandered on luxuries that seemed like necessities. Dinners, vacations, fancy cars. The thought sickens me.

"And as for the marital domicile, you may buy out Mr. Martinez's share, should you so desire," she says, a preposterous proposition. "If you cannot, as an alternative, he is willing to keep you on the title as joint owner, but he will pay the mortgage and live there. If he sells, he will split any profit with you. As for personal effects, you will work together and submit a written inventory to the court of who wants what."

That's it? I get half of everything? No war? No tit for tat on every last pot and pan out of spite? I agreed to sign whatever he wanted, but I didn't expect he'd make that easy to do. But why? There has to be a catch—I frittered away way more than him, and he can prove it, if he wanted to.

"One last thing, Mr. Martinez will sign a building on Sistrunk over to you."

I feel lightheaded.

"Ms. Locke? What do you think?"

Each time I open my mouth speak, the words stick in my throat, the vocabulary of conciliation not my strongest suit. "It's...the terms are...more than acceptable."

Bucknell pushes some papers across the table. "That's wonderful, dear. I'll ask Ms. Knight to prepare the final divorce decree based on Mr. Martinez's offer. If you could please sign these copies of the offer already signed by Mr. Martinez, one for each of you, that would be good. The divorce will be final one week from today."

Signed paperwork in hand, Bucknell sprints from the room, leaving me staring at Manny's signature on my copy, a signature I've seen so many times alongside my own, on mortgages, loans, checks. It looks alien to me now, like a commonplace word that appears to be misspelled.

***

I find Manny staring out a window by the elevator bank.

"Grace," he says, the sharp edges of his features softened by the fading light of day. He holds out a single key, strung on a red ribbon. "I hope you'll find happiness."

I stand mute, searching his face for any vestige of anger or regret, but all I see is peace, a peace of which I am envious.

He takes my hand and sets the key in my palm. "It needs some work, but it's all yours."

"I don't get it," I say, a quaver in my voice.

"Don't get what?"

I turn away to look out the window, over the city, a steel-and-glass skyline of towers filled with dreamers and hustlers, all looking for their piece of the American dream. Just like we had been. "Why are you caving?"

"It's not caving. Marital property rules are rules. No sense arguing for the sake of it. It's time, time for both of us to forgive and move on."

I curl my fingers around the key, the steel cold in my sweaty palm. My father loved to say, "Nostalgia is a seductive liar" as justification for leaving the past behind, for not gilding memories made fond only by the healing passage of time. I'm quick to heap scorn on people who indulge their regrets, wish for the roads not taken, loves not found, who think the good old days were always brighter, instead of getting on with the now. Is my sudden reticence to walk away simply that? Nostalgia?

Or maybe I *am* getting soft.

I pocket the key.

"You might not believe it, Gracie, but I want the best for you. We're just not the best for each other, anymore."

When the elevator arrives, he steps aside for me to get in.

"Thanks, I'll take the next one."

He leans his back against the doors. "For what it's worth, you're doing a great job on Zoe's case."

I feel my chin tremble. "I'm putting up a fight. It's all I can do."

"Take care of yourself, Ms. Locke."

"You too, Mr. Martinez."

He points outside. "And stay out of the storm. I know how you hate thunder and lightning."

"And change," I mumble, as the doors slide together, the words painful given the lump in my throat.

A hand on my shoulder. "Ms. Locke, how unusual to see you here, back in my neck of the woods."

Hackles spike on the back of my neck and I wheel around, fists balled, hyper-aware of being unarmed.

"Whoa, there!" A man's voice, one I know all too well.

I blink hard and find myself staring into the face of Robert Britt, my former boss and the State's Attorney, the guy who had my possessions dropped on our doorstep with a letter of termination taped to the box mere minutes after my mug shot hit the news.

"Jesus, you scared the crap out of me!"

"I come in peace," Britt says, hands up.

He may be skinny, bald, and as pale as a sheet, a seemingly benign force, but Britt's a two-headed snake. He tolerated me when I was a winner, a foot soldier in his war against crime—his bread-and-butter platform come election time. He was the one who nicknamed me "Locked and Loaded," but he never much appreciated what he called my "gunslinger" ways of prosecuting cases. He hired me because, like him, I went to Ivy League schools, but what he got was a law-and-order zealot with a bum leg and the use of dubious judgment in her personal life.

I pick up my briefcase and walk away, the potential for an altercation a risk I cannot afford.

"You're one lucky lawyer, Grace."

I freeze.

"Getting hired on the Slim case, I mean."

I resist the urge to turn around.

"That's the kind of case you would have been champing at the bit to handle back when you were working for me. A high-profile murder. Funny thing, isn't it? You must have pulled a few strings to get on that gravy train." He clucks his tongue. He's closer now, right behind me. "Bet there's one helluva good story there. The register of his voice drops, his tone conspiratorial. "One you surely don't want getting out, would you?"

I hammer down on the emergency bar and step into the stairwell, acid rushing up my gullet from my churning gut. After the door slams, I grab onto the handrail to steady myself.

It was Reilly taught me you're not paranoid if they actually are out to get you.

Chapter 17

The bus driver is straight out of central casting for a zombie apocalypse flick. A razor-edged beak for a nose. Black stringy hair. A reflection of the windshield wipers slapping back and forth in his glassy stare. He turns on the radio and the Bob Marley classic "I Shot the Sheriff" comes on. I chomp hard on my gum when it gets to the part about a capital offense.

The air conditioning's on full blast which, given the ambient air temperature outside of ninety-five degrees and ninety percent humidity, has fogged up the windows. I clear a porthole with my sleeve and survey the aftermath of the deluge. A few diligent homeowners are sweeping detritus from the patios of their beach-front mansions. Palm fronds, coconuts, empty beer cans, mangled beach chairs, all coated in sand. No matter how rich you are, Mother Nature is always in charge and she treats everyone equally.

The only vehicles on the road are cops and Florida Power & Light trucks, except for one optimistic hooker trolling her turf in a too-tight miniskirt and ripped fishnet stockings. Normally

I wouldn't venture out so soon after a storm, but the endless wind and rain have jangled my nerves and have me searching for relief. A reprieve from the four walls of #7 after mowing through the two-hundred-plus pages of discovery on Zoe's heretofore defenseless case wouldn't be bad, either. Then again, maybe I'm riding the bus on a Sunday morning in the wake of a storm because Jake the bartender is not so hard on the eyes.

Miranda's seated at my feet, ears pricked up as if I've said something to her.

"What? Those words were all in my head. No way you know what I'm thinking."

I pull the cord above my head to signal the driver one stop before the jail complex and the Star. The walk will do my head good. Every visit up here since my release has given me nightmares. Given I'll be spending a lot more time behind bars seeing clients, I need to inoculate myself against the debilitating fear in my gut every time I hear iron gates clanking shut.

We get off at the intersection of Powerline Road and Martin Luther King Boulevard under a bruised slate sky. The streets are deserted. The metal grates on Fancy's Pawnshop are closed up tight. Mr. Prince, the owner, a Jehovah's Witness, never opens on the Sabbath. Otherwise business is twenty-four seven, no matter the weather. Downed tree limbs litter the rutted sidewalks. The only people around are a couple of women smoking at the side door of Garnet Girls, a strip joint, wobbling like baby birds on skyscraper heels, their skeletal bodies trussed into black bustiers. When the back door opens and a hand beckons, they stamp out their cigarettes and disappear inside.

Miranda tripodding along at my side, I construct a mental map of the junkyards, auto body shops, and abandoned lots strewn with trash, to familiarize myself with the geography of the area, to render it less like Fallujah. All war zones freak me out, even if the only ones I see now are on TV, or in my dreams. I wonder if Miranda is equally anxious in this domestic wasteland, one also marred by violence and death, albeit one devastated by homegrown poverty and despair, not war and jihad. Probably not. The dogs with us in Fallujah thought sniffing out explosives and chasing bad guys was a game, not their job, even though the consequences for them could be fatal, a fact about which they were blissfully unaware.

I catch Oscar's toe on a bulbous tree root that has erupted through the sidewalk and stumble forward, catching myself on a lamppost. Reflexively embarrassed, I look around, but no need. No one out here but us girls.

I stop outside the Star to free my hair from the ponytail holder, slip inside, and hop onto my stool.

"Counselor Locke, people are going to talk. If you keep coming in here, they may think it's not the booze that keeps bringing you back."

I feel myself blush for the first time in I have no idea how long.

"And who do we have here?" Jake asks, peering over the bar.

"This would be Miranda."

"Of course it is. What else would a dog of yours be called?"

"I think it's a perfect name."

Jake circles Miranda. "Well, she is a beauty." He freezes. "Wait, she's got only one back leg."

"That makes two of us. Two old war dogs. Not a good set of legs between us."

"Can I pet her?"

"Her vest says no, but I'll make an exception for you. She deserves a little spoiling."

"What service?"

"Marines."

"Semper Fi," he says, smoothing the fur along the length of her back in one long stroke.

"What? You were a Marine?"

He slings a towel over his shoulder and slips back behind the bar. "That's a story for another day, Counselor. But for now, what can I get you? The usual?"

"Roger that and make it a double."

Jake wags a finger at the ease with which the words roll off my tongue.

"I still like to say that. Even if double nothing boozy is just that, nothing."

"And I'll get some water for the little lady, too," he says. "Hey, quit that, would you? Thing's unplugged," Jake shouts to a shaggy looking guy poking at the buttons on the jukebox.

The man pulls a cigarette from behind his ear, looks at it as if he's surprised such a thing would be there, and shuffles outside.

Jake places the keg-sized mug of Coke in front of me and waits for the espresso machine to sputter to life.

I jerk my head at the jukebox. "Who is that?"

"That would be Moose."

He places two steaming shots of espresso in front of me and then places a water bowl on the floor by my feet. I drop both shots into the Coke one at a time and take a sip.

"What brings you up here on a Sunday?"

"Change of scenery. The walls in my tiny hole of a place are closing in on me."

"And you came all the way up here from the beach for this?" he asks, the note of suspicion in his voice well-deserved. If I were a betting woman, one vice I've not acquired despite my love for playing poker, I'd wager Jake has had an unprofessional thought or two about me too, based on the fact that I'm the only customer he allows to run a tab when I don't have cash. And I can't deny it, he has what the French would call *je ne sais quoi*, what I call danger. And while I have a history of being just fine with danger—dangerous men, dangerous places, dangerous habits—Jake's one of the good guys, and good guys don't need a gimp with recurring nightmares and a bad habit of flirting with disaster.

I pat my laptop. "The discovery on Zoe Slim's case that needs reviewing. I needed a homey place to face the brutal facts and not make me wanna drown my sorrows."

"So, you chose a bar? My bar?"

I shrug.

"Should I be worried?" he says, which I take as a reference to my frequently patronizing a bar.

"You're the one barkeep in this town who won't serve me. Besides, it would take more than a few months in the pokey and a trashed career to take me down again. Just too damn stubborn to crawl into a hole and die. So, here I am. In a bar. Your bar. Where the company's good, even if the case sucks."

Unconsciously, I rub the hot spot on my right thigh where the shrapnel is buried.

"You doing okay?" he asks, his warm smile replaced by concern.

"Yep, all good," I say, although my mind is full of my old boss, State Attorney Britt, and the havoc he could wreak for me if he had any inkling about how I maneuvered my way onto Zoe's case.

Jake leans against the back bar, his broad shoulders reflected in the mirror behind the rows of liquor bottles and waits until I look up from the screen.

"I'm good. I am," I say, conscious that my tone rings less confident than intended. "I've been going to meetings every day, got me a sponsor, and—"

"The case, I mean." He snaps the towel at me. "Are you doing okay with your new case?"

"Since you asked..." I jab at the power button on my laptop, imagining it as Britt's eye. "The cops found the murder weapon in Zoe's locker with her prints on it. And it turns out the gun is registered to her father."

His face contorts into a scowl. "Not good at all."

"You're the master of the obvious, Jacko. But since you're so nosy, another reason I'm up here is to do a meet and greet across the street with two new court-appointed clients. Figured I wouldn't have to waste my very valuable time waiting to get in."

"Yeah, what idiot has nothing better to do than to shoot the shit with a couple of criminals the morning after a storm?"

"Just me, I guess, but I need the chump change." I poke my tongue in my cheek. "And they are accused, Jake, accused."

"Now you think they're all innocent."

I bark out a laugh. "Shoe on the other foot is what I've been told."

"And how does it fit?"

I tip my head from side to side. "Jury's still out."

"I'll leave you to get on with it. I've got paperwork to do in the back. If you need me, holler. Or if some unrepentant drunk, other than Moose, wanders in here looking for his next drink, holler louder."

"Roger that."

***

Serial killer or petty thief, the format of the State's discovery packet never varies, but given how big this computer file is, Hightower appears to be covering all the bases and then some.

The first page is the case identifier: State of Florida v. Zoe S. Slim, case number 09-007878CF10A, Division FB/Judge Twietmeyer. Next, the bones of the State's case—a list of witnesses, along with physical and other evidence, including exculpatory evidence, if any exists, but I can't remember even one time I handed over anything that might have let a criminal walk. I'm sure Hightower has also left a few things out accidentally on purpose.

Law enforcement witnesses: Detectives Sorenson and Reilly, Officers Lynch and Bond, and a long list of uniforms on scene at St. Paul's. Next: Wendy Struppe and Jason Oliver, crime scene technicians; Vincent Owen, M.D., the medical examiner; Albert Simpson, fingerprint technician. Civilians: Elaine Bannister and Serena Price. No alibi witness. No surprises.

"She's screwed."

"What?" Jake yells from the back.

I ignore him and get back to reading.

A big fat blank space under the heading Williams Rule/ Exculpatory Evidence.

"No surprise there, I guess."

As much as it used to pain me, the prosecution is required by law to turn over anything that might suggest the defendant might not have done what he or she is charged with. But no such luck for Zoe, the omission of any good news further cementing the hopelessness of my first big case back.

Dr. Owen's grisly autopsy report follows: "Conclusion— cause of death was two gunshot wounds, one to each of the head and groin. Manner of death—homicide." To the point. No need to say more.

The crime scene photos, some of which I saw at the bail hearing, are horrific to the point of being pornographic. Sinclair's body sprawled back in his chair, knees wide. Sinclair's exploded head, clumps of brain tissue on the chair and splattered on the bookshelf. His once white button-down saturated with so much blood that the polo man on the chest is now a gruesome shadow. Sinclair's pants bunched around his ankles, the white rubber toes of his Converse high tops frosted with crimson, topped off with boxers, a repeating pattern of cupid and his bow. I'll say they're too prejudicial, but that won't fly with Twietmeyer. He'll admit them into evidence.

I expel a sigh strong enough to blow several cocktail napkins off a pile and along the bar.

"What's wrong?" Jake says, between swipes at the array of bottles with his squirrel-like feather duster.

I turn the laptop around.

"Nice skivvies," he says.

"You guys always go for the low hanging fruit first," I say, the pun sending Jake into paroxysms of laughter.

"Hey, pay attention here. This is important. What else do you see in the picture?"

He leans in. After a few seconds his eyes widen. "What

a creep! The way the papers talk about him, he was the next coming of Jesus Christ."

I turn the computer back around and hone in on the simple gold wedding band on Sinclair's left ring finger. "Exactly. Maybe our Mr. Sinclair was a regular guy after all, just one who got caught with his pants down."

"So to speak."

"Could be I've got something to work with there," I mumble to myself as I click through the pictures of the Glock 19. A close-up of the serial number. Anton's firearms registration. A grid of shadowy black-and-white images of fingerprints lifted from the gun accompanied by Simpson's conclusion that the prints match Zoe's. I plug earbuds into the headphone jack and click on a file labeled Zoe Slim/Video and hold my breath.

Zoe appears, dressed in her school uniform, a white polo shirt and pleated plaid skirt, seated at a table at the FLPD. Reilly reads her the Miranda warnings and sets a written waiver in front of her, telling her to sign. Zoe ignores him. He makes several more attempts to get her to talk and sign, his efforts ranging from the good cop line, "It'll all be okay if you tell me what happened," to the more heavy-handed version, "You better tell me what happened, why you killed Brandon Sinclair. I'm going to find out anyway." Nothing worked, praise the Lord. She didn't say one word in response to any question during the two-hour interrogation. Didn't ask for her parents, to go home, for a lawyer. It was if she wasn't there at all.

Getting nowhere, Reilly stands, but something she says turns him around. I back up the video and increase the volume.

"Is Mr. Sinclair going to be okay?" she asks. A ploy to suggest she had no idea Sinclair was dead? Or maybe she didn't know he'd died at the scene? Or didn't know if she had killed him. If she had shot him.

I suck down the rest of my drink and cue up the videos of Serena Price and Principal Bannister's sworn statements. Serena was saying she came to Sinclair's office for her weekly counseling appointment, scheduled for 8:30 a.m. on August 24. She says she was late "because my car got a flat tire on my way to school."

Sorenson: "So, what time did you arrive?"

Bannister: "Around nine, maybe."

Sorenson: "What happened next?"

"It was really dark when I opened the door. I thought maybe he'd left because he thought I wasn't coming. I flipped on the light and—" her voice cracks. "That's when I saw...saw..." Wailing. "There was blood everywhere. It was simply awful."

Asked what she'd done when she found the body, Serena says, "I screamed and ran for the door, but Principal Bannister came in. She wouldn't let me leave. I wanted out of there. I didn't want to look at him."

Bannister stating she'd been greeting students when screaming erupted from Sinclair's office. "I burst in. Serena was screaming."

Sorenson again. "What did you do next, Mrs. Bannister?"

"There were dozens of students outside, on the way to class. I didn't want anyone else to...to see the body. I made Serena stay with me. I tried to get her to calm down, and I called 9-1-1."

Not much more than hasn't already been in the news, front and center for potential jurors to prejudge Zoe based on the gun. Other than Zoe's question about Sinclair's being okay, I have little on my side. Nothing at all to suggest Zoe's innocent, or at least not guilty. Worst of all, nothing to create any doubt, not even an unreasonable one.

The next fifty pages are phone and text message records from Zoe's cell phone for the six months preceding the murder. A couple of numbers repeated with great frequency identified as belonging to Gretchen and Anton. Numerous other calls to local numbers in Broward's 954 area code, but none exceeding a minute or two in length. All short, to be expected given that kids prefer text messaging to actual talking. Manny's niece, Rosa, once told me, "Tía Garcia, calling on the phone is so 2001."

An onslaught of texts follows the call logs. Typical kid stuff. Meeting at the mall or the movies. Which boy is cute. Which girl is a slut. Pages and pages of teenage angst.

Jake dips his head in front of my face. "How's it going in there?"

I rub my eyes, burning from staring at the screen. "I should ditch the shrink and the sleep meds and just read this stuff. It's deadly."

"So to speak."

"Sorry, another bad choice of words. I'm just tired. Didn't sleep at all last night."

He leans towards me, elbows on the bar. "I was thinking maybe..."

I reread a text from Zoe's number, (954) 555-1666 to (954) 555-1341. "its me he likes skank not u, stay away or else i warn u." Delivered 10:45 p.m., August 22, 2009.

"Maybe you and I could—"

"Holy shit, that's the night before Sinclair was murdered!"

Jake leaps back. "What are you—"

"That's what Sonny was talking about when he told me to ask Zoe about the texts!"

Jake shrugs and goes back to wiping down the bar.

I run a finger down the screeds of texts on the screen until I get to the reply text from (954) 555-1341 at 10:47 p.m., August 22, 2009. "LMAO ur a real buzz kill. sexy serena is what he needs now baby"

"I've seen that number (954) 555-1341 somewhere." I repeat the number out loud.

I scroll back to the witness list which includes the witnesses' names, addresses, and phone numbers. I scan down to (954) 555-1341, beside which is the name, Serena Price.

"No way!"

"Miss, did you say something?" Moose back at my side, another cigarette behind his ear.

"Leave the lady alone," Jake calls from the kitchen, which

sends Moose back to punching buttons on the jukebox.

I toggle back to the texts.

Zoe to Serena: "he thinks ur an ugly twat leave him alone"

Serena to Zoe: "he aint got no sugar 4 u go 2 ur corner and b blue without him better die"

The oldest texts between the two girls date back to February 1, 2009, hundreds about clothes, shopping, boys, parents, going to the beach, mani-pedis. All things best friends would talk about. YouTube clips of cats.

"What is it with cats?"

Miranda emits a grumbly growl, even though she looks like she's asleep.

So far, all standard adolescent nonsense. Then all communication ceases—nothing from August 17 until the night before the murder.

I use my phone to log onto St. Paul's website and pull up the academic calendar. "Holy moly! August 17 was the first day of school."

"What did you say?" Jake says, his nose propped on top of the screen to get my attention.

I bat his nose away, power down the laptop, and shove it into my backpack. "What time you closing up shop today?"

He surveys the empty bar. "Soon, I guess. Given the obvious lack of interest."

"What about old Moose over there? Isn't he a customer?"

"Nope. Moose never pays. Does odd jobs around here, cleans up after I close, and I pay him in liquid currency. Miller Lite, mostly."

"It's about time for him to earn his keep." I hop off the bar stool. "Moose, you're in charge." I scoot around the bar and grab Jake by the arm, Miranda by the leash. "You two want to take a ride?"

Jake doesn't answer, but the goofy grin is all the evidence I need that he's a willing participant.

Miranda? She just wags her tail. It's all a game to her.

Chapter 18

Traveling east from the Star to the coast, it strikes me that Broward County is a ghetto sandwich. To the west, the suburbs, a sprawl of cookie-cutter homes and chain stores stretching to within spitting distance of the Everglades. To the east, beyond downtown Fort Lauderdale, the beach, with its waterfront mansions and high-end condos and a dwindling number of old-timey Florida places like The Hurricane. And in the middle, the 'hood, as Vinnie calls it. Block after desolate block of dilapidated buildings, pawn shops, and desperation.

"Hey, Counselor," Jake says. "You're the navigator here, so navigate."

"What?"

"Where are we going?"

"Next light, take a left."

I stuff the crime scene photos I've been studying in my backpack. "Not like anyone deserves to be shot in the crotch or anything, but can you believe the dude was found behind his desk with his pants down? Not exactly what's expected of a faculty member at an elite private school."

"I guess," Jake says. "But what would I know? I went to public school, and you know how much shit happens there when no one's looking, don't you?"

I shift in my seat.

"I forgot. You're Miss Fancy Pants. Private school all the way."

"Let's get back on topic, why don't we? You saw the wedding band."

"So?"

"Men, you're all the damn same."

I check over my shoulder on Miranda.

"What's she doing back there?" Jake asks.

"Sleeping with one eye open. Or maybe she's awake with one eye closed. Hard to tell. One thing I can tell you is she's listening to everything we say."

"How can you know?"

"Take my word for it."

Miranda emits a confirmatory woof.

Jake's eyes widen. "Scary."

"Next right."

"Your theory is the wife killed him?"

"Maybe, maybe not, but the spouse is the obvious place to start. I know I've wanted to kill Manny more than once."

"I can't imagine why."

"Yeah, yeah. I'm sure he's felt the same way about me." I say. "Take a right here. And then there was how Sinclair was found. Either he was...er...finding some pleasure in his own company, which normally doesn't result in getting shot in the groin and the head, or he had other company that morning."

"Come to think of it, I think that close-up shot with the skivvies showed he was shot in the balls, and that his—"

"Do not go there! Besides, that doesn't mean anything."

"What do you mean it doesn't mean anything? The guy had a hard-on, for Christ's sake!"

"Happens a lot when someone dies. It's called angel lust. I've seen it a dozen times in murder cases and suicides. Can happen with fatal gunshots to the head. In hangings too."

"You see some weird shit in your job, Grace. No wonder you drink."

"Used to drink."

"True, because if you still drank, I'd be making more money off your sorry ass every time you come into my place."

"Hey, turn left here!"

We screech into the turn.

"Take it easy. We don't need the cops to pull us over."

"A little advance notice would be nice, Ms. Navigator."

"Sorry."

"You're pretty demanding for someone asking for a ride."

"I *said* sorry."

"Can I assume we're going to visit the weeping widow? She'd be all pissed off if he did have company."

I pat his knee. "You'd make a great investigator, Jacko. Damn straight that's where we're going."

"The police report says Sinclair lived at 456 Poinciana Court, Lauderdale-by-the-Sea." I pull my crumpled copy from my jeans pocket. "And it lists his Social Security number. Can you believe that? The state still put socials on public documents. I guess it drums up business for the State Attorney's identity fraud unit."

"Not that you ever spent any time there, did you? From what I hear, you were top-shelf cases all the way."

"That's ancient history." I jab my finger at the Poinciana Court street sign. "Turn left," I say, in time for Jake to jink into a two-block-long street running east from A1A to the beach.

"Jesus, Grace! A little notice, please?"

For Sale – Foreclosure signs litter the street, one on almost every lot, pallets of bricks piled high behind chain link fences marked Keep Out. No Trespassing. Plywood-covered doors and windows of unfinished McMansions, concrete victims of the real estate bubble bursting all over South Florida.

I wave the police report in the direction of a contemporary home, all angles and glass. "There. Number 456."

"Pretty nice for a guidance counselor. Those palms alone are worth more than my bar."   "Which might not be saying much."

"Always the smart ass. And, by the way, at least it's paid for." I bite my tongue.

"Oops, my turn to say sorry."

"No need. I got myself into the hole, I'll get myself out."

"Nice ride," he says, referring to a black Corvette parked in the driveway.

"Park down there, on the opposite side."

"Yes ma'am," he says, pulling a U-turn and parking down the block. "How do you know if the wife is even home? Maybe you should've called."

"No warning means no time to get her story together."

"Or maybe not. Maybe we should be looking at Serena. And maybe there are other girls and Serena was jealous. Or maybe..."

I let the police report flutter to the floor. "Or maybe Zoe did it—end of story."

"That's not what I meant. But this woman just buried her husband. She may not want to talk, especially to you. What are you gonna say? 'Hello, maybe you can help me. I'd like to know why your husband was caught with his pants down. Maybe you had something to do with it? And by the way, I represent the person accused of ruining your life'."

I flinch.

"I didn't mean, I know you and...never mind."

I survey the graveyard of half-finished homes. "Look, I have no clue where this is going, but I have to follow the evidence, and it's telling me there was more to Sinclair than meets the eye." I pull back and look Jake up and down as if I'm seeing him for the first time. "Hey, handsome. I bet a guy like you'd be able to get the widow talking."

He sticks a finger in his chest while raising an eyebrow.

"Yeah, you."

"Handsome?"

"Maybe, maybe not," I say, trying my hardest not to grin like a schoolgirl. "What do you say?"

He gives me a time-out sign. "No way. I agreed to drive you. And that's it. Nothing else. Come on. Nothing's happening here. Let's go."

"Calm down, cowboy. Please. A little assistance here," I say, thumb and forefinger no more than an inch apart.

He bumps his head on the steering wheel. "If you want to talk to her, you go."

"Or we could do it together?"

He gives me a crooked grin.

"Like I said—men!" I clear my throat. "We can say we're investigating and that we'd like to ask her a couple of questions. Maybe not say exactly who we're working for?"

"We?"

All conversation stopped as we saw a man leaving the house, carrying a couple of boxes stacked one on top of the other.

"You got any binoculars?" I flip open the glove box.

"Do I look like a perv to you?"

"Don't play all innocent with me. You deep-sixed a few of my cases with your surveillance skills."

He pulls a pair of binoculars from under the driver's seat, exhaling hard through clenched teeth.

I grab the binoculars. "I knew it!"

I blow a layer of dust from the eyepieces and hone in on the man, bull-necked, with white skin tinged pink like an albino. His muscular bulk is stuffed into his jacket, an odd fashion choice for the Florida heat, until I see why. A bulge at his waist. "He's carrying."

Jake scoots farther down in his seat. "Another good reason to get out of here."

The man deactivates the Corvette's alarm with a key fob as

he pans up and down the street.

"Duck!" I shove Jake's head down low and tuck in beside him, but keep the binoculars rested on the dashboard like some cartoon detective.

"What the— What are you doing?"

"He might spot us! Whoever he is."

"Maybe Sinclair was his buddy? Maybe he's here to pay his respects. Maybe he's a plumber. Damned if I know, Grace, but can I please take the gear shift out of my right nostril now?"

Boxes deposited on the passenger seat, the man slides into the driver's seat and drives away. "All clear," I say, pulling Jake out of his crouch by his collar.

"What does he have to do with any of this?"

"No idea."

Jake flips the driver's seat back. "Let me know when the next brilliant idea pops into that pretty little head of yours, why don't you?"

I shove the binoculars into his chest. "Let's go. I think I'll cut the grieving widow a break. Maybe come back another day."

"Why? Things seem to be getting interesting."

"Maybe I want to know a little bit more about the Sinclairs before I go busting in like a bull in a china shop—like why some meathead with a gun's taking stuff out of the widow's house, and like what Sinclair might have been up to in his free time."

"And like why there's an unmarked cop car following the 'Vette?" Jake says.

Chapter 19

A colleague of mine once referred to Everglades State Hospital by its nickname, the Alligator Farm, and earned himself a night in jail courtesy of the judge for causing a mistrial. The name is squarely on point, however, given ESH sits on a verdant hundred-acre campus, a stone's throw from the Everglades.

The buildings, like the name of the place, are benign looking enough, bland government architecture circa 1970, but ESH gives me the creeps. I've been out here before on a tour led by administrators bent on extolling the humanity of the place, despite the barbed wire fences, padded rooms, and orderlies armed with stun guns. As we walked through the facility, I stepped over one man curled up on the floor of a common room in plain view of staff and other patients watching The Weather Channel. I left that day wondering what life was like at ESH if what I saw was the sanitized version.

Lauderdale West is only a receiving facility, a term more suited for the post office than a psych hospital. Once the patient's crisis has passed, she gets warehoused here if she's still a danger, like Zoe. When the Slims found out Zoe was being shipped off to a state psychiatric hospital, and not some private Club Loony, they were appalled, in the presumptuous way rich people get appalled when they find out money can't buy everything.

"We will spare no resources to make sure Zoe gets whatever help she needs," Anton said during our confab in the stairwell. And he better have meant it, because Dr. Michaels doesn't come cheap. I hired him to do a private competency evaluation, "private" being the operative word. If the results are bad, meaning Zoe's looking very much like the cunning criminal the State says she is, I'll bury them, and the State will be none the wiser. If the results are favorable to Zoe's case, I'll milk every last mitigating diagnosis and rationale as to why Zoe isn't in any shape to go to trial, let alone prison.

I hesitate to call Michaels a defense whore, one whose opinions can be bought, paid for, sculpted like putty and made to sound like they were written on stone tablets delivered by God himself, but that's what he is. I saw it more times than I care to remember when I was up against a defense attorney representing a guilty client with deep pockets. The subtle craft of diagnosis is a fine art, not a science, and one man's psychosis is another's creative nature in the hands of the right hired gun. Michaels is a nice enough guy, though. But, like Zoe said, it's easy to be nice when the money's right.

ESH's lobby, a cavernous yet seemingly claustrophobic space, is decorated in shades of brown and beige. Walls. Furniture. Floor. All the color of shit.

I flash my Florida Bar card to a big-haired receptionist, a ringer for Amy Winehouse.

"Attorney Grace Locke here to see my client, Zoe Slim."

Amy hunts and pecks on the keyboard.

"Ms. Locke, are you sure about your client's name?"

"Yes ma'am. Last name Slim. Like skinny," I say, trying not to sound snarky.

The beehive hairdo shifts forty-five degrees to the left, which makes it look like it's about to pull Amy's head off its stalk, hunting and pecking some more.

"Slim? Here she is. Zoya Zoe Slim, a.k.a. Zoe Slim. On the Dolphin Unit. Please take a seat, someone will be right with you."

Zoya? Zoe has three names? Like Lee Harvey Oswald or John Wayne Gacy. Zoya Zoe Slim. Criminals are always referred to using their first, middle, and last names on police reports, but it makes them all sound like serial killers or presidential assassins.

In lieu of sitting, I browse the patients' artwork on the walls. Some pieces resemble kindergartners' finger paintings gone wonky, others are complex and beautiful, like a delicate line drawing of a butterfly emerging from its chrysalis. Most depict pain, like the black and red watercolor of a spider clawing at a decapitated head.

A voice from behind jolts me out of my disturbing, yet somehow soothing, reverie. "Ms. Locke."

I turn and find myself face to face with a forty-something man in a blue blazer and gray pants.

"I'm sorry. I didn't mean to startle you," Dr. Michaels says, a wide smile revealing teeth like Chiclets, chalky white blocks his mouth seems too small to contain. "Nice to see you again. But on the same side this time."

We shake, his grip sure, like one who would never doubt his own opinion, even if compelling evidence to the contrary were served up on a silver platter. Money and power can do that to a person.

"Dr. Michaels, thanks for coming on such short notice," I say, although I'm under no illusion he's doing me any great favor. Beyond being a fan of exorbitant fees, he's an unadulterated media hog. That Zoe's case is high profile would have been incentive enough for him to clear all manner of common car thieves and drug dealers from his schedule.

"My pleasure. I understand there was quite a scene in

Twietmeyer's courtroom."

"Yes, indeed, but I'm sure I don't need to remind you, Doctor, you were retained on a confidential basis."

"Understood. I shall submit my written report to you and only to you."

"And, by the way, Dr. Slim sent over copies of Zoe's records. I believe you have them too?"

"I received them this morning."

"Have you seen Zoe?"

"Yes, I have."

"And your conclusions?"

He takes a quick look around. "Let's step outside," he says, which we do, beyond the reach of a surveillance camera mounted above the entrance.

"I'm not sure if this will be good or bad news for you, but your client is not incompetent. She is indeed competent," he says, wiping beads of sweat from his forehead.

I find myself nodding. The bar for competence is low—basically all a defendant has to be able to do is find her butt with both hands to go to trial—and Zoe, while a little whack-a-do, seems to me to be on the ball enough to face a jury.

"But you knew that already. Am I correct?"

"I suspected as much." I feign a concerned frown. "But I am ethically obligated to be certain, which is why you're here."

"And?"

"Excuse me?"

He peers down his nose at me. "And you're buying time to keep your client out of jail."

"Doctor, it seems as if you *are* a mind reader," I say in my best Southern belle drawl.

"I've been doing this for a while, Ms. Locke," he says, smirking. "Yet, I do feel for Ms. Slim. A place like this may not be not five star, it's better than the county lockup for an individual who is not without her, let's just call them, challenges."

"Agreed. She's so fragile one minute, so volatile the next."

He gives me a big wink. "Yes, even when she is not being encouraged to be so."

"Exactly how bad off is she?"

"I suggest you review the records with great care. There's plenty in there to work with. Your client may be competent, but she is a profoundly disturbed young lady. And if bipolar disorder with psychotic features and an anxiety disorder is bad, then she's bad. But that can be good too, if you know what I mean, Counselor?"

"Your diagnosis is the same as Dr. Kesey's, the attending at Lauderdale West?"

"And also Zoe's regular psychiatrist's."

"She's got a regular psychiatrist?"

"Thank goodness. Numerous incidents of self-harm and striking out at others, add to that an early diagnosis of Oppositional Defiant Disorder, not a good omen for the development of the criminal personality. And then there's the fact she's adopted, all of which doesn't bode well for Ms. Slim."

As he drones on, I turn the litany of horribles over and over in my mind, trying to reframe them into some sort of mental state defense for the child of Manny's lover.

"You knew that, Ms. Locke, didn't you?"

I ignore the jab.

"Doctor, did you discuss her suicide attempt?"

"I did, and she insists she didn't take an overdose of Xanax as the medics reported. She did admit to taking Xanax that evening, but only the prescribed amount. But you know how that goes," he says, looking at me as if I'm an example of what happens when Xanax becomes like candy. Or maybe it's my paranoia talking.

"When I followed up, she became hysterical. I'd advise you to stay off that topic for now since you'll require her cooperation in preparing her defense."

"I'm sure I don't have to remind you that if it were to become public that Zoe tried to kill herself, it would greatly impact her ability to get a fair trial."

He gapes at me. "Do I look like I was born yesterday? That goes without saying. You can count on my discretion. And, Ms. Locke, I'm available to discuss this further, but right now I have to get going to another appointment. I'll have my written report to you within a couple of days. And, please, as I said, do take a careful look at the records. They are self-explanatory, even for a layperson like yourself, and enlightening, if not a little frightening. Don't hesitate to call if you have any questions."

If I had a dollar for every shrink I've seen since Iraq, I'd be living the high life on a tropical island with an umbrella drink, the nightmares and heart palpitations behind me.

And if I were a lay person, I wouldn't be out here in the swamp trying to find a way to turn Zoe's mental illness into a positive.

***

An orderly shepherds me across a courtyard ringed with several empty benches, over a shuffleboard court, and through a byzantine web of corridors and locked doors, selecting a different key for each one from the dozens on a life-preserver-sized metal ring on his belt.

I point at his ID badge. Etienne Dumas.

"Where are you from, Etienne?" I ask, employing my best French accent. My father insisted I take four years of high school French because it's the "language of diplomacy." Or maybe it was when he was young, because the only benefit I've ever reaped from the forced march through verb conjugations and Molière was knowing what wine to order and what the lyrics "*Voulez-vous couchez avec moi, ce soir,*" meant when my mother sang along as if she were ordering a pot of Earl Grey tea.

"Here," Etienne says, in a tone which implies, "Where the hell do you think I'm from?"

"Okay, then."

He hangs his head. "I'm sorry. Haiti, originally," he says, perhaps embarrassed due to the misconception some in South

Florida have about Haitians being a lower class of immigrants. Haitians get sent back if they're caught washing upon shore. Cubans set a foot on dry land and they're in.

"I'm called Eddy now." He fingers the ID, rubbing at his name, as if trying to blot out his past. Likely one where crossing shark-infested waters in a rickety raft seemed preferable to hunger and persecution.

Eddy delivers me to the nurse's station on the Dolphin Unit.

"I'm here to see Ms. Slim," I tell the duty nurse, omitting Zoe's first name to avoid any further confusion.

I turn to thank Eddy, but all that's left of him is a door sucking shut to hermetically seal me in to the locked psych unit, a sound with which I am not unacquainted.

The nurse catches me looking over her shoulder through a window into a tiny white cave where a man in tightie-whities is twirling like a dervish, hitting the deck only to rise up and twirl some more. She whisks me off to a meeting room clearly designed in the prison version of Bauhaus, with the added design feature that the rectangular table and four chairs are bolted to the floor.

Zoe, dressed in green scrubs, is seated in the chair nearest the door, her body listing to one side.

"Ms. Zoe, your lawyer is here."

Zoe doesn't bat as much as one eyelid.

"I can take it from here." I slide onto a chair next to her.

The nurse points at a red HELP button on the wall. "Press, if there's any trouble."

I dip my head to see Zoe's face beneath a tangle of hair. "How're you doing?"

She flips her hair back to reveal a purple egg-shaped bump protruding from the middle of her forehead like a third eye.

"Jesus, how'd you get that?"

A shrug. "Just happened."

"You okay? Did you have someone look at that?"

I make a move to take a closer look, but she waves me off.

I make a note to tell the nurse my confidence in the medical care shaky in this place where a bump on the head is not a priority.

"Look, this is only temporary," I say, but the words ring hollow, the bars on the window a reminder of the opposite—the real possibility she might never be free again.

Reading my mind, she says, "Until I go to prison," words slurred, eyelids droopy like baggy pantyhose, clearly she is doped to the gills.

During the tour, I asked what kind of therapies were available. The administrator replied, "Drug therapy is our go-to therapy," and rubbed his thumb and forefinger together to indicate other options were too expensive. Whatever therapy Zoe's getting, it's robbing her of any last vestige of energy to help herself, the urge to fight like she did in front of Twietmeyer, without which our defense will fail, regardless of any smoke and mirrors I can conjure up.

"Like I told you at the jail, I watch the news," she says in the flat tone of one for whom all hope is gone. "Everyone thinks I did it." She looks down at her hands, fanned out like palm fronds, nails bitten down to the quick. "But what do you think?"

I sit back. "What matters is what the State can prove, and that's what I came to talk about, but I do also want to listen to whatever else you have to say. I'm sorry I didn't do that in the jail."

Her eyes brighten enough for me to see they're flecked with gold. "Thank you, Ms. Locke."

"It's Grace, remember? Would it be okay if I asked you some questions, first?"

She crosses her legs, knobby knees protruding out over the chair. "Shoot," she says, an unfortunate choice of words, but one which makes us both smile, albeit nervously.

"You said before you weren't there. What did you mean?"

The standard teenage eye roll. "You won't believe me."

"Give me a chance, okay?"

"Fine," she says, with a tired sigh. "I couldn't have killed Mr. Sinclair because I wasn't there."

"Where were you if you weren't at school?"

Her brows draw together. "That's not what I mean. I was at school, but I got there late. I slept through my alarm and got there just in time for first period English, so I missed my regular appointment with Mr. Sinclair."

"Did you call to tell him you couldn't make it?" I say, hoping against hope there might actually be some useful phone records.

She bows her head. "I was going to go by later and apologize. Maybe if I hadn't..." she pauses for a deep breath. "Maybe if I hadn't missed my appointment, he'd still be alive. Maybe if I'd been there, maybe whoever killed Mr. Sinclair would have, I don't know, just gone away."

"In my experience, Zoe, killers who mean to kill someone don't give up that easily."

"Yeah, or maybe whoever it was would have killed me too." Her shoulders sag. "But maybe that wouldn't have been so bad."

My heart sinks. "Don't say that. You're a smart, beautiful young woman with parents who love you," I say, although I'm unsure of the parent part.

"You're only being nice because my parents are paying you," she says, swiping at an errant tear.

Her cynicism shocks me. But, then again, Russian orphans ordered up like pizza don't exactly have the luxury of believing there's such a thing as something for nothing.

"I can understand why you might think that. But no matter who pays me, it's my job to make sure you get the best defense possible."

She tilts her head to one side as if I've asked her to solve a complex math problem. "You're saying you're one hundred percent in my corner?" After a second or two, she lets a full smile bloom and raises a clenched fist, knuckles forward, for a fist bump.

"It's settled then. All for one and one for all," I say, surprised to find myself knocking my knuckles against hers, surprised her mood shifted so fast.

"*Three Musketeers*, right? I love that movie."

I reel back. "Really?"

"I know it's a book too, silly!" she says, as an ungodly ruckus erupts out on the unit.

"What the heck is that?"

"I've been here a couple of weeks now and, I'm not kidding, every afternoon the same two nut jobs get into a screaming match because one wants to watch Jerry Springer and the other Judge Judy."

"Hilarious. But maybe we shouldn't call them nut jobs?" I say, trying to keep the tone light.

Her quick smile is replaced by an even quicker grimace. "It gets a little scary sometimes."

"I can imagine." I hold her gaze. Is she testing me, to make me believe we're a team? Or worse, maybe just plain crazy, her mood shifting like the wind? "Okay, so you say you weren't there, and—"

She slams her fist on the table. "I wasn't! I told you you wouldn't believe me."

I press on. Backing down in fear will rob me of credibility and will do her no good either, a cowed defense lawyer being about as useful as tits on a bull. "That's not what I meant. I was just repeating what you said. But let's move on from there, why don't we? We need to talk about your father's gun, the one the cops found in your locker with your fingerprints on it."

I brace myself for her reaction, but, to my surprise, no sooner are the words out of my mouth than the emotional floodgates open. "That's not possible. I didn't kill Mr. Sinclair, and I would never bring a gun to school. St Paul's has metal detectors. And I would never...He helped me...He was the only one—"

I pat her arm. "Hey, slow down there, kiddo. We've got all the time you need."

Her chest's heaving as if she's run the hundred-yard dash.

"First, did you know your father had a gun?"

"Yes," she says, gulping in air.

"Had you ever seen his gun?"

"Yes."

"When did you see his gun?"

"A few times."

"A few times, like when? How many times?"

"I don't remember. Not exactly."

"Try. This is important."

"There was a break-in at our house a few months back. After that, Dad said our security system wasn't enough anymore."

"And he bought a gun."

"For protection."

"What did they take?

She raises her eyebrows. "They?"

"The burglars, what did they take from your house?"

"I'm not sure. Some of Mom's jewelry, maybe. Not that she'd miss it. She's got so much."

Her gaze drifts out the window to a column of patients in mismatched clothes shuffling past the window.

"Did they ever find who did it?"

Her head jerks back. "What?"

"Find who broke in?"

"No, they didn't," she says, her tone becoming more firm with each answer. "Another reason Dad wanted more protection."

"What kind of gun did he get?"

She doesn't miss a beat. "Glock 19. Two of them."

"Two? Why two?"

"He wanted both of us, Mom and me, to learn how to use them since we're home alone a lot."

"Did you see the guns?"

"Of course."

"Handle them?"

"Sure."

"Both?"

"Yes."

"Dad took me out to the gun range at Markham Park to learn how to shoot."

"Your dad's familiar with guns I take it, since he was giving you lessons?"

"God, no. He needed lessons, too. Some off-duty cop came with us to make sure we were doing it right."

"From the Fort Lauderdale Police Department?

"No idea. He wasn't wearing a uniform."

"Do you remember the cop's name?" I ask, confident there are few cops working for FLPD or the Sheriff's Department I haven't heard of, or that haven't heard of me.

"No."

'What did he look like?"

"I can't remember exactly. Tall, maybe. Not too old, but not young."

"So, you did shoot the gun? One of the two your dad bought?"

"Yeah."

"Only one time?"

"More. We went to the range a bunch of times. I liked shooting. Going to the range with Dad was fun." She raises her arms out in a shooting stance, hands clasped. "Bang, bang. Like in those cop shows. We always went for pizza on the way home at Anthony's."

"I love Anthony's," I say, in an effort to redirect her attention.

"Me too. Pepperoni's my favorite. But I like plain cheese too. What's your favorite topping?"

"Veggie."

"Yuck!"

I smile. A normal kid talking about normal kid stuff. As it should be.

"Did your mom go with you guys?"

A dark shadow crosses her face like a rain cloud across the sky at the very moment you're pitching your tent. "No, Mom doesn't eat pizza."

"I mean did your mom go with you to the range?"

"Hell no. Thank God."

I suppress the urge to laugh. "Why do you say that?"

"It was our thing. Me and Dad. She won't go anywhere where there's no A/C."

"Did your mom learn to shoot?"

"Dad got her private lessons for her birthday."

What a guy. If Manny had given me marksmanship lessons as a birthday gift, I might have left him. Or shot him.

"Where'd your father keep the guns?"

"In a safe in their bedroom. At least, I think so."

"Okay, this may be painful, but I have to ask. How were you feeling around the time Mr. Sinclair was killed? Your trip to Lauderdale West wasn't the first time you'd been in bad shape, was it?"

Her lower lip starts to tremble, and she bites down on it so hard she draws blood.

"You know what I mean," I say, pointing at the wound on her head, trying not to look down at the scars on her forearms, too many to count. Some scabbed over, others healed long ago. The medical report from Lauderdale West said the concussion happened when she fell off her desk chair and passed out, collateral damage from downing a bottle of Xanax, but slicing her wrists up hadn't been accidental. Did she actually want to kill herself? To get attention? Or was she just damaged at her core?

"I was taking meds, but nothing helped. My head hurt all the time. I couldn't sleep, and then I'd fall asleep in class. Half the time I was trying not to explode, the other half I wanted to die. Sometimes it's all too much, you know?"

It's a rhetorical question, but I find myself answering, "Yes, I do know."

She shoots me a quizzical look and opens her mouth to speak, but I cut her off. "Why did you feel that way?"

"Stuff. Everything," she says, clenching and unclenching her fists. "But, like I told Dr. Michaels, I didn't try to kill myself. I only took one Xanax, not the whole bottle, no matter what they say. I would never do that!"

"Mr. Sinclair was your counselor. Did you speak to him about how you were feeling?"

"Every Monday morning at eight."

"Did it help?

"He listened, you know? I mean, really listened."

"And you didn't see him the morning he died? Or talk to him, maybe on the phone?"

"No. I said that already, didn't I?"

I run my finger down my list of questions to ensure I'm not missing anything. "About the pills you took after your folks left for the gala?"

She flops back and sets about plucking hairs out of her head, one strand at a time.

"Please answer my question."

"Can we not talk about that? Like I said, I didn't take all those pills," she says, her words slurring again.

"Do you need to take a break?"

"I'm okay. I don't want to talk about any of this anymore."

"Just a few more questions."

She groans.

"Did you talk to your mom about what was going on with you?"

"I tried, but she doesn't get it, you know?"

"And your dad?"

"God, no!"

"What do you mean, 'God, no'?"

"If you haven't noticed, he's not exactly Mr. Touchy Feely." She lets out a snorty laugh. "He tries, but he comes from what he calls the school of hard knocks."

"You don't get along with your dad?"

"No, I do. He's old-fashioned. He's doesn't talk about feelings much."

"For some people, feeling too much isn't good," I say.

"Huh?"

"Feeling too much isn't part of being a surgeon. It's not good to overthink things when you're cutting into someone."

"Gross," she says, wrinkling her nose, which makes me laugh. "And how would you know?"

I push back from the table and unveil Oscar.

Her eyes go from droopy to wide. "What happened?"

I drop my pant leg. "Story for another day. Let's just say I know a thing or two about surgeons."

"I guess," she says, in a way that implies, "Duh!"

"Getting back to it, I understand you were adopted. From Russia."

She swallows hard. "If it weren't for Mom and Dad, I'd probably be some sex slave."

"Why do you say that?"

"Because that's what happens to girls like me. Girls who don't matter."

Her matter-of-fact assessment stuns me into silence.

"I was six when they got me. Most people want newborns. But they chose me anyway. Without them I'd be God-only-knows where."

"Do you remember much about it? The orphanage, I mean?"

"You know what I remember? I remember getting a new winter coat the day Mom and Dad came to get me to look nice when they arrived. At least nice enough for them not to change their minds and ask for a refund. It was the only new thing I'd ever owned. Only the chosen kids got a new coat. The rest? The ones who stay behind? They just keep wearing worn out hand-me-downs that don't keep out the cold."

She walks to the window and runs her hands across the bars, and I wonder if she's trying to divert my attention. "Dad was poor when he was a kid, too."

"Let's get back to your case, okay?" I say, conscious of the possibility, she's playing on my emotions. "There were some texts the cops got off your and Serena's phones."

She stiffens.

"You and Serena are best friends?"

"Were," she says.

"What do you mean, 'were'?"

She crosses her arms and sits. "Story for another day."

I look her in the eye. "I hate to ask this, but I have to. I've seen Serena's texts. She knew you had a crush on Mr. Sinclair, didn't she?"

Her face flushes bright red. "No, I didn't! He tried to help me. Nobody else cared."

"Did Mr. Sinclair ever touch you?"

In a flash, she lunges at me, grabbing me by my jacket lapels. "No! He never did anything like that to me!"

I flip into tactical mode. I plant my feet, crook my elbow, twist my body around, and put her in a choke hold. After a few seconds, her body turns limp and I guide her down onto the chair.

"You're strong," she says, half crying, half smiling.

"I think that's enough for today. You need to get some rest."

Tentative, I hold out my hands to pull her out of the chair. She takes my hands and lets me pull her up.

"And you're strong, too. I bet you're stronger than you think." I wipe a giant tear from her face. "Things might not look so good, I understand. But hang in there. I'll do everything I can to get you out of this mess."

She glances down at her disheveled clothes. "I'm a mess. Mom would freak. Not a beauty-queen moment."

"We can never lose our sense of humor, can we?" I say, pressing the button to call the nurse. "It gets us through when nothing else does."

She gives me a crooked, sniffly smile. "Thanks, Ms. Locke."

"It's Grace, remember?"

At the door, I turn. "Hey, they have you registered in here under the name Zoya. What's with that?"

"That's my real name. It was my name when I was adopted from the orphanage in Solnyshko. Zoe's my nickname."

"Zoya's a beautiful name."

"Zoya means 'sun' in Russian."

"Even better. From now on you're Zoya The Warrior Princess to me. And warriors do matter. They matter a lot."

Chapter 20

"**D**inner tonight? Red's at seven," Marcus says, but before I can reply "Roger that," he's already hung up. Marcus calls, I come. And vice versa. No questions asked.

Beyond being a man of few words, Marcus Jackson is my closest friend and everything you wouldn't expect in a brainiac prosecutor appointed by the Republican Florida Attorney General to head up the South Florida Office of the Statewide Prosecutor. Marcus is black, from the ghetto, and gay, facts well-disguised by his Brooks Brothers suits and spit-and-polish wingtips. He is not, however, "out," other than to a few close friends. A former foster kid schooled in the ways of the street at Miami's Northwestern High School, Marcus survived his youth by hiding his superior intellect under two hundred and fifty pounds of defensive back muscle. He got a scholarship to play football at the University of Miami and transformed himself into the warrior philosopher. Two national championship rings, an English and Philosophy double major, and a 4.0 GPA got him a free ride at the University of Miami School of Law and a job as a professional ass kicker with the Florida Attorney General upon graduation.

The year before I got myself fired from the State Attorney's Office, Marcus and I worked on several Statewide projects together. The last one was a task force to shut down organized crime, the task force that netted Vinnie. We became fast friends, developing an ease and mutual respect in our interactions that stood in stark relief to my relationship with Manny, one characterized by unpredictable cycles of intense desire and abject hate. I admired Marcus's tenacity for ferreting out the bad actors, and Marcus said he envied my outspoken nature and foul mouth.

I arrive ten minutes early. Red's is already a beehive of activity. An iconic watering hole located in the heart of Wilton Manors, a small and predominantly gay city adjacent to Fort Lauderdale, Red's serves as a social hub for all sorts, regardless of sexual orientation or political persuasion. On any given night, aspiring politicos and judges can be seen rubbing shoulders with patrons dressed in body paint, while business types discuss the relative merits of Pinot Noir and Cabernet with sports stars.

I take a seat at a quiet table on the patio to decompress. In a park across the street, a father and son are playing catch. The boy can't be more than four, all soft-limbed and uncoordinated, like a newborn deer.

At seven o'clock on the dot, I detect the rumble of Marcus's motorcycle.

"You look like Lord Vader in that helmet," I say, as he pulls me in for a bear hug.

"Flattery will get you everywhere, my lovely. But look who's talking about having gone to the dark side."

He slings his black leather motorcycle jacket on the back of the chair. He's wearing indigo designer jeans, creases knife-edge sharp, and a starched blue-and-white-striped dress shirt, open at the neck.

"You look great, as always. A little bad boy in that jacket, but all buttoned up underneath. Too bad you play for the other team."

The well-worn joke makes us both smile. Manny had been jealous of the countless hours we'd spent working together on the task force. At least until he found out Marcus is gay, a fact I'd kept in my back pocket just to rankle Manny.

"Your gorgeous mug in the papers a lot these days. How is it sitting on the other bench?"

"It's work."

"Everyone deserves a defense, right?" he says, smoothing the napkin on his lap. "Tell me, how's it looking for your girl's defense?"

"Now that would be telling tales out of school, wouldn't it?"

He leans in. "Come on, you can tell little ole me."

I hold out my hand and count down the reasons Zoe's case sucks. "First, my client is a rich kid, who is as bratty as she is batty, for whom I have no defense, at least not one that isn't made up out of thin air. Second, she says she didn't do it, that she was somewhere else when it all went down, but don't they all say that? And, third—surprise, surprise! There's no alibi witness in the discovery. Oh, and how can I forget? I got the case through my ex who may or may not be still sleeping with my client's mother."

He flings himself back in his chair. "Now why don't you tell me what you really think?"

"It's a loser. I know it."

A waiter wearing a red satin bow tie appears. "What can I get for you?" he asks, with the emphasis on the "you" and looking only at Marcus.

"We need a minute," I say. The waiter doesn't budge. "We need a minute here, okay?"

The waiter flares his nostrils at me, smiles at Marcus, bowing in retreat.

"The bow tie is a bit over the top," Marcus says.

"Ya think?"

"Okay, so it's not a slam-dunk winner."

"Who would have thought I would end up defending the types of scum we used to lock up?"

He reaches for my hands across the table. "Don't let it get to you. It's just work, remember?"

I fix Marcus with a stare. "I need to talk to someone about this, or I'm going to explode. But you are sworn to secrecy."

Marcus draws his thumb across his lips. "Do go on."

"There's a mountain of texts between my client, Zoe, and her former best friend. Seems Zoe had a crush on the victim."

"Not good."

"It gets worse."

"The BFF stole Zoe's boyfriend, and, while Zoe didn't say it, I get the feeling the BFF may have been sleeping with the victim, and the BFF was the one who found the body."

"Very soap opera."

"What does all of that say to you?"

"It says your girl had some pretty strong motives for murder."

"First big case back, and this is what I've got." I make a zero with my hands.

He raises an eyebrow. "You know most defendants are guilty. At least you used to know that," he adds with a wink.

"Stop making fun of me. I'm serious. I'm going to lose, which is bad enough. It's not that I need Zoe to be innocent. It would be nice to have a theory, any theory, that doesn't involve her being the only possible killer. I'd like one shaky leg to stand on so I have something to say in court that doesn't sound like freakin' fantasy land. I need a plan B, Marcus."

"You used to love raking attorneys over the coals for their outlandish defenses."

"Asshat." I kick him under the table. "Thing is—the victim was the only person who listened to her. Why would she want to kill him?"

"Jealousy knows no bounds, my friend."

I stare out at the parade of cars. Regular people with regular lives. Why is it that looking from the outside in has a way of smoothing the rough edges of life? In all likelihood, some of them are in the middle of ugly divorces, or nursing ailing parents. But from the outside, their lives are bathed in a warm, comforting glow of routine. I'd settle for a little of that illusion at this point.

The waiter reappears.

"Burger for her, hold the bun. New York strip for me, rare," Marcus says, shooing the waiter away with the menus.

"To make matters worse, she's a total loon."

"Meaning?"

"Meaning she has a history of hurting herself and fighting."

"More not good."

"And pot. And who knows what else."

Marcus covers a sly grin.

"But, guess what? She may be a psychological train wreck, but wait for it...She's competent. At least that's what Michaels told me today."

Marcus stuffs his fist in his mouth to stop himself from laughing. "I guess you do get what you pay for."

"Zoe was adopted. From Russia. And by Gretchen. You remember her, don't you? What a start in life."

"I watched a program about the problems the kids adopted from orphanages overseas can have. Maybe that's got something to do with her behavior."

"Thanks, Oprah. What? You thinking about adopting?"

He gives me an exaggerated eye roll. "'No' and 'Hell no' would be the long and the short answers. Heck, I haven't even had a date in months. Working too hard."

A taught silence descends between us. The real reason Marcus called is about to surface, an intuition confirmed by the change in his tone from jocular to serious as a hanging judge.

"I want nothing more than to see you succeed. I was quite concerned about you when you fell off the edge last year. I wasn't sure I'd get you back."

"And?"

"I have certain obligations not to talk about cases I'm working on, just like you."

I look away, guilt bubbling in my gut for having said too much about Zoe's case.

"And?"

"And if I said maybe I saw something that rang a bell, you would believe me, right?" He leans his bulk across the table. "Maybe you should go back and look again at everyone involved in the case with fresh eyes."

"Why? What am I missing?"

"Exactly! You're missing something, but I can't tell you what. I wish I could. You've spent a career thinking accused equals guilty. But sometimes that's not the case, even though it can seem that way at first blush."

I scoot my chair in close. "What are you saying, exactly? Do you or do you not you have anything to help me? I sure would like to see it if you do. As it stands, I got zippo, nothing, nada. And I'm running out of time."

"Think about the types of cases we work on at Statewide. We investigate and prosecute crimes that impact more than a single jurisdiction and—"

"Thanks for the lecture, so how's about telling me something I don't know?"

He hangs his head. "I can't do that."

I stifle a sigh of frustration and stare over his shoulder at the bar crowd, drinks and voices raised, without a care.

"Stop for a second and think about what kind of crimes those are? What kind of task forces did we work on together?"

"Organized crime. Drugs. Crooked politicians." I ball up my napkin and throw it on the table.

"Look, all I'm saying is try to see outside the little box of your case. Look into the wild *blue* yonder and see what's out there in the *blue* sea of death that might help you find your defense."

"And by 'blue,' can I assume you're referring to OxyContin?"

I say, referring to the street name for the pain killer?"

Marcus shrugs.

I give an exaggerated wink. "Don't be coy with me, my friend."

"And don't put me in a bad spot. I take the confidentiality obligations very seriously. There's only so much I can say about certain things. Same as you. I mean, if I asked, did she do it, even if she'd told you she had, you wouldn't tell me, would you?"

I look at my hands. "No, I would not."

The waiter places Marcus's steak in front of him with a flourish and flings my burger in the general direction of my place mat.

"Angry queen," I say, sticking my tongue out the moment the waiter's back is turned.

Marcus chokes on his water. "You haven't changed a bit, have you?"

I stick my tongue out at him too and he raises his hands in surrender.

"Let's do Trial Prep 101. What do you do when you get a witness list from the State?"

"Okay, I'll play along, but this riddle better have a solution. First, I check out the witnesses' backgrounds, see if they've ever been arrested, convicted, whatever. Where they live, work...I don't know."

"Go on," he says, making a churning motion with his right hand. "Look, take off those myopic prosecutor glasses that see the defendant as Satan and the victim as a saint."

"Pretty please. Give me a hint. Just an itty-bitty one. Nothing that would compromise you, but, maybe a crumb for old times' sake?"

Marcus puffs out his cheeks and expels the air in a rush. "Okay. Let me make it simple, and this is the last I'm going to say on the topic. Someone is never on the witness list in a murder case."

I shrug, palms up.

Marcus throws his arms in the air. "I give up. Give it some thought. I have faith in you. But in the meantime, let's enjoy our dinner like the old friends we are."

"Who you calling old?" I point an accusatory finger and he points one right back. "We made a great team, Grace. And don't you ever forget it. You may be playing for the other team now, but you will always be the same person in my book."

"Thanks."

Cheering erupts from the bar.

"The Dolphins must be winning," I say.

"The 'Fins are a lost cause. They may be cheering now, but they'll be crying later," he says with a shake of his head.

"Yeah, tell me about lost causes."

***

After leaving Marcus at the bar making small talk with a male hair stylist from Coral Springs, I retrieve Miranda from Vinnie's place, where he's teaching her to fetch beer from the fridge, one trick I hope she fails to perfect.

Now, she's sprawled on the floor, getting the sleep I desperately need.

Page by page, I review the discovery.

Nothing.

"What am I missing? I already aware I'm missing an alibi witness because, as my luck would have it, Zoe doesn't have one because she slept late and was alone while doing it."

Miranda raises her head.

"But what else?"

Miranda hops up and rests her shiny snout on my stump, eyes fixed on the laptop screen.

"How can I find something that isn't here? What did Marcus mean with his cryptic comments?"

On the verge of abandoning the search, I freeze, mouse hovering over the file labeled, Autopsy Photographs. Victim, Brandon Sinclair, DOB 4/23/1974.

"The victim! The murder victim's name is never on the

witness list."

Miranda's opens one eye.

"Why you might ask? Because, my furry friend, the victim is dead. And dead men can't tell tales." I close the laptop. "But nosy defense lawyers can."

Chapter 21

The doors don't open until 7:30 a.m., but I'm first in line, shifting from foot to foot, like a racehorse in the starting gate. Actually, I'm the only person in line outside the courthouse, but I'm on a mission. The answer to Marcus's riddle lies in Sinclair's past. He might be six feet under, but whatever official records exist on him may have a story to tell.

I pop a stick of gum into my mouth to keep from grinding my teeth. I wanted to bring Miranda along as a calming influence, but an enormous wolf dog, no matter how tame, is not exactly the way to fly under the radar. This mission is one which requires stealth, not to mention luck. Any inkling I may be onto something to help Zoe, and the State will find a way to turn the screws even more. That's how the system works. The strong get stronger and the weak perish under the government's heel.

Two people fall in line behind me. A mother and son. First timers for juvenile court is my guess. I give mom a quick study. Jaw clenched, eyes boring holes into her boy who is squirming inside navy-blue polyester. It may be a new suit, but his is an old story. Next time, and there will be a next time, mom won't be able to convince him to wear a suit, and he'll be looking her straight in the eye, his contempt the only defense he'll have.

Deputy Brian unbolts the Attorney's door at 7:30 a.m. sharp. At least I remembered this one's name.

"The early worm better watch out for Ms. Locke. She looks to be on a quest for justice," he says, placing my briefcase into the scanner.

He points at my leg. "Best if you come around this way," he says, guiding me around the side of the metal detector. "Too early to get the natives all twitchy with alarms and such."

"Thanks, Deputy Brian. Much appreciated. But how'd you know?" I ask, pointing down at Oscar.

"Word gets around here fast as clap on a...You know what I mean."

"Roger that."

He hands back my briefcase. "Now, you have a great day, Ms. Locke."

"There are things in our control and things that are not, Deputy. But I'll give it a try."

I head for the offices of the Clerk of the Court on the first floor, a rat trap of a place prone to flooding in the most timid of storms. Last year, the *Sun Sentinel* ran a picture of clerks in rain boots hanging pages of court files to dry on clothes lines after a summer squall inundated the file room.

The space is split in two by a wall of glass partitions, behind which sit minimum-wage file clerks charged with retrieving documents, and if requested, making copies for twenty cents a pop, cash only. Since I have no idea what I'm looking for, their services will do me little good today. My business is with the Clerk's database, which contains information about every matter under the jurisdiction of the Seventeenth Judicial District: criminal, civil, municipal, and traffic; the names of plaintiffs and defendants; court filings, and hearing dates; and all manner of progress notes.

Given the early hour, I have my choice of terminals and select the newest and, therefore, fastest—fast being a relative term when talking about government resources.

I type in Brandon Sinclair. Nothing. Then Sinclair Brandon. Still nothing. His date of birth, 4/23/1974. No records. Not even a traffic ticket.

I stuff another piece of gum in my mouth and run the searches again with various misspellings of his name, a common occurrence in court records.

Still nothing.

If Sinclair had any involvement in a case at some point, as a party or a witness, his name would have come up. It hasn't. Dead end.

Maybe Marcus wasn't referring to the victim at all. Maybe he meant some other person not on the witness list.

I survey the airless space. In front of windows labeled Attorneys, Law Enforcement and Probation Officers, and Public, long lines of people are fidgeting, checking phones, reading the newspaper. One guy is picking his nose with a sharpened pencil, a risky habit if ever there was one. Everyone's dressed the part, no need to look at the signs to know who's who. Attorneys—suits. Cops—guns and swagger. Public—anything from saggy pants to hundred-dollar manicures. A woman, her front teeth but a distant memory, keeps yelling at the clerk, "That case was dropped. Why's it still on my record?"

I focus on the empty screen. Marcus as much as told me to look into Sinclair. But why would Marcus send me down that rabbit hole if there's no record of him? Statewides file their cases in the Seventeenth, just like the State's Attorney for Broward County. If there's a Statewide case involving Sinclair in any capacity, witness or defendant, it should show up in a search.

I pound on the keys, searching for my own name.

And there I am. My name, Grace Kelly Locke. My knees weaken. Some said I got lucky, that is, if you can call six months in jail lucky. But there it is, in black and white. Reilly skated, but my whole sorry mess will be with me forever, for the whole world to see, an indelible, shameful reminder of what I became. DUIs are like tattoos. They're with you forever. They cannot be expunged, sealed, or erased from your record no matter how many *mea culpas* you say.

"That's it!" I bang my fist on the counter, causing a shaggy man in the Public line to shout "Bingo." Several heads turn to stare, my level of animation a rare sight in this place where endless waiting causes hope to die, if it hasn't done so before you walk through the door.

Cases disappear when they are made to disappear. Sealed or expunged. And there's only one way that happens—by court order. One stroke of a judge's pen and the case is gone, like magic.

I log off and scoop up my belongings. No need to wait in line today. What I need won't be found buried in the back in some old file box, but I have an idea of where I might be able to find out if there was a case involving Sinclair. One that was sealed or expunged—one Sinclair needed to keep off the radar to keep his job at a fancy private school.

***

The light for the sixth floor blinks on with a pinging sound.

"Excuse me, excuse me," I say, muscling my way from the back of the elevator through the crowd, extruding myself into the reception area of the State Attorney's Office like meat from a grinder.

As if trapped in amber, Maddy, the receptionist, is still at her post. Just as she has been since decades before I was a newbie prosecutor, fueled by the belief that truth and justice go hand in hand and that I would serve justice up to those who deserved it like I'd done in the Army.

"Well, I'll be, Ms. Grace. Is that you?" Maddy says, her melodic twang announcing, "I'm from the real South."

Maddy always knew who was doing what or whom at the office, and where the political bodies were buried, but her demeanor never deviated from that of a grandmother who wanted nothing more than to make you feel welcome by serving you some sweet tea out on the porch.

"How are you, Maddy?" I say, blood pounding in my ears.

"I'm fine," she says, the kindness creases around her eyes crinkling. "But how are *you* doing, honey?"

A warmth spreads through me, followed by a sharp shot of regret. "I can't complain. Even if I did, I'd only have myself to blame."

"While it is wonderful to see your pretty face, you didn't come 'round here to jaw with me, so, tell me, what can I do for you? And why don't we get you going to where you need to be getting to? Maybe not best to stand around here for too long."

I look right then left, but no one in sight. "Too true, Maddy. Can you check and see if Rita's in?"

"Sure thing." She picks up the phone and pecks a few digits into the phone with the eraser end of a pencil.

"Rita, honey, guess who's standing here? Your former partner in crime."

Long pause.

"Yep, she sure is. Right here in front of me."

Another pause.

"Sure will." Maddy hangs up. "Follow me, young lady. Let's go in the back way."

She guides me to the end of the hallway and through a door she unlocks using a keypad. I note that the code is still the same and enjoy a private moment of humor about the false sense of security complacency begets.

Maddy ushers me into the first office on the left with the nameplate ASA Margarita Morales on the door.

"Sweetheart, now you take care of yourself," Maddy says, easing the door closed.

I pan around the cramped space. "I can't believe we shared this coffin."

I lean in to give Rita a hug, but she retreats behind the desk.

"I'm sorry," she says, eyes downcast. "It's been a while."

"Don't apologize. I know how this place is. No fraternizing with the enemy. Even if the enemy is, well, was, a friend."

I remain standing, briefcase clutched between both hands like a fig leaf. "And, for the record, you're not the one who has something to apologize for."

She points at one of the two guest chairs. "Sit down, for heaven's sake. You're standing there like you've been called to the principal's office."

I perch on the edge of one of the chairs. "I stayed away. I didn't want to call. Didn't want my crap to spill all over you."

She holds her nose. "I see you haven't lost your powers of description. And I surely don't want to be covered in yours. Mine's about all I can handle."

"I've missed you, Rita."

"I've missed you too, but I do keep seeing you in the news. You've gone big time on me."

"If being the captain of the Titanic is big time, then I guess I'm big time, but the ship's still sinking." I clear my throat. "Which brings me to why I'm here. I'm hoping you can help me."

She sighs. "I knew it. You drop out of sight and then reappear asking favors."

I raise my hands, palms out. "Hear me out, please."

"Spit it out."

"I'm trying to check a name to see if he's been a party to any case in Broward."

She pushes back from the desk and crosses her legs. "The Clerk's office is on the first floor."

"And I see you haven't lost your penchant for sarcasm."

"Touché," she says, with a tight smile.

"I already ran the name through the Clerk's database, but nothing came up. And the thing is—"

Rita holds up a hand. "And your point?"

"I scoot the chair in close to the desk and lean in. "When a case is expunged by court order, the Clerk and all law enforcement agencies, even your office, have to destroy all of its records, paper and digital, for the case, right?"

"Again, and your point would be?"

"But sealed records still exist—they just go into hiding and can only be seen by certain agencies."

Rita raises a finger as if to test wind direction. "That's what you want. You want me to do a search of our private records."

I look away.

"For you," she continues. "You, the one who was fired from this very office. By my very boss. The one who signs my paychecks."

I bite my lip.

"You sure you're still the same person I knew? The one who thought everything in life divided neatly in two categories—right or wrong? And you know this is wrong, don't you? Woman, you're not exactly in friendly territory here."

"And how is Mr. Britt by the way? I saw him just the other day."

"Still the same jackass he always was."

She stares at the door as if Britt will materialize at any second. "He's one vindictive sonofabitch. He still thinks your embarrassing episode was what almost cost him the last election."

I grunt. "If only. *That* would have made getting arrested worthwhile."

"Back to why you're here. You want me to run a name for you, don't you?"

In my mind's eye, I envision Rita grabbing for my car keys outside the Ragin' Cajun, insisting I should call a cab.

I stand to leave. "Forget it."

Rita's eyes widen. "It's really not the same you, is it? The Grace Locke I knew would never give up so fast."

"People change, Rita."

"Apparently. So, sit your ass back down, why don't you. Name?"

"Brandon Sinclair. Try Sinclair Brandon too. The cops just love to mess up people's names on police reports."

"And you think this Sinclair's case was sealed?"

I nod.

She stops typing. "Wait a minute. Is Sinclair the guy who got killed? The one your client murdered?

"Allegedly."

She bangs hard on the keyboard. "Sure. Now I know you've changed."

After a few keystrokes, she shakes her head.

"Damn."

She chews on her thumb for a couple of seconds. "But like you said, that may just mean his case was expunged, and we were ordered to destroy the file."

"And it's gone forever, and I'll never know if Sinclair had a criminal history." I flop back.

"Think, woman! Just because a case evaporates from the official records, doesn't mean one never existed. If there was a case and it was sealed, we'd still have a file. We don't. Therefore, no sealing. If it was expunged, we wouldn't have anything because we got a court order to destroy everything. But let's go back to the basics. If someone is arrested in Broward, what happens?"

"He or she appears before a magistrate within twenty-four hours for a hearing to make sure there was probable cause for the arrest."

"And who represents almost every defendant at that point, because almost nobody, except for the richest of the rich, has a private criminal defense lawyer on standby?"

"The public defender?"

"And who isn't ordered to destroy its records in an expungement order?" Head bobbing, coaxing the answer, obvious to her, out of me.

I palm my forehead. "The PD. The PD may have a file for Sinclair even if it was expunged and, if they don't, chances are there never was a case for Sinclair and my source is wrong."

I rocket out of the chair and squeeze behind the desk for a hug. "Thanks, *chica*, I owe you one."

"No, I owe you one. That night, I should have—"

I grab her shoulders. "Stop right there. *I* shouldn't have. You did everything you could. That night is all on me."

Extricating myself from behind the desk, I stumble against the wall and, reflexively, redirect my prosthetic leg.

She catches sight of the metal ankle and drops into her chair. "You did it. You finally got the operation."

"It was time. It was never going to be right. And I was never going to be right if I had to keep taking those damn pills," I say, smoothing down my pant leg.

As I am about to leave, she puts an arm around my shoulder. "Grace, what's past is past. It's time to move on. Now go show them they can never take away what you got."

"And what is it I've got?"

"Fight, my friend. You're a fighter from way back."

Chapter 22

The waiting area outside the Office of the Public Defender resembles a casting call for *The Wire*. On one side of the room are the cops, some in uniform, others in plain clothes, faces pinched, as if they've just eaten something that doesn't agree with them. Going to the Public Defender's Office is a trip to the place cases go to die because of what law enforcement calls "technicalities" and it isn't exactly a cop's idea of a good time.

On the other side sit the PD's clients. Some wearing saggy pants and flat-brimmed hats, legs splayed. Others have chosen Walmart church clothes in hopes of making a good impression. One young woman, holding a wailing infant wrapped in a dirty blanket, chews on her nicotine-stained fingernails. Lines of people wait in front of three windows behind which sit attendants, all with eyes which say, "I've heard it all before."

I lean against the wall by the entrance and fidget with my phone to avoid eye contact. I had called ahead to Joshua Jacobs, the Broward County Public Defender, to avoid waiting too long face-to-face with defendants I may have prosecuted, or cops I may have ripped a new one for blowing a case with an illegal search or a confession extracted without Miranda warnings.

After a few minutes, the security door buzzes and a short man in cowboy boots and a string tie appears. He rushes me, hands outstretched. "Ms. Locke, how the hell are you?"

All heads swivel in Joshua Jacobs's direction. Cops shake their heads. Defendants chuckle. One guy with a gold medallion the size of a pizza hanging around his neck lets fly with, "Hey, bro. I saw you on TV."

Jacobs has a weekly spot on the local news called Jacobs's Justice, in which he rights legal wrongs suffered by Average Joes. Price-gouging roofers, home-health-care aides stealing old ladies' Social Security checks, contractors absconding with deposits, they're all up Jacobs's alley. My favorite episode was his straight-faced analysis of whether it was unconstitutional for Toys "R" Us to sell only white, and not black or Hispanic, Barbie dolls. Laugh as I might, Jacobs's Justice has made him a darling of the underdog, not to mention a household name when election day rolls around.

I let myself be hugged, a prop in his performance. Maybe it's my puritanical upbringing, but I've always found his "man of the people" theatrics a bit over the top. Still, I owe him big time, and have to admit he isn't without a certain charm.

Showmanship aside, it was Jacobs who stepped up to help me when everyone else, including my own husband, had written me off as a self-inflicted train wreck. Manny had cut off my access to our bank accounts. With no money for a lawyer, Jacobs was my lifesaver, representing me himself, something he rarely did. He had little to work with, but he managed to engineer what he did have into a plea agreement that spared me a felony on my record and disbarment—two things State's Attorney Britt wanted.

Not that Jacobs went to bat for me out of the goodness of his heart, however. An old hippie from way back, he stepped in because he hates cops, and never misses an opportunity to go to war with authority, a quality which made me despise him when I was a prosecutor, but which saved my ass when I was looking down the barrel of a long prison sentence.

"Josh, good to see you."

"Back at you, my friend," he says, his stubby legs taking two steps to every one of mine as we head toward his office, his curlicue ponytail bouncing side to side.

He points me to an upholstered client chair opposite his desk.

"Your face is on TV as much as my own these days," he says, propping his feet on a wide mahogany desk. "Things seem to be looking up for you. So, what brings you to my humble abode?" he asks, motioning at the view of the New River from his corner office. It's a location that would go for thousands a month if it weren't paid for by the taxpayers.

I puff out my cheeks.

Jacobs tents his fingers in front of his face, a maze of tanned wrinkles punctuated by probing blue eyes. "Start at the part where you tell me what you want."

I take a deep breath. "You're familiar with the Slim case?"

"Of course. Who isn't? Like I said, it's all over the news."

"Maybe the victim wasn't quite the angel the media is making him out to be."

He drops his feet to the floor and paddles his chair to the desk. "Do tell. You know me, I always like a little tattle and a little tale."

I can't help but smile right along with him. A bit of a caricature he may be, but he is amusing, not to mention an effective advocate for the powerless and the just plain crazy.

"It appears that Sinclair, the guy my client is accused of killing, was involved somehow in a criminal case."

"Your client, by the way, is a shit show."

I laugh along with him, but only for a second, more of a reflex than an expression of agreement.

"A shit show she may be, but she's a profoundly mentally ill young woman in a fight for her life."

"That, she is."

"You enjoy being a champion for the underdog, don't you?"

He gives me a time-out sign. "Enough flattery, for now."

"You'll help?"

"You had me at underdog." He drops his feet to the floor and leans in. "And you know this, how? The thing about Sinclair being involved?"

"I ran Sinclair through the Clerk's computer, and nothing. Not a party to, or a witness on any case, not even a freakin' traffic ticket."

Josh shrugs. "It's always the ones with no history who do the worst shit."

"True, but starting with the assumption that he was involved in a case somehow, which I have on good authority—"

"Get to your point, will you?"

"Bottom line, the State Attorney has no records either, which means either my information was wrong and there was no case, which I doubt, or he had a case that was expunged. If it were just sealed, the State would still have the records, but they don't."

His eyes light up as if someone's just turned on their power source. "Seems as if you still have at least one friend over at the conviction factory, former ASA Locke."

"Maybe. Well...anyway..." I study the ceiling, searching for a way to frame my favor.

"Your point? Please."

"Since your office represents ninety-nine percent of everyone arrested..."

Taking full advantage of my pause, Jacobs points at me. "Yes, and me," I say with a sigh. "Since your people are in magistrate court for every first appearance hearing, you get the complete docket every day and log every possible defendant's name in case they need counsel later."

He bats his eyelashes. "And you want to know if your guy's

name is in our database."

"Exactly."

He shifts in his chair. "Let me put this another way, maybe a way that would make me feel more comfortable? The State, your former employer and now archenemy, may not have given you all the goods on Sinclair, correct?"

"Maybe not."

He wheels around to the credenza behind him and punches at a keyboard, screeds of names appearing on the screen. "Which is why you came to me, given my fondness for poleaxing the State."

I stick my tongue in my cheek. "Is that so? I'd never have guessed."

"Humor me a little so I can get even more comfortable with this whole, I won't say, conspiracy, but what shall we call it? Let's just call it an evil little plan, shall we?" Jacobs rubs his hands together. "Would you agree that, if we have anything in our database about Sinclair, it wouldn't be a violation of attorney-client privilege for me to share? After all, he wasn't actually our client. He never signed an engagement letter."

I jump on board. "And court dockets are public records, after all."

He swivels around. "Brilliant point!" He turns back and motions to the screen. "I think I have something for you."

I walk to his side of the desk and look over his shoulder.

"Brandon Sinclair, DOB 4/23/1974, arrested December 2, 2008, one count of Trafficking in oxycodone, seven to fourteen grams."

I am rendered speechless. That's what Marcus meant! The wild blue yonder. Sea of blue. Marcus meant blues, slang for oxycodone—OxyContin's generic name.

"You ever watch late night TV, former ASA Locke? When some Benihana type is trying to sell you Ginsu knives you don't need?"

"If I had a dime for every late-night commercial I've seen

when I can't sleep, I wouldn't be defending criminals to scrape out a living."

Josh flaps his hands. "And what is it they say when they keep adding more crap to the deal for nineteen ninety-nine?"

"And that's not all folks?"

"*Correcto mundo.* Add this little nugget to what I just told you. Brandon Sinclair, DOB 4/23/1974, arrested May 25, 2009. Any guess on the charges?" His smile widens, revealing coffee-stained teeth.

"More drugs?"

"You get the prize. Yes! Trafficking in oxycodone, but this time the quantity was greater, twenty-five to one hundred grams.

"No way," I say, my mind racing. "Meaning he was facing some major prison time."

"No way that amount could have been for personal use. That amount of blues would kill an elephant. And, as you know, having put away a dealer or two yourself, that amount will send you up the river for a minimum of fifteen years. So, unless your victim was a superhuman addict, I'd say he was a dealer. Says here, the second case was filed by Statewide."

He clasps his hands behind his head and leans back in his chair. "Any of that make sense to you?"

"Sinclair was popped in a task force drug sting."

"I'd say you have pulled back the curtain on the great State of Oz," Jacobs says. "Cases come, only to go bye-bye when a rat is willing to help the cops catch the bigger fish."

"So says the wizard, otherwise the whole system would come to a grinding halt."

"And then where would we be? Fewer people convicted. Fewer going to private prisons. Fewer dollars going into reelection campaigns so those same elected officials can allocate more tax dollars for more prisons."

"And I thought I was cynical."

He shrugs. "The truth is the truth, Grace, no matter how you spin it."

"Sinclair flipped."

"Would explain why his case evaporated, why he has no record in the database. It would've kept him out of prison."

"And employed."

"That too." Josh gives me a lopsided grin.

I bury my face in my hands. "Thank you, Josh. Thank you so much."

"But remember, my friend, you aren't in Kansas anymore."

I drop my hands. "Meaning?"

"Think about it, Dorothy. Doing the right thing by old man Vicanti cost you dearly. And now you find yourself in the same position again. Standing up to the almighty State's version of things, which is that these arrests don't exist, is not without risk." He takes a deep breath. "Sometimes it's not so easy speaking truth to power, even if it is the truth and the life on the line is a kid's."

I exhale hard. "Why is it I always have to do things the hard way?"

"You and me both, sister. You and me both."

The printer starts to hum. "Here. Take these. There may be something in them that will help. Our people scan all of the police reports into our database after magistrate court every day. That way, if we end up appointed on the case, we can get straight to work without waiting for the State to provide the reports in discovery when they damn well please." He covers his mouth. "Oops, I keep forgetting you used to be one of *them.*"

We share a full-throated laugh this time. "'Used to' be being the operative phrase."

"Amen to that." he says, flopping back into his chair.

I scan the papers. Two identical arrest reports for Sinclair. Each one written poorly. The earlier of the two, dated December 2, 2008, states: Subject arrested when he attempted to sell thirty-five pills of Oxy to Det. Sorenson who was plain clothes. The second, dated May 25, 2009, reports in similar pidgin English, that Sinclair was arrested for "attempting to sell a hundred and fifty Oxy for fifteen hundred."

"Seems as if Mr. Sinclair was not only a murder victim, but a twice-arrested drug trafficker," Josh says.

"And, interestingly, one without a criminal record."

"If only we could all be so lucky," he says. After a long pause, he adds, "Like you."

I grab my backpack and head for the door. "Again, thank you."

"Not at all. Always glad to help an underdog," he says. "And if the high life of private practice ever stops suiting you, there's always a place for you here, Grace. I can always use another bull in a china shop."

"I appreciate that compliment, but for now I need to make some real money. I'm broke and a PD's salary won't cut it."

"It's a standing offer, no expiration date, but in the meantime, keep those eyes in the back of your head wide open, young lady. I'm not interested in going down the yellow brick road with you ever again."

Chapter 23

I jab my finger at the windowless, concrete-block structure. "That's it! 1447 West Sunrise Boulevard."

"What is that place? Looks like the death row at Starke," Vinnie says, his top lip curled back.

"That, my friend, is a pill mill, also known, in more polite circles, as a pain clinic."

A low growl from the back seat.

"Maybe we should have left her in the crate back home?"

Another growl.

Vinnie shoots me a look that could strip paint. "No one's getting locked up in a cage again. Not on my watch," he says, docking Carmela in one of the few empty parking spaces outside the pill mill.

Many of the vehicles in the jam-packed lot are multi-passenger vans with out-of-state license plates. Most of the cars with Florida plates are beaters, some rusted out, others with mismatched quarter panels. All appear to be on their last legs, not unlike the dozen or so emaciated, jittery people pacing back and forth outside the entrance, smoking cigarettes and chomping gum.

A white, middle-aged man exits the building and hones in on a skeletal woman in skin-tight jeans and a bikini top leaning against the fender of a tan pickup with West Virginia plates. The woman sucks on a cigarette and forages deep in her pocket as if it contained untold treasure. Cash in her hand, the man shoves something at her, grabs the money, jumps into the truck, and guns the engine. The woman stays behind, swaying, staring at whatever is in her hand.

"If I had to guess, I'd say they're giving away blue candy in that bunker."

"Huh?"

"The blues, baby," I say, affecting a dreamy tone.

"That a music club?" Vinnie asks, the furrows in his brow carved deep by time and a hard life.

"For a former made guy, you sure can be naive. No, not music, silly. Drugs. Pain pills. OxyContin. Called blues because of their color. Hillbilly heroin. Whatever you wanna call it, it's pure evil on steroids."

A young couple, hand in hand, walk inside. Her hair's in pigtails. He's wearing a Nirvana T-shirt.

A young woman gets out of her car and straps on a back brace, before limping inside with the help of a cane.

"More grist for the pill mill."

"I read about them pill mills in the paper. It said Broward is the epicenter of the opioid epidemic. Whatever epi and opi are."

"They mean this is where people come to die at the hands of those sworn to do no harm."

"Meaning what?"

"Meaning doctors in white coats pushing drugs. All legal. All made out to be a regular medical office. Except the patients, most of them at least, as just looking for their next fix."

"Back in the day, we weren't no pushers. We had our rules, and drugs were against them."

"Only girls and gambling. Isn't that the party line?"

"A little of this, a little of that," he says, examining his age-spotted hands on the steering wheel. "But that's all another lifetime ago, sweetheart."

"Check that out. Dude over there in the brown Toyota. He's shooting up right there, out in the open!"

"Mother of God." Vinnie covers his eyes, but peeks though his fingers at the man tightening a rubber band around his arm with his teeth. "Thought it was pills they're sellin'."

"Yeah, but the high is twice as special if you crush the pills and shoot or snort the powder."

"Jesus, Gracie. Enough. I ain't got the stomach for this. And neither do you," he says to Miranda, along with a command to lie down.

"Thank God, nor do I. Anymore," I whisper to myself.

"Why is it we're here again? You said Sinclair got arrested here. But for what, if all this is on the level?"

"Sinclair was arrested here for drug trafficking. He got caught trying to sell some pain pills to an undercover cop."

"Oops," Vinnie says with a shrug. "But why here?"

"You ever heard the saying that bank robbers rob banks because that's where the money is?"

"Sure."

"Drug dealers deal drugs at places like these because it's where the drugs and the consumers are. Here in the Sunshine State, not only can you get pain pills prescribed at a pain clinic, but you can also get that very prescription filled there too at an on-site pharmacy."

"One-stop shopping. How convenient."

"Exactly! But it gets better. One pill that costs three dollars at the on-site pharmacy goes for as much as eighty out here on the street, or even twenty times as much out of state where the laws don't allow doctors to prescribe and dispense drugs from the same location."

"Big bucks," he says, with a faraway look.

"Big business. The height of junkie entrepreneurship."

"Yeah, until you get caught. Sinclair. He got caught and then he got dead, right?"

"Maybe Sinclair got greedy. Says here he tried to offload thirty-five pills. Over thirty-one, it's a minimum mandatory prison sentence of three years and a fine of fifty thousand dollars."

His eyes bulge like a frog's. "Fifty grand? And a three year bit?"

"The more pills you get caught trying to sell, the more prison time you get and the higher the fine, until you go away for life."

"You said he didn't have a sheet."

"No way to know for sure, but I'd guess Sinclair agreed to help the cops."

"You tellin' mean he was a rat?"

"If he was in the business, he could finger other dealers to save himself. And if the cops dropped the case, Sinclair could have all evidence of his arrest erased. It's called an expungement. Presto, all gone from his record. And the fancy folks at St. Paul's are none the wiser."

"Snitches make enemies, sweetheart."

I rub my chin. "Maybe you're onto something there. Maybe he paid the ultimate price for trying to save his own ass." I wave the second police report. "But why would he risk everything—his job, his freedom—a second time?"

"People do stupid shit for money. That's why you stayed with that creep for so long, remember?"

"That's not why, Vin."

"Sure, I forgot. You loved his sorry Cuban ass."

"That's ancient history. I pinch his arm. "Let's get back to why we're here."

Vinnie slides down in his seat. "Whatever you say, boss."

A group of twenty-somethings emerges from the pill mill, all emaciated with skin so white it's translucent, like parchment paper. They get into a white panel van, the type we used to call a pedo van at the State due to the fact they are the vehicle of choice for pedophiles. Before climbing in, each one hands the driver a brown paper bag. They'll get their cut later, as well as a few bills for their trouble. The rest goes to the big boss, back wherever they came from.

"Not that I'm a fan of cops or nothin,' but why don't they shut these places down? Look at this circus. Kids going in an out like it's a candy store."

"Pain clinics are legal."

"Shameful."

"And you want to know the best part? Anyone can own one of these places. All you need is to hire one doctor with a medical license and a DEA number to order narcotics, and you got yourself a cash cow. Doc writes the script and it gets filled on site. Everyone goes home rich or high."

"What gives with all the out-of-state plates?" He points at a Tennessee license plate with the dubious state slogan, Sounds Good to Me, above the number.

"Tennessee, West Virginia, Kentucky, they're all just a day's drive away. It's gotten so bad the cops call I-75 in and out of Florida the Blue Highway to Hell."

"I had no idea."

"There's a flight every Monday into Fort Lauderdale from Huntington, West Virginia that never has an empty seat. The Oxy Express."

"Where the heck is Huntington, West Virginia?"

"You get my point."

"How's it you know so much about this?"

"I once prosecuted a woman who testified she was sponsored by a guy back up in Nowheresville, Kentucky, who ran five vans packed with addicts down here every week. Did the circuit of all the pill mills. Addicts got their visits and drugs paid for, and got to keep some of their prescriptions. The rest, the guy sold back home for ten times what he paid for it down here."

"Doesn't anyone keep track of who's buying what?"

"Nope, our good old governor has blocked a statewide database to shut down doctor shopping."

"Jesus. What's this place called? There's no sign."

"They don't need to advertise."

After a half hour of watching zombies parading in and out with brown paper bags stuffed with enough pills to anesthetize a small island nation, I've got a pretty good idea of what Sinclair was up to. Just as I'm about to tell Vinnie to get us out of here, a young woman strolls in front of the car.

I snatch Vinnie's threadbare Marlins World Series cap from his head.

"What? What you doin'?"

I aim both index fingers at the young woman. "That's Serena Price! Zoe's BFF."

"Who?"

"The girl who found Sinclair's body."

"You sure?"

"Damn straight, I'm sure."

"Wait here," I say, bolting out after her.

"Wait! Maybe I should come...Wait!"

***

By the time I get inside the pill mill, Serena's nowhere to be seen. Two giants stand sentry outside the only door off the interior hallway, their otherwise trim suit jackets bulged out with handguns. One has a tattoo of a teardrop under his left eye.

The man without the teardrop holds out his tree trunk of an arm. "Phone?"

I nod.

He signals for me to deposit my phone in one of the pigeon holes on the wall. "Frisk her," he says to Teardrop.

More than a little uncomfortable about having the monster's paws on me, I widen my stance and extend my arms like a scarecrow for Teardrop to pat me down. I ball my fists to refrain from clocking him when he spends way too long on my chest.

"Go," Teardrop says, waving me through.

Douche bag.

Florida Center for Pain is stenciled on the inside door in benign, small black letters. I step into a room which looks like a warehouse, not a waiting area. I pull the ball cap low and walk around, as if I'm looking for a place to sit. No Serena. Rows and rows of folding chairs are set up in the middle of the space, like at the DMV. At the far end is a door to the clinic's inner sanctum with a No Entry sign. The cement walls are bare, except for a poster, a twist on the classic Florida mantra: No shirt. No shoes. No problem. Instead, it reads: No Weapons. No Phone. No Cameras.

Those waiting are in various stages of deterioration. It's obvious some are too far down the road to survive much longer, their bodies shriveled, teeth mostly gone along with any hope for a better tomorrow. Today, along with whatever they can swallow, snort, or shoot, is all they have, all they will ever have. There are a few bright faces, young, for now. They too will look as old as time soon, the light in their eyes extinguished by what will become their single-minded obsession—the next fix.

On the side wall there are three bulletproof-glass windows: Check In—Cash Only, MRIs—Cash Only, and Prescriptions—Cash Only. Dozens of people are lined up in front of each, not one of whom is standing still. All biting nails, scratching skin, sniffing and sighing, every second getting closer to their next high. Behind the glass are women wearing scrubs decorated with pictures of *Winnie-the-Pooh* characters. Yellow background for Pooh, pink for Piglet, and blue for Eeyore.

I join the Check In line. The attendant takes two hundred fifty dollars in cash from each patient and drops the bills into a large red garbage bag labeled BIOHAZARD. A heap of identical bags is piled behind her chair.

"You have appointment with doctor, miss?" asks a young Asian woman in the Piglet scrubs seated behind the glass.

"No, but I'd like to see a doctor."

"Not today, sweetie. We too busy."

"I just want to get some information. I was thinking about making an appointment, but—"

The woman shoves a clear plastic bag through a slot under the window. "Here, information. Cash only, no insurances, fill in forms before come. Next please." She flicks her wrist for me to step aside. I grab the bag and step back.

A cheer rises from the crowd when a woman wins a car on *The Price is Right*, playing on an ancient TV mounted high in a corner. A security camera is bolted to the top of the TV. I count seven other cameras.

I sit and tip the contents of the bag onto my lap. A photocopy of an ad from South Florida Weekly, a free local newspaper, saying, Chronic Pain? Stop Hurting and Start Living!, along with a list of all Florida Center for Pain locations: Miami, Fort Lauderdale, Delray Beach, Riviera Beach, and Orlando. Coupons offering a free first visit and twenty-five dollars cash for bringing in a new patient. The final item in the bag is another ad, this one for a fifty percent discount on an MRI at Mobile MRI.

On the far side of the room, a crowd has gathered around something. Shouts of "Out of the way. Out of the way!" burst from the center of the group. Four paramedics from the Fort Lauderdale Fire Department charge in and load a woman onto a stretcher, a twig of an arm dangling off the side.

I approach one of the medics who is packing away equipment. "That was scary. That happen a lot in here?"

The medic slings a heavy pack over her shoulders and shakes her head in disgust. "Every damn day. We're over here every damn day. Overdoses, fights, you name it, it happens here in Zombieland every damn day." She trots away to catch up with her colleagues toting the stretcher.

I sink onto a chair beside a sleeping woman, head tipped back, mouth open, no doubt one of the few moments in her day when she's not trolling for her next high. In her lap, an open purse, a pill bottle visible on top, its contents a brownish color through the amber plastic. I don't need to see the blue to know they're oxycodone.

It would be easy, wouldn't it? Just one pill. She'd never miss it. At least not until long after I'm gone. A moment of relief, the feeling that all's right with the world. It would be easy.

No one will ever be the wiser, will they? Tomorrow will be just as good a day as today to rebuild my life as today. I deserve a break, a few moments of euphoria, don't I?

Easy maybe. But also, wrong. So wrong.

I stand and shake myself so hard the woman awakens.

"One day at a time," I say under my breath, a non sequitur which results in the woman clasping her purse to her chest.

"You okay, honey?" she asks.

I nod and walk away, forcing myself to focus on the task at hand—how to defend Zoe.

I clasp my shaking hands and close my eyes. When I open them, Serena and a stocky man are emerging out of the restricted area. He hands her a duffel bag. It's the albino guy from the Sinclair house.

I stuff the paraphernalia back into the bag and take off after them.

At the exit, I tap Serena on the shoulder. "Excuse me, you're Serena Price, aren't you?"

Serena keeps walking, the man's beefy arm around her waist.

"If I could talk to you for a minute. I'm Zoe's lawyer. You guys were friends."

The man deposits his bulk between me and Serena. "Who she is ain't none of your business."

I grab my phone at the entrance and chase after Serena, the man having disappeared back inside the clinic.

"If I could just ask you a couple of questions, I'll get out of your hair."

Serena keeps walking. "Crazy bitch killed Brandon. No way I'm gonna do or say anything that could help her. I'm not telling you nothing."

"But you guys were friends."

Serena tucks the duffel under her arm.

"Why are you at a place like this?"

She clicks her key fob in the direction of her white BMW.

"You know anything about Brandon Sinclair selling drugs?"

Serena whips around, her eyes spearing me like dual daggers.

"How about you?" I point at the duffel. "What you got there?"

She shoves me aside and drops the duffel in the trunk. "Get away from me."

"From what I hear, you were pretty close with Brandon. Maybe too close, is what I hear. I bet that's something your parents might be interested in." I step back. "You can't avoid me forever. You're going to have to answer my questions in a deposition."

"Screw you," she says, before getting in her Beemer and taking off.

Back at the car, Vinnie's fiddling with the radio. "Why can't I get the Marlins on this thing?"

I change the frequency to AM and tune in the Marlins game.

Vinnie grabs my arm. "And next time, give me a heads-up when you're thinking about doing something stupid."

"What?"

"This place ain't exactly safe."

"You mean for someone like me?"

"I mean for anybody."

Chapter 24

West Sunrise Boulevard is a panorama of ghetto landmarks: a cash exchange, a Dollar Store, two pawn shops, and an establishment called Pussies Galore.

"You see the MGM behind us?" Vinnie asks.

"The what?"

"MGM. A Mercury Grand Marquis. The dead giveaway undercover cop car? What, you forgot the lingo already?"

I check the side mirror. "Wise ass. And no, I can't see any MGM."

"Maybe nothing."

I pat his arm. "Old habits die hard."

"You can't never be too careful," he says with another peek in the rear view. "Who was that girl you said was stupid enough to chase back there?"

"Serena Price. The girl who found Sinclair's body."

"She tell you anything?"

"No, but she sure as sh— Let's just say she really wanted to get rid of me, though, so I must be on to something."

"Nice save, sweetheart. You, too, can learn new tricks." He glances at Miranda. "But not anywhere near as fast as you."

"Zoe's trial's around the corner, so I better learn a lot more soon or she's going down, along with my chances for a big payday."

"I thought the blonde paid you."

"She only gave me a retainer. We agreed I'll get the rest for the trial. Or more when it pleads out—more likely given the evidence. There's always the risk they'll stiff me, but given all the attention the case is getting, it's one worth taking."

"The bloodsucker who had my case made me pay him everything up front."

"It's never easy to collect from someone on the inside. Maybe he thought you were going down."

"And I did. At least until you came along," he says, his hands flexing and unflexing on the steering wheel.

I count off the street numbers, in search of 6555 NE 6th Avenue, regretful for my failed attempt at humor.

"Coming up, stop number two on our whirlwind tour of the pill mills of South Florida. If I'm not mistaken, this next place was one of the places we raided when I was working with Marcus on the task force for the Florida Department of Law Enforcement and the Feds."

"Way too many cops in this world," Vinnie says, a renewed twinkle in his eyes to remind me, while he may owe me his life, he reserves the right to rag on me for having once been a military cop and a prosecutor.

"Wise ass."

"Yeah, yeah. Whatever. But why's this place still open if it was raided?"

"We closed it down, but another owner stepped in and picked up right where the old one left off. It's a game of whack-a-mole. Didn't even change the name. Sunshine Pain. Sinclair was arrested here by the same task force Marcus and I worked on together. They caught Sinclair red-handed with a boat load of Oxy. He was going down for a long time."

"What happened?"

"Nothing. That's the point. The case mysteriously disappeared."

"Don't tell me. He ratted again?"

"Seems that way. Maybe the task force didn't even know about his other bust by Lauderdale PD at FCP. Or simply didn't care. Who knows? The only thing for sure is if St. Paul's had found out about the arrests, they would have fired him."

He turns right onto NE 6th Avenue and rolls to a stop in front of 6555, an old Florida-style house, yellow striped awnings shading jalousie windows. Carport. A hand-lettered sign on the front porch reads Sunshine Pain.

I double check the list the FCP attendant gave me to make sure Sunshine Pain isn't part of the FCP pain clinic industrial complex. It isn't. Looks like Sinclair went doctor shopping to lay in inventory.

"Wait here. We'll be back." I clip on Miranda's leash and she leaps down in a single, fluid motion.

"Walk time, pretty girl. And no biting, okay?" I say, thankful she's not a drug sniffer dog, or she'd be alerting to every vehicle and person in sight.

The street's a junkyard. Cars, trucks, vans, and even a battered old yellow school bus, all squeezed in nose-to-tail. We walk down the block, checking license plates undisturbed because everyone moves out of the way when they see Miranda. Maybe they've seen one too many police dogs in their lives.

When we get back, Vinnie's leaning against the hood of the car, arms crossed across his favorite Guy Harvey T-shirt, a picture of a blue marlin in full flight. He's only wearing it because I gave it to him for his birthday. Vinnie hates to fish. Despite his prior occupation as an enforcer, he can't bring himself to kill an innocent creature. He once told me a story of how back in the day, when he was the superintendent of an apartment building in Chinatown, a Chink—Vinnie's words not mine—kicked an orphaned kitten he'd been bottle feeding. "I taught that piece a shit a lesson he'd never forget. Never did come back for his security deposit."

I jerk my chin at the line of shifty people spilling out the clinic's front door onto what had once been a lawn, a space long ago given over to weeds and ant hills.

He shakes his head. "Same caca, different place."

"Bet you can't guess what I saw back there?"

He gives me a self-satisfied smile. "A guy getting a blow job."

I stamp my foot like a willful child. "How'd you guess?"

"Because I saw the same thing over here."

He motions with his head to an ancient Cadillac with purple neon rims which are spinning even though the car is parked. Inside, a woman is hunched over a guy in the driver's seat, head bobbing up and down like the drinking bird toy I won at a carnival when I seven.

"Now we've confirmed Sinclair was a scumbag, what next?"

"We? Taking this investigator role seriously, are we?"

He gives me a crooked salute. "At your service, ma'am."

I plop the Marlins cap on Vinnie's balding head and settle in to observe the macabre, hypnotic rhythm of the scene. The living dead shuffling in and out, faces full of anxiety on the way in and vain hope on the way out.

Before he sits down beside me, I notice a bulge in the small of Vinnie's back, the place where a person might stash a gun. If one were in need of protection. If one were not a convicted felon and, as such, prohibited from carrying a weapon.

When a woman stumbles on her way down the steps, landing on her knees, several customers step over her. She closes her eyes, face raised to the sun in supplication.

It's Beth from the NA meeting.

I resist the urge to run over and help her. "Only you can save you now, sweet Beth."

God, grant me the serenity to accept the things I cannot change, the courage to change the things I can, and the wisdom to know the difference.

Chapter 25

I spend the next morning hammering out a plea bargain for a court-appointed client. The fee for indigent cases sucks, but it's better than zippo, and it's fast money when you can meet them and plead them all on the same day.

The client of the day is Willy Grass, charged with—what else—marijuana possession. Just another moment to add to my notebook of You Can't Make this Sh...Up observations.

Deal done, I consider my options. I could do some work organizing my very own new office courtesy of Manny. Then again, a day at the beach might be good for my state of mind and my ghostly white skin which makes me look like I just got sprung from the slammer. It has been a while since I've played tourist—so the beach it is. I head for the bus stop.

To spite me, my phone vibrates. Gretchen. So much for getting sand between my five toes.

She's panting, gulping out the words. "Doctors say Zoe's ready to come home. Doing better. New meds."

More panting.

"Where are you?"

"On the treadmill."

"You run?"

Maybe she's not so bad after all.

"Yeah, but I hate it. Best way to keep the pounds off."

No, she's worse.

"If it's okay, I'll pick her up this afternoon from ESH."

"Fine. I'll call the bondsman to reinstate the bond like the judge ordered."

Treadmill belt winding down. "I talked to her a few minutes ago."

Gulping something. Likely some designer alkaline-infused-ionized water or some such ridiculousness marketed to rich people as the a newly improved version of something they can already have for free.

"She sounded nervous."

"A few days at home and she'll be fine. But remember, she's only allowed out of the house for school, church, and medical appointments."

"I understand. We've decided to get a tutor for Zoe instead of sending her back to St. Paul's, so that's not an issue."

"Wise choice."

"As for church—we don't go. And doctors? I think she's had her fill of those for a while." After a painful pause, she adds, "I'm grateful for what you're doing, Grace."

I force myself to say, "You're welcome," although being the source of Gretchen's gratitude is a bitter pill.

"Call soon. Bye."

When my bus arrives, I wave the driver off. The walk to the office will do me and Oscar good.

***

A few steps north of Broward Boulevard, the glass-and-steel skyscrapers give way to low-slung concrete-block buildings that once housed thriving businesses, now abandoned, their paint faded by decades of neglect, their purpose forgotten to time.

Next, Florida pine cottages, once home to children who played outside without fear of death and parents who believed in Sunday best for church and hope for the future, are now crack dens tagged with gang graffiti. Lot for Sale signs dot the landscape in the shadow of dilapidated billboards touting the Community Redevelopment Association, an organization that failed despite millions in government funding. I count five churches in less than a mile, all denominated by some variation of the words Prophet, God, and Ascension, not one of which applies to the surrounding blight. Two young men, bodies propped up in the doorway of a liquor store, flick cigarette butts at a stand of dead palms, trees planted for "curb appeal." The decay of the neighborhood is suffocating.

Turning left onto Sistrunk Boulevard, I hear steps behind me and pick up my pace. After a couple of blocks, I turn around. Only a tree branch blowing in the wind.

And there it is—#1301 Sistrunk, wedged between Booker's Bail Bonds and Ivory's Soul Kitchen, a run-down two-story building as much in need of a face-lift as I am a tan. Manny bought the place as an investment at the height of the excitement about revitalization which, in the end, was nothing but another unfulfilled dream.

I uncurl my hand and stare at the key. I've been it gripping so hard it's made an impression on my palm.

"Surprise!" Jake and Vinnie, Miranda in tow, jump out from the doorway.

I double over, trying to recover the breath they scared out of me. "Sweet Jesus!"

Smiling like kids on Christmas morning, they point up at a banner over the door: The Law Offices of Grace K. Locke, Esq.

I pull them into a group hug. "You two about gave me a freakin' coronary."

Vinnie holds up a toolbox. "We thought you might need some help getting this place ship shape."

I stare at the banner and choke back tears.

"Why are we all standing out here like dopes? Let's check this place out." Jake sweeps his arm wide for me to enter. "Welcome, Attorney Grace K. Locke 2.0."

I slide the key into the rusty lock and turn, but the door doesn't open.

Vinnie stiffens. "That piece of..." he mumbles under his breath, his aborted statement a reflection of my paranoia.

I give it another go, this time pulling up on the handle. The door creaks open. I hold my breath and fumble around for the light switch, anxious my credit card payment to Florida Power & Light was declined, but the light comes on, revealing three pieces of furniture—a steel desk and two chairs, one of which is missing a leg.

"Now look at that," Vinnie says. "A chair to match you and your dog."

Miranda's perks up at the word "dog."

"Don't say that about her. You'll give her a complex. She thinks she's perfectly normal."

"She must have inherited that delusion from you," Jake says.

"Everyone's a comedian." I drop my briefcase on the desk and pan around the room. "It's not much, but it's a start."

"Nothing a little TLC can't fix," Jake says, dragging in a box of cleaning supplies.

"You guys, you don't have to do this."

"Yes, I do," Vinnie says with a finality I wouldn't dare question. "This and a whole lot more. Without you, I'd be swabbing the decks at Starke, waiting to die. Not here helping you clean this rat trap." Tears start to wet the old man's eyes. "Let's quit jawin' and get to work."

"First, let's take a tour." I slot my arm through Vinnie's and motion Miranda to follow me into the back room. "And this here is the kitchen complete with chipped enamel sink and..."

Vinnie casts a sideways glance at the adjoining toilet with no door and coughs. "We'll need to fix that eyesore first. Can't be makin' coffee in the same place where you...Well, you know what I mean."

We climb a rickety wooden staircase to the second floor which is empty except for cobwebs the size of hammocks.

"Hey, can you give me a hand?"

Downstairs, we find Jake hauling in two chairs, a coffee maker, and a microwave from the bed of his truck. "Housewarming gifts from the staff of the Star," he says with a flourish, like a game show host.

"You have a staff?"

"Hey, you met Moose."

"Thanks, Jake. Totally not necessary, but much appreciated."

For the rest of the afternoon, our little merry band scrubs, mops, and dusts, cleaning away years of neglect. We position the desk against the back wall, facing the storefront window which has also been relieved of decades of grime. Jake even manufactures a makeshift bathroom door with a blue tarp, the type used to cover damaged roofs after hurricanes. It's the most joyous afternoon I've spent in a long time, the perennial knot in my gut replaced by what might be hope.

"How about we go back to The Hurricane and I'll put some food on the grill?"

I drag one of the chairs behind the desk. "Thanks Vin, but I think I'll spend some time getting settled in."

"Just us boys then, Jakey. Let's go. I'm hungry after all this slave labor."

***

After they're gone, I venture out with Miranda to survey my new neighborhood. As twilight descends, junkies huddle in doorways of abandoned buildings, grubby coats pulled around their wasted bodies, like nightcrawlers waiting in the shadows for nightfall to troll for their next fix. A group of young men crowds around a milk crate playing cards and talking trash. A mother drags a toddler away from a blind man who's weaving hats out of banana leaves when he tries to stick one of his creations on her head. Like I said, it's not much, but it's a start.

And it's all mine.

We've only been gone thirty minutes, but by the time we get back, at least a dozen handbills have been wedged in the door jamb, offering everything from tarot card readings to silicone shots to plump up your butt. I unlock the four deadbolts Jake insisted on installing. Miranda bounds inside and settles herself in a dog bed Vinnie left by the front door. I pull the snub nose Smith & Wesson from my jacket pocket and put it in the top drawer of the desk. Firepower beats locks every day of the week. And so does a huge canine with sharp incisors.

I connect to Ivory Soul Kitchen's guest Wi-Fi network, log onto the Broward County Property Appraiser's website, and type in the address for the Florida Center for Pain, and scroll down to the sections labeled Property Owner and Mailing Address. I repeat the process in the counties for each of the FCP clinics and find the property owner and mailing address to be identical for all five locations listed on the flyer: Doloris Holdings, Inc., 1001 Federal Road, Suite 310, Fort Lauderdale, FL 33301. I Google the address and find it's a UPS Store. Doloris Holdings looks to be a shell company, but one set up by someone with a maudlin sense of humor, Doloris being the Latin word for pain. Six years of prep-school Latin did not go for naught.

I search for Doloris Holdings on the Florida Department of Corporations site—incorporated in 2005, same Federal Highway address and owner.

I rub my eyes to make sure I'm not hallucinating.

"Holy roller! Gretchen owns the FCP pain clinics!" I yell, causing Miranda to leap from her post by the door and race to my side.

"No way! The FCP clinics are owned by Gretchen?"

Right there in black and white—Doloris Holdings' most recent annual report lists only one officer, its president, Gretchen Post. Post, Gretchen's maiden name. At least one good thing came of cyberstalking Gretchen back when I was trying to figure out who Manny was sleeping with.

I slump back in my chair, hands on my head. "But what, if anything, does Gretchen have to do with Sinclair, other than the fact that Zoe goes to St. Paul's?"

Miranda sits back on her haunches, eyes fixed on me.

"Maybe it's just a coincidence that Sinclair was arrested at one of Gretchen's clinics, the same place I saw Serena? Or are they all connected? And what would that matter? There's still the proverbial smoking gun and then the fact that Zoe had a crush on Sinclair, who was sleeping with Serena, and..."

I glance down at Miranda, her gaze so earnest, as if what I'm saying is of the utmost importance to the future of mankind.

"Gretchen owning FCP doesn't change a thing, does it? It makes her a shady lady, but it doesn't mean Zoe didn't kill Sinclair."

A low growl.

"I hear you. I don't think she did either."

"Aghhh!" I get up to switch off the overhead light, which sounds like a dying fly. "More damn questions than answers at every turn."

I sit back behind the desk and pull the chain on the green banker's desk lamp, a law school graduation gift from my father which Vinnie nabbed from my home office and brought over.

"I need to get some blinds for that thing," I mumble, feeling exposed in face of the window which spans the entire front of the building.

Outside, the dregs of daylight are fading and it's raining, making my ghetto look less ghetto, softening its rapier-sharp edges as in a moody black-and-white photograph from an earlier time, one where men in trench coats waited under lamp posts, faces obscured by fedoras.

A fire engine siren pierces my reverie, sound waves attenuating as it vanishes into the night on its way to someone's misfortune.

I pace around, trying on a few theories for size. Why had Sinclair been able to escape charges twice? If he was dealing dope, maybe something he said or did got him killed—like flipping? But for two agencies? Nobody gets that lucky. Sonny's a by-the-book cop, and Marcus Jackson is a true believer in making people pay for their mistakes and pay even more for their bad decisions. They wouldn't let Sinclair walk for no reason.

And then there's Reilly. He's one who would trample the truth for a conviction in a high-profile case like Zoe's, but he wasn't Sonny's partner back when Sinclair was arrested. He was fighting his own battles, trying to stay out of prison for lying about Vinnie.

And the damn gun. Could someone have planted it? But how? And why?

After endless arranging and rearranging of the chess pieces, I'm still stumped. No way Twietmeyer will give me more time to investigate. Not unless I have a damn good excuse. But where can I find one of those?

Marcus made it clear—he's said all he's going to say.

Fortunately, however, I still remember Sonny's number by heart.

Chapter 26

I leave Miranda with her godfather, Vinnie, and walk the mile to Primanti's Pizzeria.

I choose a sidewalk table and watch as a woman in a spangly mini dress lets herself be pulled into the embrace of a twenty-something man wearing a half-tucked shirt and the kind of spark for a smile that says he's sure he'll get lucky later. No doubt he looks better to her now than he will in the vicious light of day, but she doesn't care. Now is now and tomorrow, well, tomorrow is not now.

A jolt of jealousy courses through me. Was I ever so carefree? So sure that no matter what dubious choices I made, no matter how many times I tempted fate, everything would be fine? Truth is, I was, and it nearly killed me.

At the thought junction of "I am sure I never was so carefree," and "I wish I were now," a "Hey, pretty lady," brings me back to why I'm here.

Sonny.

He rests both palms on the table and leans in. "Sorry I

couldn't get off earlier. Total nightmare shift. One dead guy and two home invasions."

"That's what I call job security."

"And since when do you look on the bright side?"

I grab a grease-stained trifold menu from under the shaker of hot peppers and hand it to him along with a twenty. "I'm buying."

"You know I can't be taking gifts." He hands back the cash. "But there's no rule against me buying you a slice."

"Veggie, please."

He wrinkles his nose.

"Can I assume the usual sausage for you?" I say. "You're nothing if not a creature of habit, Sonny."

"Much like you're nothing if not a smart ass."

"Ha ha. You do know how they make sausage, don't you?"

"Jesus, all that clean living's turning you into the food police."

Pizza in hand, we cross to the beach and sit on the sea wall, the ocean furling out before us, a black silk sheet embroidered with dancing white lace.

"Nice night," I say to stall, while I figure out how to ask for his help. He doesn't owe me anything, except maybe a tongue lashing for how I treated him. But he's too nice for that.

"You didn't ask me here to talk about the weather, Grace," he says between bites.

I wipe my mouth with a crinkly paper napkin. "Am I that transparent? I must have lost my touch."

"I seriously doubt that."

After inhaling a few more bites, he stops chewing. "I heard what happened at the bail hearing. You got ambushed. The ASA didn't need to pile on about the gun."

"Forget it. And come on. It's a freakin' smoking gun! I'd have done the same thing in Hightower's shoes. But..." I bat my eyelids.

"But, what? I should have known there was a catch to

meeting you."

"But maybe you could do me a teeny-weeny favor."

He gives me an I-told-you-so grin.

"I get it. You guys believe you got the right person, but if you would clear one thing up for me?"

"Believe? We *know* we got the right person, and I gave you everything we have, early even, before you had a right to it."

"But not everything."

"Meaning?"

"Meaning Sinclair. You arrested him some time back."

Sonny stops chewing. "What does that have to do with anything? The guy's six feet under, his record's irrelevant. He's the victim here."

"Thing is, Sinclair didn't have a record, so I was hoping you could tell me why. Cops like you don't ditch a solid case unless your fingernails are being pulled out one by one."

"Cops like me? What does that mean?"

"By-the-book cops. Cops who want more than anything to put bad guys away, but not if it means breaking the rules."

"You think my job is to do yours now, too? I want that client of yours behind bars where she belongs, no matter how much you flatter me. You're killing me here, Grace."

I raise my hands in surrender. "Look, I don't want to miss anything. That's all."

Sonny nods as he chews. "We all have jobs to do. That's what makes the system work."

"Yeah, as if it does."

"Shoe on the other foot now, is it?"

I slap myself on the side of the head. "If I hear that one more time I'm going to scream."

"Settle down. You chose to do what you're doing."

I look away, his eyes following mine to a couple, hand in hand, strolling along the breakwater, the tide licking at their bare feet. "I need this case, Sonny. If I do a good job and lose in the end, I'm good with that. But I need to turn over every stone, which is how I ended up getting the arrest report for Sinclair. Your report."

"Where'd you get— Never mind."

"Sinclair tried to sell you Oxy at FCP."

He wipes his mouth with the back of his hand. "Police business is just that, police business. Not Counselor Locke's business."

"Come on, what I found is public record. Or was. Until it somehow disappeared."

He glances over his shoulder.

"Are you that afraid of Reilly? Afraid he followed you here."

He stiffens. "Hell, no. I'm not afraid. I don't like going behind his back is all. He's a good partner. Much as you want to deny it, the Vicanti fiasco changed him."

I grunt and inhale the last of my pizza as he stares at me, unblinking.

"People make mistakes and some of them deserve second chances. And some even get them. The trick is to not fuck up the second chances. And I'd advise you to try not to do the same. Second chances don't come along twice."

"Thanks for the advice, Detective. But I'd still like to know why you or your partner didn't clue me in on the fact that Sinclair was arrested at FCP, or at least mention it in the reports on Zoe Slim's case."

"Like I said, it's irrelevant. We've got your girl dead to rights."

"Maybe, but it might have been nice to know that the victim was a dealer. And why'd you single out Sinclair? There's a line of dealers outside FCP as long as my list of debts waiting to deal their stash."

He drops his head to his chest. "Jesus, you're a pit bull."

"Coming from you, I'll take that as a compliment."

"Okay, but you didn't hear this from me. I collared Sinclair at FCP. People were selling their prescriptions. Then one guy OD'd in his car in the parking lot. That reporter, what's her name? Sharon Posner. She shot video of a bunch of drug deals out in the open, in FCP's parking lot."

"And?"

"And the chief put the heat on us to make some arrests over there, to get the media and the public off his back. Sinclair just happened to be one of the lucky ones. Tried to sell me thirty-five Oxy. All on tape. Legit bust. End of story."

"That's a lot of dope, enough to put him away for a long time. So, what did Sinclair agree to do for you to avoid having a record?"

"He sang like a canary at the station. Scared out of his mind he'd lose his job. He fingered a few mid-level guys and one high-level dealer we put away for twenty-five to life, and the State dropped his case. Period. End of story."

"But then the canary ends up with two holes in his body, one in his head and one where his prick used to be. Don't you think it might raise questions about who it was who might have wanted him dead not named Zoe Slim? Did you check out other higher-ups in Sinclair's network? They would've had a good reason to want him dead if they found out he was cooperating."

"No need." He clasps his hands behind his head. "We have the murder weapon. Bullets in the body matching the gun. And fingerprints. Your client's fingerprints. And to wrap it all in a neat package, we've got the threatening texts. Why would we even think about crawling down another rat hole?"

"Zoe's the obvious choice. No need to look at anyone else. Kind of sloppy police work, don't you think? Especially since you had to know your confidential informant Mr. Sinclair got himself arrested again during the time he was working for you, working off his bad behavior to keep it on the down low."

His eyebrows shoot up. "What? No. That's not true."

"Oh yes, it is."

"If he was arrested again, it wasn't us."

"If? I assure you there's no ifs about this. Same facts, different pill mill. Ring any bells?"

A definitive shake of the head. "No way. What agency?"

"And, as luck would have it, while I was doing my field research, I happened to bump into," I pause, "wait for it...Serena Price."

"The girl who found the body?"

"One and the same. Thing is, for the life of me, I can't figure out why a key witness against my client, the same person who found the dead guy, is a customer at the same place you arrested the victim. Now what are the chances?"

"Coincidence, I guess."

I crack my knuckles. "You know what coincidences mean to me, Sonny?"

"No, I don't. What do they mean to you, Grace?"

"Coincidences are explanations used by liars. They mean the real story, the truth, is a lot more complicated."

"Shit, Sinclair could've been Pablo Escobar and Serena his right-hand man, and it wouldn't matter for shit for your client. Do the best job you can for Zoe Slim and move on. Sometimes you can win more by losing. Her case has already boosted your profile. You'll hook some other sleazeball clients with deep pockets on the heels of this one. Besides, when your guilty client goes down, you'll be able to sleep at night. You won't have to worry about walking a murderer."

I stand and face him. "Maybe, but what keeps me up nights are the ones who didn't do it."

"Come on, you think she's innocent? Don't let the pressure mess with your head." He points at me. "And most of all, don't let the kid play you."

I look up at the full moon, a ghostly cloud drifting over its face. "I'll try not to."

He reaches out a hand and, gently, strokes the tattoo on the top half of my left arm. "Between the service and the job, I've seen a lot of tattoos, but never another one like yours. Me, I got your standard eagle when I was in the Navy."

He hops over the sea wall onto the sidewalk. "I'll be seeing you in court, Counselor."

"That's one thing we can both count on," I say, but my words are drowned out by the waves crashing onshore.

Walking home, I stroke my tattoo, my mind drifting across the chrystalline waters to Stiltsville. The place I want to be buried. At sea. At peace. I wanted there to be no doubt.

Chapter 27

Vinnie's customary knock. Four times: three hard, one soft. "Mail call. Open up."

The sight of the large envelope causes my heart drops faster than an anchor in calm seas.

"The FedEx guy left this for you."

I stare at the envelope as if it's radioactive.

"Go on. Take it, would ya? I'm busy here." Vinnie digs deep in his pocket for a doggie treat. Without being asked, Miranda gives him a paw, takes the treat like a delicate treasure, and crunches it into rubble.

I grab the envelope and drop it on the futon.

"I take it you know what's in there."

"Final divorce papers."

He puts a hand on my shoulder. "Endings are never easy, sweetheart. Maybe think of it as a new beginning."

I wipe my nose on the back of my hand. "It's just..." I drop onto the futon and rub the fading tan line where my wedding ring used to be. "Who am I now, Vin?"

"You are still you. And stronger than ever. And if it makes you feel any better, I was married and divorced three times, and not one day do I want any of them back."

I let out a snotty laugh. "You sure it wasn't the other way around?"

"Always with the smart mouth. Like I said, you're still you, Gracie."

He looks deep into my eyes, his own flinty. "You're better off without that cheatin' rat bastard, kid. You're a force of nature. You're smart. You'll figure it out."

I rip open the envelope, grab a pen, and scrawl my signature on every line marked with a Sign Here sticky arrow, and stuff everything into the enclosed return envelope.

"Can you take this for me?"

"You mean keep it for you?"

"No, I mean send it for me."

"Sure. I'll take it to FedEx in the morning."

"First thing, okay?"

"Sure. Anything you need."

"Can you look after Miranda while I take a run?" I glance down at Oscar. "Or more like a hobble."

He grabs the leash and dashes out before I can say "Thanks."

***

The beach is a black desert, the scorched tourists all back in their hotels, dining on stone crabs and key lime pie. I close my eyes and inhale, the air a cocktail of salt, magnolia, and a blanket of dense humidity. It's the kind of air tourists spend thousands to breathe, the kind that made me fall in love with Florida.

Obscured from prying eyes by the darkness, I start to jog, the odd outward sweep of Oscar something I'm still not used to. I pass couples making out in parked cars. And a homeless woman pushing a shopping cart, searching for a safe place to sleep out of sight of predators.

Farther south, the Strip, several blocks of touristy restaurants and souvenir shops emerges, the ferocity of its garish neon in stark contrast to the night. Flashing signs promising 2-4-1 and The Biggest Margarita on the Beach. A tattoo parlor called Pink's Inks wedged between a frozen daiquiri bar and a psychic offering readings for five dollars, three for ten. On the corner of Las Olas, the Elbo Room is humming along as it has since World War II, the overflowing crowd corralled by a rope line monitored by off-duty cops. Beers in hand for locals, weak umbrella drinks for tourists, all sway along to the strains of the ubiquitous Jimmy Buffet wannabe playing the unofficial state song, "Margaritaville."

From the top of the Las Olas bridge, I look west, to my destination, Idlewyld, a finger of coral rock lined with mansions. Perhaps I'm doing this to feel pain, to feel something other than regret, but I tell myself it's to close the book on my old life once and for all.

I wail into the night like a banshee. "Face up! You need to get on with your life, soldier!"

The four-story contemporary looks more like a modern art museum than a home. I'd wanted contemporary, Manny, Mediterranean. We flipped a coin and I won. And while the money came pouring in from his real-estate-development business to build the house and fill it with designer furnishings, more than we'd ever imagined as broke students, the kids never arrived to sleep in its many bedrooms.

I stand in the shadow of the huge banyan tree and take a deep breath, the scent of night jasmine filling my lungs. It's been less than a year, but it feels like much longer since I was last here. I lean my face against the stainless-steel railing atop a half wall, like a kid at the zoo, and take inventory. The sun-bleached Florida pine bench by the front door. The banana palm I planted is still there too. The foliage in the courtyard is neatly manicured, although Manny loathes anything to do with the garden. Clearly, he's hired a new gardener, one to replace the one he fired because he saw the guy spying on me out by the pool.

I recognize the outline of my Jaguar under a tarp in the driveway, alongside Manny's black Mercedes S Class, its high polish reflecting the sharp, geometric lines of the house.

A light goes on in the master suite upstairs and I crouch out of sight.

Manny stands in the window, staring into the night. He's wearing the robe I gave him on our last Christmas together, a few weeks before I was arrested. Crimson silk with his initials AAM, Armando Alonso Martinez, monogrammed on the breast pocket. After a couple of minutes, he recedes into the bedroom. I'm about to stand when he reappears, scanning the street.

A chill blooms inside me, my sweat-soaked running clothes stuck to my body. I need to get moving. As I jog away, crickets accompany my retreat, chirping their night music. I forgot about the crickets. I am enchanted by the sound, until a white Bentley convertible rolls to a stop in front of the house, a halo of blonde hair in the driver's seat.

***

The 11 p.m. NA meeting at St. Anthony's is always a macabre circus, but I need to go. For the Bar, yes, but more for me. The late hour brings out the most broken, the most bold in their denial, the ones who cannot help but tempt fate. I cross the parking lot, drawn by the light streaming from Fellowship Hall. Two police cruisers are parked outside the entrance, driver's side to driver's side, the cops busy shooting the breeze in plain view of two drug deals and one couple screwing against the dumpster.

A hand yanks me by the arm as I am about to step inside. I turn, right arm ready to put my attacker in a choke hold, but the person backs away and raises both hands.

"Stop, Grace. It's me."

I squint into the darkness. The voice is familiar, but the person isn't. It is Hachi. But not the Hachi I know—the strong Hachi, my sponsor, my friend, the one who held me together when everyone else, including me, was tired of trying to save me. No, this is another Hachi. This Hachi is destroyed. Eyes bloodshot, hair a bird's nest. Her skin a dusty gray, cheeks sunken. She may be forty calendar years old, but in addict age she looks double that.

"Jesus H," I say, grabbing her and pulling her away from the entrance. No matter how loaded, how done, how stupid you are outside NA, inside you need to follow the script. No drugs and no drama inside.

"What happened?" I say, frantic at the thought that she's flushed eight years of sobriety down the drain.

She buries her face in hands that haven't seen soap in ages. "I messed up," she groans, her whole body quaking like a withering leaf in the wind.

I open my arms and she dissolves into my embrace. A good six inches taller than her five-feet-four, I lower my head on top of hers, my long black hair cascading over her raggedy, brown braids, shielding her face.

"What did you take" I ask, afraid.

"Smack. Can't afford the pills no more."

Exactly what I was afraid of—heroin, the last stop on the addict's highway to hell.

I shudder. "But you're here, aren't you?"

"I can't do this again. Can't start all over." I try to lead her inside, but she yanks her hand away. "I just can't."

I wipe her face using my shirt tail and smooth her hair back from her face.

"I look like shit," she whimpers.

"You kinda do, but this isn't a fashion show. Let's just go on in."

She turns her back and starts to walk away. "No, I can't. I won't."

I grab her arm. "Yes, you can. You think I'm going to believe you came over here not to get help? Let me help you this time."

She drops her head to her chest. "I can't."

"I'd have had to come looking for you. Find you in some gutter with a needle in your arm. That's what you would have done if you'd really given up."

She raises her head and sniffles, eyes so puffy they appear glued shut. "Guess I'm not real good at giving up either."

"You and me both," I say, taking her by the hand and leading her to an empty row of seats in the back of the hall. "But failing at giving up isn't so bad, is it?"

She rests her head on my shoulder. "Damn, woman. Did anyone tell you you're a pain in the ass?"

"What do you think?"

The slightest of smiles to crawls its way onto her lips, but soon fades when a woman in a waitress's uniform starts to share how her three-year-old son drowned in the bathtub because she went to the corner to buy crack.

I clamp my eyes shut against the brutal image and squeeze Hachi's hand hard, as if the pressure will save her from seeing the drowned child.

Hachi stands to leave. "I can't. I'm not strong enough."

"Yes, you are," I say pulling her down by the sleeve. "You're going to do what I'm going to do, and what we're going to keep doing. We're going to keep coming back here, keep saying the words. For as long as it takes."

"What words?" she asks, words slurred.

"The words we need to say every day, my friend. My name is Grace, my name is Hachi, and we are addicts."

***

The second he hears the squeaky gate, Vinnie explodes from the office, arms waving. "Get in here. You gotta see this!"

"I'm exhausted. I'm going to bed."

"Trust me, sweetheart. You need is to get in here."

I peek around the door, the tiny, dark office illuminated by the light from an ancient TV.

I point at the rabbit ears. "You might wrap those suckers in foil to get a better picture. Or maybe even buy a new TV?"

Vinnie drags me in front of the grainy screen.

A news ticker crawls across the bottom of the screen. "Body of young woman found on Fort Lauderdale beach."

"They've been replaying this non-stop on all the channels," he says.

A shot of the beach. The scene a jumble of swings, ropes, monkey bars, and two people drifting by on floating mattresses in the background.

"That's the playground on the beach at Del Mar Way," I say. "That's the one the city had to close the sides of with two-by-fours because a homeless family was living under there. But one of the boards has been pried off."

"That's where they found the girl's body."

An image of Detective Reilly limboing under crime scene tape.

I lean in close to the screen. "Holy shit! That's Reilly."

Another plain clothes officer.

"Wait. That's Sonny. I just saw him a couple of hours ago."

Reilly and Sonny standing beside a body covered by a white sheet next to Dr. Owen, the county medical examiner.

"He never said anything—"

"Keep watching, will ya?"

The screen reverts back to a live shot from the newsroom.

"We have breaking news. The body found late this afternoon on Fort Lauderdale beach has been identified as that of Serena Price, eighteen, a resident of the Rio Vista neighborhood. Ms. Price had been shot twice. Once in the head at point blank range and once," the newscaster clears his throat, "and once in the groin. Ms. Price was to be a key witness at the trial of prep schooler Zoe Slim for the murder of a much beloved guidance counselor at St. Paul's Prep, Brandon Sinclair. The weapon used to kill Ms. Price has been recovered from Ms. Slim's bedroom at her home. Prints lifted from the gun have been identified as those of Zoe Slim, currently out on bail for the murder of Brandon Sinclair, a counselor at St. Paul's Prep. Ms. Slim was taken into custody this evening."

Chapter 28

The guard leaps to his feet and salutes.

"Evening, Counselor," he says, as my possessions pass through the magnetometer without a second look. "On the late side, isn't it?"

"Crime never sleeps."

"Ain't that the truth."

Before proceeding through the arch, I point at Oscar and he nods. "Come on through."

Given the late hour, I'm processed and locked into one of the attorney's rooms within fifteen minutes of my arrival, so quickly it takes another ten for Zoe to be brought from the holding cell where she'll be kept until she's booked on her second capital murder charge tomorrow morning.

She's still in street clothes, jeans and an oversized St. Paul's hoodie emblazoned with a football. "I told you someone's out to get me!" she screams at the top of her lungs as the guard locks her manacled feet to the bail on the floor. "You have to believe me, I—"

I put a finger over my lips to silence her and leave it there until the guard steps out.

"I didn't do it! I didn't kill Serena! I didn't!" she yells, the gold flecks in her eyes incandescent, her face contorted into a mask of abject terror. "You have to believe me. I, I didn't kill anyone, I—"

I reach across the table and grab her cuffed hands, aware my eyes are bugging out of my head. "Take a deep breath and let's starts at the beginning."

She closes her eyes, her breaths shallow and choppy.

"Where were you tonight?"

"At...At home. But listen, there's something I need to tell you," she says, her speech pressured. "I didn't sleep late the day Mr. Sinclair was killed, like I told you before. I was with Joe."

The speed with which the words come tumbling out leaves me gasping for air, too. "What?"

"I was with Joe. At school. Well, outside. In the parking lot."

I reel back, taking all of her in—the crazed eyes and disheveled clothing, the utter panicked sincerity of her emotions.

"You were at school when Sinclair was killed? In the parking lot?"

A definitive nod.

"And who is this Joe?"

"Joe Harper. My boyfriend. Well he was. Until—"

"Until what?"

"Until Serena took him. I mean, I know she's the prettiest girl in school. And Joe's the school's star quarterback, so I guess it's no surprise. But I thought he was a nice guy." She drops her head to her chest. "And I thought she was my best friend. I'm an idiot."

"I thought you had a falling out with Serena because she," I pause, searching for a more sensitive way to say a teacher was molesting a student, if such a thing exists. "Because she was involved with Mr. Sinclair."

"I never said that!"

I pull back and rerun our meeting at the Everglades State Hospital through my mind.

I look away, chastened by my cynical assumption. "You know what Zoe, you're right. You didn't say that."

I should have asked why their friendship ended, but I was way too busy assuming she was guilty. I had already made up my mind.

Her eyes harden and I can't help but look away "It's not fair. But girls like Serena always get what they want."

I feel lightheaded, like you do when you've jumped out of a plane but have yet to open your parachute. I was prepared for murder defense number two, not an alibi defense for murder number one. I take a moment to reframe my thoughts, reconstitute them into a scenario in which Zoe might not be the killer.

"Help me out here. Joe Harper was your boyfriend, and then he hooked up with Serena. But, if that's the case, why were you with Joe in the parking lot the morning of the murder?"

Silence.

"Zoe, answer the question—why were you with Joe?"

"What does it matter?"

"Because the answer to that question might save your life. And like it or not, as soon as I leave here, I'm going to inform the ASA that you have an alibi, but he will ask who Joe is and why and where you were with him." I slam my fist down on the table. "Tell me dammit! Why were you with Joe?"

She pulls her head down into the neck of the hoodie, as if hiding her face will protect her from the impact of whatever else she has to tell me.

I will myself to wait, let her answer in her own good time, although I'm tempted to lunge across the table and shake it out of her.

"Joe has a younger brother, Sam," she says, her voice muffled. "And last year he hurt his knee playing lacrosse and had to have surgery. The doctor gave him pain pills. And then—"

"And he got hooked," I say, causing Zoe to extract her head from the hoodie.

"How'd you know?"

"Just a good guess. Go on, what about Sam?"

"His parents did everything they could, sent him to rehab a few times, but nothing worked. When school started back after summer, Joe suspected Sam was using again. He said Sam would disappear after school let out, when Joe was supposed to give him a ride home—Sam had lost his license when he got busted the last time for pot. Anyway, one day Joe followed him. And..." her voice cracks.

"And what?"

She shakes her head. "Grace, I can't."

"Yes, you can, Zoe. You are stronger than you think. I am not letting you take the fall for something you didn't do." I take a second to catch my breath. "And you didn't do it, did you? You didn't kill Mr. Sinclair," I say without any hint of a questioning tone.

"No, I did not."

Her words wash over me like a soothing wave, the knot in my gut unclenching for the first time since we met. "Tell me what happened. The whole truth and nothing but the truth."

Whispering as if she's telling me a secret, she continues. "Joe followed Sam to a pill mill. You know, one of those places addicts go to buy drugs. They're always on the news."

"Do you know which pill mill?"

She swallows hard. "Florida Center for Pain, on Sunrise."

The fear in her eyes conveys only one thing, the one thing she feared the most—nothing will ever be the same. But she has no choice. The secret she must now share will change her life, her family, forever.

She wipes her eyes on her sleeve. "Joe saw my dad there. And Mr. Sinclair."

"What were they doing?"

"He said they came out the back together."

"What else?"

"He said there was another guy there too. A big dude loading a bunch of bags into the trunk of my dad's car and—"

"Did he say what kind of bags?"

She sits back, eyes half closed, trying to recreate the conversation with Joe in her mind.

"Red garbage bags. Joe said the big dude dropped one of the bags and it burst and a whole bunch of cash fell out. That Dad slapped the guy and made him and Mr. Sinclair pick it all up."

"And did they?"

"Yes." Her face turns ashen. "And Dad drove away with all the money."

"They only accept cash at pill mills."

She lowers her head onto the table and starts to cry. "I thought my dad was a plastic surgeon."

I stroke her hair. "Did Joe say why he wanted to tell you about that?"

"Wouldn't you want to know your dad has been lying to you?" I hesitate long enough for her to add, "That he's a drug dealer? That the house we live in, the cars we drive, the vacations we take, they're all paid for with money from selling drugs that kill people?"

She raises her head, a deluge of tears raging down her cheeks, spattering onto the hoodie. "Sam's drug problem's tearing his family apart. Maybe Joe wants to tear mine apart. Maybe that's why he told me." She lets out a sob so gut-wrenching it shakes me to the core.

"Oh, Zoe, I doubt that. He was your friend," I say, but she might be on the mark. Addiction can turn those closest to us from decent folks into avenging angels when they run out of options to save their loved ones from themselves. "He probably was at the end of his rope, didn't know what to do to save Sam."

"Maybe. He said he wanted me to know what my dad was doing, that he didn't want me anywhere near that shit. That's what he said, but he might have been lying just like everyone else."

"I understand this is all incredibly upsetting, but why didn't you tell me before? Your life is on the line."

"I did. I told you I wasn't there when Mr. Sinclair was killed."

"But you didn't tell me the whole truth. You have an alibi. As far as I know, no one knew to talk to Joe. He didn't give a statement. Not yet, anyway. I need to let the State Attorney know immediately."

"This is going to sound stupid. Now things have gotten even worse, but I didn't want my dad to get in trouble. I just thought things would work out in the end."

"Oh, Zoe," I say, the sad irony of her protective impulse a punch to the gut. "You should have told me."

"I didn't kill Mr. Sinclair, and I thought Joe would say I was with him and it would all be over with and no one would have to know about Dad."

"In my experience, no matter how much we might want to keep secrets, the truth comes out sooner or later."

"I guess," she says, her tone resigned, yet freighted with regret.

She slams the cuffs into her forehead. "I was so stupid to ever think I could have a real family!"

I grab her cuffed hands. "You're not stupid, Zoe. You deserve a family. We all deserve people, *our* people, people who love us no matter what," I say, the force of words so strong, I'm out of breath.

She opens her mouth to say something but stops herself.

"What is it, Zoe?"

I stand. "I'm going to track Joe down and get him to talk."

She turtles her head into the neck of the hoodie, muffling her voice. "Grace, do you think me telling you about the pill mill was the right thing? I mean, my mom and dad, I mean they—"

I rest a hand on her shoulder. "One thing I learned in the Army is sometimes doing what's right hurts."

Her eyes pop open. "You were in the Army?"

I stand at attention and salute. "Yes, ma'am, Specialist Grace Locke reporting for duty."

"Wow! So that's where..." she points at Oscar.

"Yep, that's where."

I signal the guard to unlock the door. "Want to know the other thing I learned in the Army?"

She nods, unblinking eyes still trained on Oscar.

"That things aren't always what they seem."

"I think I'm learning that, too." Her gaze loses focus. "So, who *do* you think killed Mr. Sinclair?"

"I have no idea. And finding out is not my job. My job is making sure the wrong person doesn't go down for something she didn't do."

The tension in her shoulders slackens under my grip.

"And do you know why I want to do that?"

"Why?"

"Because you matter, Zoya. You matter a whole lot."

Chapter 29

"Kinda tight, don't you think?"

Vinnie rolls his eyes and squeezes the Crown Vic in between a Porsche Carrera and a Maserati Quattroporte.

"You live in the city long enough, you learn to park by Braille. A little bump here, a little shimmy there, never hurt no one."

"Nice work, Vin. I wasn't sure this tank would fit."

"We were gonna fit, sweetheart. Or I was gonna make us fit."

He twists the rearview mirror to face him and rakes his downy crown of white hair with a black pocket comb like the one my father always carried in his pocket.

I step out and shield my eyes from the sun. It's a bluebird day, not one cloud in sight, a day more suited to a beach chair and a trashy novel than a funeral. Here I am, back in church for the first time since Iraq, the hellhole which robbed me of all faith and almost my life.

"You don't have to come in with me."

"You kiddin' me? I don't ever get to dress up these days," he says, jumping out. "But, now that you mention it, what is it you think you'll learn from this bunch of stiffs?" He claps his hand over his mouth. "Sorry, bad choice of words."

I stifle a laugh. "I need to speak to a kid called Joe Harper. I figured, since he was Serena's boyfriend, he'd be here at her funeral."

"Who's Joe whatshisname?"

"Zoe said she was with him when Sinclair died."

"Holy Mother of God. Like maybe she didn't do it?"

"Seems that way." I straighten my pant leg so Oscar's hidden.

Vinnie straightens his tie. I'm warmed by the openness in his face, a look of peaceful acceptance that comes only with forgiveness. I can't say I'd feel the same in his shoes. I'd probably still be raging at the years stolen from me. But all I can do now is keep the promise I made to myself back then, that no matter how guilty a person looks, I'll never stop asking questions until I find the truth. Or at least until I'm sure no one's lying. It's the least I can do to make my amends.

We slip in the side door of First Presbyterian Church and into a rear pew, one of the few that's unoccupied. I've never seen him in a suit before. Head held high, he's debonair, an international man of mystery.

The sanctuary is packed with black-clad mourners of all ages. Teenagers sit book-ended by their parents, pulling on starched collars or pantyhose, the mourning attire a far cry from their usual rock band T-shirts and skinny jeans. A pimple-faced boy waves at a girl, only to have his hand swatted down by his father.

It's been a long time since I darkened the door of a church, but I'm no stranger to Presbyterian décor, and First Pres, as the locals call it, is no different from the New England churches of my youth. Not spartan, but not fancy either, restrained enough to make the well-heeled congregation believe their generous offerings are going to worthy causes, and not into gilded pulpits.

A minister clad in a simple black cassock and purple tippet stands in front of a carved marble altar, arms wide, and proclaims, "Welcome, family and friends. Welcome one and all to celebrate the life of Serena Price." His tone is one employed by all preachers in times of grief, one intended to reassure the faithful that the sad event is but another inevitability in the circle of life. A tone intended to console, but also to celebrate the life of the deceased, whatever that means for the eighteen year old lying in the white casket up front, for a life cut short before there was much at all to celebrate.

I wonder what the rows and rows of mourners are thinking. What trite condolences they will offer Serena's family in the receiving line after the service, when the only thought on their minds will be, "This could have been my child." Are they hankering for Zoe's head, as if such a thing could ever set things right? Still, an eye for an eye does bring with it a certain reassurance that justice does exist.

In the five days since the discovery of her body, Serena Price has become a national obsession. Even the national morning shows sent reporters to recount how Serena, a beautiful young woman and star student, who played the violin and led St. Paul's soccer team to a state championship, was murdered in cold blood. How she was shot by a friend, a classmate at a fancy private school. How the bullet had been fired from same type of gun Zoe is accused of using to kill Brandon Sinclair. How Zoe threatened Serena by text. It goes without saying, they sidestepped the issue of the OxyContin found in Serena's system, a fact that would have been front and center had Serena been a black kid from the projects, not a white one from Rio Vista. But they didn't skip the part about Zoe being mentally disturbed, not to mention about to be tried on another murder committed with the same *modus operandi*.

Still nagging at me like a hangnail is what, if any, connections were there between Sinclair and Serena? Were they, in fact, involved, or is Zoe imaging it? And Gretchen. Is it a coincidence she owns the clinic where Sinclair was arrested, and is also the mother of one of his counseling clients?

I stand and sit and pray with the congregation, on automatic pilot from years of forced practice at boarding school, but my mind's zig-zagging all over the place like a lab rat on speed.

Reilly summed up his theory in a glib sound bite on NBC6 News. Asked why Zoe would have killed Sinclair, he said, "We don't have to prove motive. No matter what they say on TV, it's not an element of the crime of murder. After almost thirty years on the job, I've learned that murder always comes down to one of three things—money, jealousy, or just plain evil. In this case, I'm going with jealousy." A nice sound bite for sure, but something about what Reilly said strikes me as too convenient. He has a penchant for the CliffsNotes version of crimes. The easy answer, facts be damned. If he said the world is flat, I would double check. But, then again, like Sonny said, Reilly and I have a history, and I'll never trust a word he says.

Could she have been that jealous? Angry, for sure, but angry enough to kill? Why not get rid of the gun that killed Sinclair like the one used to kill Serena, if she killed Serena?

"Everyone, please stand for the final reading, the twenty-third psalm."

"Yea, though I walk through the valley of the shadow of death, I will fear no evil..." chants the crowd, an onyx wave of sorrow, sniffling, and muffled sobbing all around.

Amens said, the Price family files out of the front pew, led by the minister. Serena's mother, a slender woman in a black dress and pearls, propped up by her husband who's blinking back tears. Mrs. Price couldn't be much older than I am, but the loss of her daughter is aging her in front of all of our eyes. A silent throng follows, row by row, heads bowed.

Outside, Serena's parents are receiving condolences from a long line of mourners. I choose a spot under the thick canopy of a gumbo limbo tree, its tangled, leafy limbs offering cover from which to observe the crowd milling around on the sidewalk. Hugs are exchanged, tissues dug from pockets. A group of younger children flies across the street to play in a park beside the New River, their bright, open faces untouched by the day.

"I remember when my Joey died," Vinnie says, his voice shaky. "I couldn't understand why life, why everything, just kept going on around me as if nothing had happened. The world should have stopped. He was a boy, *my* boy. That should've counted for something."

I hook my arm through his and rub his sun-spotted hand. "Death knows not justice nor fairness," I tell him, the phrase I used in anger at the memorial services for my fallen squadron mates. If I had to look their wives in the face and explain why their husbands, my brethren, were not coming home, why they were blown to bits by an IED on a dusty highway in Fallujah on the way to pick up Easter decorations, and why I was the only one of us to come home alive, then I'd be damned if I wasn't going to be angry at God. At the world.

I push the memory from my mind and turn my attention to a young man wiping his eyes with a handkerchief, surrounded by a throng of teens. He's handsome, not in the teen idol way, but in the way that portends good looks once he's grown into himself. His sandy hair is parted on the side, but his curls are having none of it, drooping this way and that, all over his face.

"The center of attention and upset. I bet you this month's rent that's Joe."

"Sweetheart, you don't pay rent, remember?" Vinnie wipes his nose on a handkerchief, the old-fashioned, fabric kind.

"That's something I've been meaning to talk to you about."

He closes one eye. "And you never will. Not as long as I'm still breathing."

A few latecomers jockey for position to get close to Joe.

"Funny how people get some weird kind of enjoyment from being close to suffering," I say. "Maybe it's a 'But for the grace of God' thing. Me, I want to get as far away as possible from it."

He holds a finger in the air as if he's seeing which way the wind is blowing. "*Schadenfreude*," he says, clearly amused at himself.

"You're kidding me?"

"It means you like to watch others squirm, see them—"

I pinch him in the side. "I know what *schadenfreude* means. Yale then Columbia, remember? How about you?"

He dusts some non-existent debris from the shoulder of his jacket. "Hey, I read."

"You never cease to surprise me, Vin."

"It's what I live for."

A duck boat overflowing with tourists docks on the far side of the park. "Over there, in that mega mansion designed to look like Versailles, is where Walter Hall lives," the tour guide announces over the PA system. "He used to be in the garbage business, founded Waste General and 24 Hour Video. And he owns part of the Dolphins." The tourists crane their necks and ooh and aah.

"Only in South Florida," I say. "Death with dignity is no match for tourism."

We wait in the shade for several minutes until the crowd disperses, some into waiting limousines, others their own cars.

"You wait here," I tell him, and trail Joe to a black Land Rover.

"Excuse me."

The young man pivots slowly to reveal bloodshot eyes.

"Are you Joe Harper? I was wondering if I could talk to you."

A look of recognition flashes across his face. "Hey, I saw you on TV. You're Zoe's lawyer."

"Grace Locke," I say, pressing one of my business cards into his hand.

He stuffs the card in his pocket.

"Joe, were you with Zoe the morning Brandon Sinclair was killed?"

He squirms a little inside the ill-fitting dark suit likely bought for this, and only this, occasion. "Yeah, I was. I wondered when someone was going to come around asking about that."

Stunned, I take a step back. "You were? You were actually

with Zoe?"

He shifts from one foot to the other. "That's what I said, isn't it?"

"Ah, well, yes...It's just— Well, that's what Zoe said."

"I figured she would, but when no one came to speak to me. I figured she told the cops but they didn't believe her, or something like that. Or maybe they just hadn't got around to it yet." He casts an arm in the direction of the hearse, its cargo hidden from view by black curtains. "And then this happened, and I started thinking maybe she did kill Sinclair somehow, that the cops got the time it happened wrong."

"Come on. Given what you just told me, that Zoe was with you, do you really believe she could have killed them both?"

"They were both killed the same way. And the guns had her prints on them, for God's sake. At least, that's what they said on the news."

I bite my lip and let him talk.

"Then there's the fact she's a little crazy, and she sure as hell is the jealous type. She went ballistic when she found out I was with Serena." He climbs into the Land Rover. "I have to go."

I barricade myself between the door and the car. "Joe, I'm not here to argue the facts with you, but, assuming Zoe did want Serena dead for whatever reason, why would she do it in such as a way as would point the finger right at herself?"

"You're saying she was set up? Don't you have to say that?"

"What did you talk about with Zoe that day?"

He grabs for the door handle "Get out of my way. I have to go."

I step back. "Joe, you're Zoe's alibi. Count on hearing from a Mr. Hightower very soon. He's the prosecutor, and he's going to be very interested in hearing what you have to say."

Chapter 30

If bond court is a three-ring circus, Friday calendar call is the criminal courts' ninth circle of hell, the day cases get trial dates and defendants get twitchy.

Today is the day for Judge Twietmeyer to set the State of Florida v. Zoe Slim for trial, which he will do along with arraigning Zoe on the charge of the first-degree murder of Serena Price.

Today is the day Hightower will find out his marquee case, the stuff careers are made of, is going south, way south.

I join the back of the Attorneys line outside, sunglasses on, head down, to avoid any and all questions from anyone, least of all the media who are always skulking around out here like rats in search of trash. My head feels as if it's being microwaved from the inside out by the sun. Almost Halloween and the sun's still blazing as if it were July.

To distract myself from my desire to scream at the heavens, I survey my defense colleagues in line, all of us wilting in sweaty suits and once-starched collars. They're a motley bunch. Some in two-thousand-dollar suits and Rolexes, others in off-the-rack and Timexes, but they all exude the same kind of jimmied-up confidence I used to have.

Heads high, they're regaling each other with war stories of alleged recent victories, and how they stuck it to this or that prosecutor. I overhear one guy with a man bun and a shabby, thrift-store jacket brag how he'd told that "f'ing State Attorney to put that sorry-ass plea offer where the sun don't shine and smoke it," a mixed metaphor which makes me snicker.

Maybe I could benefit from shoving my shoulders back like he's doing? Hold my head that high to announce, "I am a force to be reckoned with." Instead, I rub my temples, chew on a Tums, and contemplate how many among this pathetic crew would have the balls to put the defenses they've conjured up to the test in front of a jury. And they'll use them right up until they have to announce "Ready for trial, Your Honor," at which point they'll fold faster than an origami artist. Most will convince their clients to take plea bargains, and feel justified, not to mention comforted, given the odds most are guilty.

But there's been no need for Hightower to make any kind of plea offer in Zoe's cases. He thought he was holding all the cards. And now there's no way I'd take one.

"I like the dark glasses. They make you look..." Deputy Brian pauses and pulls the word he's looking for out of the air with a snap of his fingers. "Mysterious, Ms. Locke. Very mysterious. And you brought your entourage," he says, his eyes swinging in the direction of a bevy of reporters shoving TV cameras and microphones through the adjacent scanner.

I push my sunglasses back up my sweaty nose and scowl. "Me and my shadows."

He hands me the brown accordion file from the scanner belt, but not before scanning the label, Zoya AKA "Zoe" Slim.

He lips stretch tight into a grimace. "I guess it's go time?"

"We'll see."

"Great to see you back in the saddle, Ms. Locke. I'm rooting for you. Not sure about your client, though."

The clock above the elevator reads 8:15 a.m. Fifteen minutes to figure out how to handle telling Hightower and His Honor that I have an eleventh-hour alibi witness. Despite what happens in TV courtrooms, rabbit-out-of-the-hat theatrics are frowned upon in real life.

I find Anton pacing back and forth outside the courtroom, hands clasped behind his back.

"Where's Gretchen?"

"Sitting down inside. She's beside herself with all this—"

"Killing?" I interject, and I wonder how far off base the comment is. Gretchen may look like she couldn't kill more than a dry martini, but she's apparently just fine with selling pharmaceutical tools of self-destruction.

"Dr. Slim, did Mrs. Slim know Brandon Sinclair?"

He stops mid-stride. "Who?"

"Zoe's counselor. The man she's accused of murdering, remember?"

"Yes. Of course. Mr. Sinclair. He apparently meant a lot to Zoe. But no, my wife did not know him. Why would you ask such a thing?"

I let a few seconds pass to gauge his reaction. His purposefully blank stare tells me he's hiding something. "Well, he was Zoe's counselor. Do you know if she ever talked to him about Zoe?"

He intrudes far enough into my personal space that I can smell coffee on his breath. "I said no, Ms. Locke."

I don't flinch. "And how about Serena Price. Did your wife know her? Or maybe you did?"

His left eye twitches. "Of course, she was Zoe's best friend. She often visited our home. What happened to her is a tragedy. So young, so beautiful." He whips around to head into the courtroom. "We should be getting on inside, don't you think?"

I tap him on the shoulder. "One last question—did you ever meet Brandon Sinclair?"

His limbs stiffen inside his bespoke suit. When he turns,

his face has transformed from faux friendly into bona fide rage. "No."

I plaster on a patently fake grin. "Of course not."

***

The courtroom is unmitigated pandemonium, but despite being packed to the gills, the room is frigid. Keeping the temperature down is supposed to keep emotions at bay in such close quarters, where everyone has a lot at stake and tempers can flare at any moment.

The bench stands vacant, but every other square inch of real estate is occupied. A phalanx of defense lawyers, blathering on to each other about God-only-knows what, snakes around the well in the order in which they had signed in on a clipboard guarded by the burly bailiff. Get too near, bother him one too many times about how long it will take until your case gets heard, and he will bark, if not bite, you back into line. Three ASAs stand sentry in front of the prosecution table, gatekeepers of the stacks of boxes containing today's docketed cases. Some files have paperwork sticking out the top, possible plea deals to be offered if the spirit moves them. And, for all their bravado, defense counsel will accept those pleas with appreciation, terrified by the prospect of trying a dud case and getting hammered with a heavy sentence by the judge for having wasted his precious time.

The line of lawyers parts to allow a chain gang of orange jumpsuits to pass, one armed deputy in front and another in the rear. One inmate tries to wave to someone in the gallery and trips over the waist-to-ankle chains, crumpling to his knees. Zoe's at the end of the conga line, head buried in her chest.

The bailiff booms, "All rise. Court is in session. The Honorable Josiah Twietmeyer presiding."

"Please be seated." Judge Twietmeyer says, his gaze resting on a pod of TV cameras, a flock of awkward, long-legged birds, like great blue herons. "I am going to assume the ladies and gentlemen of the Fourth Estate are here for the Slim case. Let's get them out of here first, shall we? State of Florida versus Zoya

AKA "Zoe" Slim."

Every lawyer ahead of me glares when I step to the front of the line. Infamy it seems, mine and Zoe's, has at least one advantage.

Hightower steps up to the lectern, his face full of the earnestness of a high-school debater.

"Grace Locke for Ms. Slim, Your Honor."

"I understand your client is back in custody, Ms. Locke," Twietmeyer says.

"Yes, Judge."

Every head in the place turns to Zoe.

"Mr. Hightower, is the State ready for trial in the case of Florida versus Zoe Slim?"

The words are no sooner out of the judge's mouth when Hightower jumps in—little does he know his buoyancy will be short-lived. "Yes, Your Honor. The State is ready."

"And how about the defense, Ms. Locke?"

With a flourish worthy of a player in a cheesy medieval skit, I pull a single sheet of paper from my file. "Judge, the defense hereby files this notice of alibi. May I approach the bench with a copy for Your Honor?"

Hightower throws his hands in the air as if I've just said the most preposterous thing known to the legal profession.

Twietmeyer flops back into this throne-like chair. "Now, Ms. Locke? On the eve of trial? Really? This isn't TV."

"Your Honor, if counsel, indeed, is filing a motion, I submit that such a filing is not timely and I—"

"Enough Mr. Hightower," Twietmeyer says, hand raised. "Yes, counsel, you may approach. And make sure to give a copy to the Assistant State's Attorney before he has a coronary."

On the way back from the bench, I drop a copy in front of Hightower and watch as it drifts down like a falling leaf onto his lectern.

Spectacles on the end of his nose, the judge scans the notice. "Ms. Locke, Mr. Hightower is correct in that this filing is late per the Florida Rules of Criminal Procedure. Why is it that you're so late in sharing your alibi witness with us?"

"Because I had no idea I had one until yesterday."

Twietmeyer's shoulders sag. "While Ms. Locke's filing is late, Mr. Hightower, the rule cannot be interpreted in the hard-and-fast way you are suggesting, especially when doing so could deprive the defendant of a viable piece of evidence. I have been at the judging game long enough to have learned that the appellate courts do not look kindly upon judges who would entertain such a violation of the constitutional right to defend oneself with every tool in the shed."

"Your Honor, please—"

"Enough, Mr. Hightower. Ms. Locke, I accept your notice. And, as I have a sneaking suspicion one of you will ask, please be aware I will not be granting any continuances in this matter."

"But, Judge—" Hightower starts.

Twietmeyer glances over his spectacles at Hightower. "Mr. Hightower, I seem to recall your filing a middle-of-the-night motion yourself in this matter. To revoke bond, wasn't it?"

Hightower shuffles his feet.

"From where I sit, this makes you two all even on the gamesmanship score. Trial on the matter of the State of Florida versus Zoya AKA "Zoe" Slim is set for Monday at 9 a.m. That should give you plenty of time to get Ms. Locke's alibi witness's statement on the record."

I bite my lip to stop from smiling.

"And Ms. Locke, don't bother asking for bail on your client's new case. She's had two chances to be out on bail on the first case. Now there's a second case, I'm certainly not giving her a third. I'll enter a plea of not guilty on her behalf, if that's all right with you?"

"Yes, Your Honor. That's perfect."

"Good, I shall see you all on Monday. Have a restful weekend," he says standing, then slams both hands down on the bench. "What am I thinking, rushing along here like a steam train? I'm forgetting my manners. Ms. Locke, I assume you waive a formal reading of the charges in the new case?"

"I do," I say. I have no need to highlight the similarity of the murders for the media, eager for every last sordid detail of what they've decided is a love triangle gone fatally wrong.

"Very well. Next case is State versus..."

I find Hightower waiting for me outside the courtroom. "Nice move, Locke. You're a pain in my ass, you know that?"

"You're not the first to say that."

"I just called, and Reilly's on his way to get Joe Harper's statement."

"That must be about as fast as Reilly's ever done anything."

Hightower flashes a knowing grin. "Actually, he's sending Sorenson. As soon, as I get it, I'll shoot you a copy."

"Much obliged. But you know this is the end of your case, don't you?"

Hightower shrugs. "Maybe. But there will be others."

"Many others. That's the nice thing about working for the Man. Endless inventory."

Waiting for the elevator, I spot Britt and Gretchen in a corner, seemingly deep in conversation. I wonder what the mother of a murder victim and the chief prosecutor might have to talk about.

Chapter 31

Weekends before criminal trials all feel alike. Regardless of the case, the surreal sense that someone's life is in your hands is humbling. That a jury of human beings will be charged with determining the fate of another, that their judgment will suffice to condemn or convict, is more than a little unsettling.

The phone vibrates.

"Grace Locke, speaking," I say, cradling the phone between ear and shoulder.

"Locke, Hightower here."

"You got that statement for me?"

To say the silence on the line is deafening would be an understatement. Likely only a second or two passes, but it feels like forever.

"Grace, Detective Sorenson took the statement, but—"

"But what?" I spring up and pace around like a rat in a maze, Miranda on my heels.

"You said your witness, Harper, would say he was with Ms. Slim in the St. Paul's parking lot the morning Brandon Sinclair was murdered, but..." He draws in a sharp breath. "But the kid said he wasn't."

"What do you mean he wasn't? Spit it out!"

"Joe Harper said he was in the library before first period. Not in the parking lot with the defendant."

I grab the edge of the desk to keep from crumbling into a heap. "Wait. He told me he was with Zoe!"

Another long pause. "I'm sorry, he said he never told you any such thing. I'm sending over a copy of his sworn statement now, but I wanted to give you a heads-up."

It's probably all in my mind, but I swear I can hear him smiling.

"Are you still there?"

"Still here."

"Look, I haven't mentioned it before, because the case against your client is strong, but maybe you would consider—"

"No! I won't consider a plea."

Hightower clears his throat. "I don't think I need to remind you, she's only eighteen. She'd be out in—"

"No! No deal."

***

"Wait here," I say, as Vinnie rolls to a stop in front of St. Paul's football complex, an über-modern stadium constructed of glass and steel worthy of any Division I college team. *Friday Night Lights* may conjure up images of dusty West Texas where there are only two things in abundance—oil and football fanatics. But Florida and football are as synonymous as Florida and orange juice, more professional players produced from its high schools and universities than any other state in the Union. And since Joe's the star quarterback there's only one place he'll be on a fall Friday night—on the field. Although he won't be expecting the post-game interview I've come for.

"You're no fun. You said I was your investigator."

Were my nerves not jangled, I might make a joke in response. But, the only thing on my mind is the deadly serious business of finding out why Joe Harper changed his damn story. Either he lied in the sworn statement he gave to Sonny, which is a crime. Or he lied to me at the funeral, which means Zoe also lied to me.

"Touchdown, St. Paul's!" the announcer roars as I walk toward the locker room exit at the side of the stadium, where a few groupie girls are assembled, waiting for their gladiators to emerge.

"How long 'til the game's over?" I ask a diminutive brunette in jeans so form-fitting her panty line is visible like a tourniquet.

She pulls a boulder-sized wad of pink bubble gum from her mouth with thumb and forefinger. "Only a few minutes. It's the fourth quarter."

I park myself against the wall outside the locker room to grab Joe before his attention gets diverted by the bevy of beauties. The girls peck at their phone screens and giggle, whispering in each other's ears confidences which surely relate to boys. I'm envious I was never like them—pretty and popular and totally in the moment. My mind was always two steps ahead. On college, then law school. On war. On the future where I'd be married and happy and rich. On where my next drink would come from. Never on the frivolous joy of the here and now.

Joe emerges twenty minutes later, gear bag slung over his shoulder.

I lever myself off the wall. "Joe!"

He keeps moving.

I grab his arm. "Why'd you do it?"

"Let go of me!"

"Why'd you lie, Joe?"

"I didn't lie," he says, making a beeline for the parking lot.

I trail him, taking two steps for his every one. "You sure did. You either lied to me at the funeral or you lied to Detective Sorenson today. You do know lying to the police is a felony, don't you? And lying to me. That may not be a felony, but it could have fatal consequences—like the execution of the wrong person, a girl who thought you were her friend. But you weren't really, were you?"

He casts a furtive glance around the parking lot, and pulls me into a shadowy spot, out of reach of the beams from the lights lining the periphery of the parking lot.

"You seem nervous."

"Yeah, well, so what?"

"Why would a big strong kid like you be nervous? Maybe you've got something to hide?"

He pushes me aside. "I never should have talked to you. Go away and leave me alone."

"I'll ask again—Why are you nervous?"

He rubs his eyes with the heels of his hands, making him look more child than man.

"Why don't you tell me what's going on?"

He swallows hard several times as if he can't catch his breath, his Adam's apple rising and falling like the weight on a high striker at a carnival.

"I can't talk to you."

"Why not?"

"I can't risk it," he says, striding away.

"Risk what? Seems to me as if you're not the one with a lot to lose, like Zoe."

I run after him and block his way. "Look Joe, I don't have the time for this. You need to tell me what's going on, why you told me one thing and the cops another. Zoe's trial starts Monday and unless you help me out here, she's going to prison for a very long time, or worse."

"You don't know that," he says, eyes drifting to a young man on a motorcycle, a young woman in back, hair flying out in a golden contrail as they disappear into the night.

"Oh, yes I do. Come on, Joe. The truth. I need you to tell me the truth. You owe Zoe that much. You lied to her before, about Serena. The least you can do is to tell the truth now."

Set jaw. Clear eyes. A flicker of doubt. His resolve crumbling. I'm well acquainted with his type. For all his swagger, he's a trust-fund kid schooled in the Anglo-Saxon Protestant tradition of noblesse oblige, the obligation to help the less fortunate to allay the guilt of one's privilege, so I play to his congenital guilt, betting he won't want to seem like a total douche.

"You don't seem like the kind of guy who would let her be railroaded. At least not if she didn't do it, right?"

He drops his bag at his feet and sinks to a squat on the sidewalk.

"You were with Zoe when Sinclair was killed, weren't you?"

He covers his face. "Yes."

"Why'd you tell Detective Sorenson you weren't with Zoe in the parking lot? That you were in the library? That's a lie, Joe."

A quick glance over his shoulder to make sure no one is within earshot. "I've got this brother and he—"

"Sam, I know. Younger than you. Drug problem. Zoe told me all about him and the trouble he's been in with the law."

He stands and leans against a trash can. "He just can't stop using."

"You told Zoe what you saw at FCP, about her father and the bags of cash. You have to tell the truth."

He clenches his fists and shakes them at me, his white knuckles a stark contrast to his scarlet face. "You've got it all wrong! I didn't lie! I told that detective the truth, wrote it all out for him, how I was with Zoe. That she couldn't have killed Mr. Sinclair because she was with me."

"What? The prosecutor told me you said you denied being with her."

He shakes his head hard from side to side as if trying to erase the memory. "After I signed the statement and gave it to the detective, he ripped it up."

"What?"

"He said that if I ever told anyone about being with Zoe that day, that," he says, his voice quavering, "he said he would set Sam up, make it so he goes away to prison for a very long time. "And he said he'd kill me. And feed me to the sharks."

"Oh. My. God."

He swipes at a runaway tear with the back of his hand. "Now you understand why I can't help you?"

I give him a few seconds to gather himself, until he's squared his shoulders in a futile attempt to give the impression he's got everything under control. "I understand, but if I promise you that if you testify you were with Zoe when Sinclair was killed, I will make sure you and no one in your family is harmed, would you do it?" My words may be spoken with confidence, but it's an act, one borne out of desperation. I have no idea how I'll be able to keep that promise, given my less than cordial relationship with law enforcement.

He sighs. "Ms. Locke, I can't take that chance. My mom and dad have suffered enough."

"And what about Zoe? It's a young woman's life I'm talking about here."

"And her dad? Yeah, like he's not the cause of so many people's suffering." He lets out a sinister laugh. "I have to leave now."

I grab his bag and sit on it. "Remember Joe, lying in court's a crime."

"I'm not going to court," he says, eyeing the bag, trying to figure a way to dislodge me.

"So, what do you say? Will you do the right thing? Or will you just stick your head in the sand? Imagine how you'll feel when Zoe gets convicted, knowing you were too cowardly to tell the truth." I brace myself, half believing he'll rush me and knock me on my ass to get his bag. "I didn't take you for a coward, Joe. But then again, maybe you are. Appearances can be deceiving, can't they?"

A few of the longest seconds of my life pass, my heart aching at the thought of Zoe alone in a windowless cell for twenty-three hours a day until she takes her final breath. Then, like the light of dawn cleaving the darkness, the fear lifts from Joe's eyes, replaced by a narrow-eyed scowl of determination.

"Hell, my folks have done everything they can for Sam. I can't hide behind my brother as an excuse. Sooner or later, he's going to have to straighten himself out or he's as good as dead, but that's his choice. But Zoe doesn't have one."

"So you'll testify at Zoe's trial and go with me to the authorities to tell them about what Detective Sorenson said?"

He extends a hand to pull me to my feet. "Yes, I will."

"Thank you. And one more thing."

"What now?"

"Last thing, I promise. Were you mad because Sinclair was sleeping with Serena?"

"Is that what Zoe said?"

"Not exactly."

His cheeks redden. "Yeah, I was mad. But not because she was fucking him. But because she was dealing, just like him. I thought she was better than that."

"Dealing?" I ask, trying to sound surprised given my unconfirmed suspicions after I saw her at the clinic and the widow's place.

"To kids on campus."

"Holy shit."

That's why we broke up. She tried to sell Sam some dope. Can you believe that crap?"

Every nerve in my is body is electrified. "Sinclair and Serena were in business together?"

"Yep. Serena might have looked like a runway model, but deep down inside she was rotten. And so was he. I know it's not right to speak ill of the dead, but the pair of them got what they deserved."

"Not like that's not enough, but is there anything else you want to tell me?"

"That's everything I know. And now you know it too."

"That's more than enough. You're very brave," I say, handing him his bag. "And I'm sorry about what I said about your being a coward. Nothing could be further from the truth."

He holds out his hand to shake mine. "No worries. It's your job to do whatever it takes to save Zoe." He strides away, seemingly without a care in the world.

***

Vinnie's fully reclined in the driver's seat, window open, humming some show tune I can't quite put a name to. I bang on the windshield.

"Mother of God, sweetheart! You about gave me a heart attack."

I get in and pinch his cheek. "You're too young to die."

He cranks the engine. "Everything go okay with the kid?"

"Roger that. Good news is Zoe didn't murder Sinclair."

"And the bad?"

"Sonny's involved."

"The pretty cop who used to come sniffing around The Hurricane looking for you?"

"One and the same."

Joe's Land Rover pulls out of the parking lot followed by a black Corvette.

My phone rings.

"Grace, I need to see you."

"Why?"

"Better we talk in person."

"I'll come by your office tomorrow after court, maybe around—"

"No! It has to be tonight."

I mouth "Manny" to Vinnie who motions for me to hang up.

"Okay. I'm on the way home and going for a run. If you want to come over after that, it's up to you, but it'll be late. Around ten."

"See you then."

Chapter 32

I gulp some water from the fountain outside the public restrooms at the South Beach parking lot, the halfway point on my run. This is the South Beach in Fort Lauderdale, not the one in Miami where movie stars and hangers-on go to stand in line outside the hottest clubs for the honor of paying a thousand bucks for a bottle of booze that costs twenty-five at Royal Liquors.

For the first time in weeks, I'm not carrying around a refrigerator on my back, nor is my stomach in knots. And to celebrate, I'm taking my longest run since the amputation—six miles. Zoe will go free and, as for the rest of it—how Sonny's involved, how everything connects to drug dealing and the pill mills—I have no idea. My job is done. And well, if I say so myself.

I lean against the wall to stretch out my hamstrings.

Without warning, he's on me, forcing my back against the fountain, the steel basin frigid against the backs of my thighs.

It's as if he's just stepped straight out of my mind onto the sidewalk.

"Jesus, Sonny! What the—"

"Don't think for one minute I'm gonna let you ruin me and everything I've worked for," he says, leaning his bulk against me, the piercing blue of his eyes tinged with yellow from the light above the fountain.

He rips off the armband holding my phone and crushes it under his shoe. "You're not gonna need this, because you are never going to need to talk to anyone again. Especially not Joe Harper."

I scan the parking lot for help. Empty. Not one car, not even the homeless guy on a beach cruiser who usually hangs around after the evening AA meeting on the beach to knock back a few in peace. The lot closes at 8 p.m. and it has to be at least 9:30, maybe later.

"See, like you, Grace, I'm meticulous about every last detail. After I warned Harper that it would be in his best interest not to blab to anyone, especially you, we sent Alexi to follow him, as an insurance policy, to make sure he kept his mouth shut until the trial was over. Turns out that was a good idea. You remember Alexi, don't you? The rather large man with Serena at FCP?"

And the Sinclair home. And his black Corvette. But who is "we"?

"Alexi saw him talking to you. Had to shut his mouth forever."

A sour taste invades my mouth. "He was just a boy, for God's sake." I manage to scratch his cheek, hard enough to draw blood.

He grabs both my wrists and forces them above my head with one of his hands and jams a gun against my temple with the other. "A boy who could have taken me down. Just like you."

I open my mouth, but he smashes me in the face with the barrel of the gun. "Scream and I'll kill you right here and feed you to the sharks. Move!"

He shoves me into his ancient Jeep Cherokee, face down on the back seat which smells like a used jockstrap, and cuffs my wrists and ankles with plastic zip ties. "Don't move an inch, and don't say a goddamned word."

"Let go of me!"

"I told you to shut up!" He punches me in the kidneys. I bite my tongue to keep from crying out from the savage pain.

He jumps in and cranks the ignition. As he turns the car south on A1A, he opens the window, slaps an emergency light on the roof, and guns the engine.

I can't see a thing beyond the interior bathed in the strobing blue light. But I don't need to see to know where we are. We're passing the Bahia Mar Marina, the fire station, and the Yankee Clipper, the iconic beach hotel where my father and I watched mermaids swimming in a huge tank behind the bar as patrons sipped slushy piña coladas.

I'm able to raise my face off the floor. "Tampering with a witness, not to mention threatening to kill him, that could really sink a cop's career."

"Hah! No one's ever going to know."

When he takes the curve onto 17th Street too fast, I roll off the seat onto the floor. "You're scum, Sonny," I say, but my words are swamped by the tires screeching as he pulls a fast right at the Pier Sixty-Six Hotel and brakes hard to a stop.

I bite back the searing pain long enough to arch my back enough to see out the side window. High above, the concrete underbelly of a bridge. The deafening clanging of an electronic bell from above—the parking lot under the Seventeenth Street bridge. It's ironic. This used to be one of my favorite spots for liquid lunch breaks. Only five minutes from the courthouse, and always deserted. Like tonight.

He flings open the back door and slits the ankle ties with a hunting knife, pulling me up by the wrists, the sharp plastic edges of the zip ties sawing into my flesh.

"That hurts, goddammit!"

Holding the gun on me with one hand, he tosses an FLPD Official Business card on the dash with the other, and kicks the door shut. "Didn't I already say, shut the fuck up?"

I refuse to move, and he presses the gun into my ribs. "You never were much good at taking orders, but now you're gonna learn real fast. Move! And if you even think about kicking me in the nuts, I'll blow your way-too-clever brains out."

He marches me down a steel dock to a speedboat painted with FLPD Marine Patrol.

On board, he forces me into the chair to the left of the helm, cuts the wrist ties, and secures me to the chair with a pair of standard-issue handcuffs.

He pulls two FLPD hats from a grocery bag, and jams one onto my head. "Not exactly the high fashion you used to be accustomed to, but it'll do. In case anyone gets close, which I doubt at this time of night."

He puts his hat on. "And, one thing before we get going. Take it off."

"What? Take what off?"

He points at Oscar.

"You've gotta be kidding me."

"Do I look like I'm kidding?" he says, with a whack to the side of my head.

Gun barrel resting on my temple, he unlocks the cuffs and watches as I press the pin mechanism on the inside ankle to release the leg, revealing my stump, sausage shaped and bound in white gauze.

He wrinkles his nose. "Shit, that *is* ugly."

When I respond by spitting in his face, he strikes me in the shoulder with the butt of the gun.

Gritting my teeth, I stare down at Oscar, lying on his side like a fallen soldier, foot still inside my running shoe. I've spent months hating the damn thing, and now I want nothing more than to strap him back on where he belongs.

When Sonny snatches the contraption from the deck and hurls it into the water, I know without any modicum of doubt I could kill again—if I had to.

He double checks the line securing a Zodiac inflatable boat

to the stern, unties the mooring lines from the pilings, and fires up the engine. "At least those six years in the Navy weren't totally useless." He glances overboard at Oscar bobbing like a piece of driftwood. "And at least I came back with all my parts."

"You bastard!" I scream, my voice breaking into as many pieces as my heart. "If you're going to kill me, why don't you just do it here?"

He eases the throttle forward. "Because that would be messy. And I don't like messes."

We slide through the no-wake zone in silence, the moon a golden gong high in the night sky, the warm breeze like silk drawn over my skin. A school of dolphins rises in arcs alongside the boat, their slick, silver faces grinning as they surface and dive again and again.

"There'll be other lawyers who'll take my place and they'll find out the truth too."

"Not a chance. This time the good doctor will make sure to find a hack who'll be a little more cooperative with his..." he raises his hands off the wheel to make air quotes with his index fingers, "his goals."

"Money can buy anything these days, right?"

He sniffs the salt air. "I see it as a win-win-win. I get rich, Slim gets richer, and his Botox babes with big boobs are none the wiser."

As he pilots the boat through the channel between two skyscraper-sized cruise ships docked in Port Everglades, the seemingly unconnected details—everything I know and what I don't—assemble themselves in my mind, into the whole truth, as obvious now as the fact that I'm not getting out of this alive.

Sonny and Slim are partners.

An involuntary gasp escapes my mouth.

"You got it now? I knew you could figure it out. And that's why we're taking this little cruise."

Choking back the impulse to vomit, I focus on the towers of swaying royal palms encircling John Lloyd State Park, an isthmus of land lapped by shallow azure waters where manatees like to play, and teenagers get up to no good.

"And you know where we're going, don't you?"

I do, but I'm not about to give him the satisfaction.

At the cut of the Intracoastal and the open ocean, he slams the throttle forward and we surge ahead, leaving behind a bubbly, chevron-shaped wake. This boat's nowhere near as fast as the monster cigarette boat Manny bought without telling me, but it's plenty fast enough for what Sonny has in mind.

I yank on the steel cuffs, hoping the chair rails might detach from the seat back, but knowing they won't give an inch. What good would it do anyway? Even if I were able to launch myself off the side, I'd be fish food in no time. They never tell the tourists about the sharks, but they're out there.

Keep your wits about you. Keep your wits about you!

I repeat the mantra again over and over in my head. It had been my father's advice for almost any occasion. New school? Keep your wits about you. New job? Keep your wits about you. Backpacking through the Himalayas? Just keep your wits about you, and don't eat anything from a street vendor. Going to a war zone? You know how to keep your wits about you, Grace. You'll be fine. Percy's wits had kept him alive in more than one dark corner of the earth, a topic he rarely spoke of, even when I begged. But then, I came to understand his own shadowy time overseas was why he replaced "Keep your wits about you" for "Stay in your trench and keep your helmet on," when I enlisted in the Army.

When we round Cape Florida, the southernmost tip of Key Biscayne, just off the coast of downtown Miami, my heart seizes. Stiltsville. The coordinates on my tattoo.

"You are an asshole, Sonny!" I shout into the void, futile, like one hand clapping.

"Yeah, but you know what, Grace? I'm the asshole with the gun."

Chapter 33

It's surreal. I'm en route to my death, yet I am still enthralled by the dreamy mirage on the horizon.

Stiltsville. A clutch of pastel colored wooden stilt houses erected atop pilings in the middle of Biscayne Bay, floating like a floral wreath in the nascent glow of dawn. Seabirds hovering all around, their wings gilded by the rising sun. If you've never seen Stiltsville, you might try to blink away the image, dismiss it as the product of one too many umbrella drinks, but throughout my life, Stiltsville has been my refuge. Until now.

It's one of those "only in Miami" kind of phenomena. Made up of a dozen stilt shacks which functioned as social clubs, fishing huts, and speakeasys in the 1930s. An offshore oasis where booze, bikinis, and gambling were the name of the game and rules didn't apply. A Prohibition-era hub for wreckers, rum runners, and all manner of rascals, where ne'er-do-wells mixed with lawyers, bankers, politicians, and anyone else looking to escape the scrutiny of their landlubber life.

I count and recount the remaining shacks not yet destroyed

by hurricanes, seven in all, and cast my mind back to happier times. Winter vacations from boarding school at the family estate, Miramar, on Key Biscayne, with ready access across the Bay to this place, my secret place. As a teenager, I'd motor across in my father's Zodiac, not unlike the one tied to the stern now, to hang with friends, to drink beer and smoke. And, on one muggy night, to lose my virginity to a boy named Chad. Once, on a dare, I swam across.

Sonny steers the boat alongside the Jimmy Ellenberg House, a yellow stilt shack with a wraparound porch, a haven for pelicans and people, like me, willing to violate the trespassing ban in place since 2003, when Stiltsville was taken over by the National Park Service. He eases back on the throttle, cuts the engine, and hops out to secure the bow line to a piling covered in a stucco of bird droppings.

"It'll look like you rowed your little boat out here, like you used to," he says, tying the Zodiac to an adjacent piling.

A furnace of fury ignites in my gut, the kind of rage I haven't felt since Reilly said he'd found pills in the glove compartment of my car.

Sonny jumps back on board, grabs a duffel bag from the back of the boat. He unlocks the handcuffs from the chair and pulls me upright. An instinctive attempt to kick back at him with my good leg leaves me sprawled on the deck, looking up into his eyes, bottomless pits drilled into his tanned face.

He motions with the gun for me to get up.

Unable to get my balance on one leg, I pitch forward onto the dock, scraping my face against the rotten wood reduced to splinters by eight decades of relentless tropical sun. One arm hooked under my armpit, he yanks me up like a sack of flour and, disgusted as I may be, I have no choice but to lean on him to steady myself.

"Upstairs!"

Gun at my back, I hop up the stairs, one at a time, holding onto the handrail for balance. At the top, he reaches around me and flings open the flimsy door, its busted screen flapping in the breeze.

The shack is as I remember it—one large room with a bare board floor, ringed by windows, most of which were broken out decades ago. The only thing in the place now is an old-fashioned wooden desk chair.

As he secures my leg and arms to the chair with zip ties from the duffel, I sense the healing power of this place draining from my soul, its magic gone for me now. This was the one place that had given me hope, renewed me, time and time again. A safe place, when I was a gawky teenager bullied for my bookishness. A hideout with bad boys my parents considered "unsuitable mates." A refuge, when I came back from Iraq, broken and lost, with nothing but bad memories and worse habits.

He squats in front of me, hands clasped. "It's either me or you. And, given that choice, you lose."

I turn my head away. "It's like Reilly says, murder always comes down to the same three things."

"Money, jealousy, or just plain evil. That's about the only thing that old-timer ever said that made any sense at all, except no damn way I'd ever kill for anything but money. No upside in the others."

"Why kill at all?"

He's walking in circles around me now. "You tell me, why don't you? You're Miss Ivy League."

As loathe as I am to comply with any order he might give me at this point, I'll be damned if I'll go to my grave not knowing for certain what I've spent months trying to figure out.

"You got tired of seeing the low-life dealers driving all over town in their Ferraris and Bentleys, going home to their mansions on the water."

He keeps pacing, head bobbing back and forth like a professor evaluating a student's theory.

"You couldn't let Joe tell the truth, that Zoe couldn't have killed Sinclair, because you were involved."

"Go on."

"You and Sinclair already had a connection—you'd arrested him for dealing and turned him into a rat."

He snaps his fingers. "I prefer the term 'confidential informant.'"

"Not only did you use him for information, you also made him cut you in on his profits in exchange for turning a blind eye to his dealing." I pause. "How am I doing so far?"

"Not bad, not bad at all."

"Thing was, Sinclair got popped again. This time at Sunshine Pain. By FDLE, not FLPD, so you had no control over him. Once a rat, always a rat, correct? You we're afraid he'd sell you out, and maybe even cough up the fact that Slim's running the pill mills as a highly profitable side hustle to his fancy plastic surgery practice. Joe did see Sinclair there arguing with Slim. Maybe he wanted Slim to pay him to keep his mouth shut. Maybe too much."

"Well done. But how do you think I figure in this operation?"

"The 'we' you talked about back at South Beach, that's you and Anton Slim."

He shrugs. "You tell me."

"You said it yourself—money is your only motivator. And where's the money in this picture? In Slim's deep pockets. And where does that money come from? His cash cow – his pill mill empire. You took a page out of Sinclair's book and extorted Slim to keep hush-hush."

"So clever of you to figure all that out."

"The one way to keep the gravy train running for everyone was to get rid of Sinclair. And you kept it all in the family and took care of him yourself."

"And was rewarded handsomely, I might add."

He strolls to the window and gazes into the distance. "Greed is such an unappealing quality in a business partner. Sinclair kept wanting more and more, until it was no longer sustainable. So, neither was he."

He shoves the gun in his waistband and pulls a baggie of blue pills and a syringe filled with water from his pocket along with a length of rubber tubing. "But you're missing one crucial piece of the puzzle."

"Yeah, what's that?" I say, straining against the ties, which causes the chair to fall on its side and me to hit my head.

"You're forgetting about the lovely Serena," he says, looking down at me on the floor.

"She knew about what Sinclair was doing, given she was sleeping with him. You killed her too."

"Close, but not exactly. That one was Slim. Do you know why?"

I buck my shoulders, trying, unsuccessfully, to right the chair.

"You're a little pale. You feeling okay? Don't worry, you'll feel all better soon enough. Now Serena, there was a smart girl. Didn't even take time to mourn the poor fool. Just took over Sinclair's business right where he left off. But, as tends to happen, when there's lots of cash flying around, she got greedy too."

I focus on a pelican outside, suspended in midair by the thermals high over the pulsing Gulf Stream. "What made you go bad, Sonny?"

"I was always bad. Bad's in my blood. I'm just better at hiding it than the rest of my family. You just couldn't see it. You were blinded with your nemesis, Reilly. And he did make for a nice distraction."

"You're despicable."

He kneels down beside me, his lower lip in a pout. "You know what you get for all your big words and high-minded bullshit about the truth? You get to be dead."

My vision narrows to the tubing being stretched around my left arm to make a tourniquet above my left elbow, under my tattoo.

"This'll look like just another unhappy ending for one more

junkie."

He licks several of the blue pills to remove the time-release coating, so they'll take immediate effect, crushes them to a fine dust on the window sill, and sweeps the mound of powder onto a spoon.

My grip on reality slipping away like an outgoing tide.
Squirting the water from the syringe onto the powder.
Mixing the powder with a pinkie finger.
Dipping needle into liquid.
Pulling the plunger back.
Chamber filling.
Syringe gripped between his teeth.
Flicking the flesh to find a willing vein.
Needle piercing skin.
Overwhelming sense of warmth and well-being.
Tubing falling away.
Door slamming.
Fade to black.

Chapter 34

"Hail Mary, full of grace, the Lord is with thee. Dear Jesus, please let her live."

I will my eyes to open.

"Breathe, sweetheart. Breathe!"

The voice—familiar, comforting.

Lids apart. A face. Familiar, like the voice, but it's shape-shifting like an image in a fun house mirror.

Must get up!

"Relax, Gracie, relax," says another face.

Bongo beat pounding in my chest.

First voice: "What'd you give her?"

The second face: "Narcan."

"Stay with me, Gracie."

"M— Manny?"

"Yes, it's me. And Vinnie, too," Manny says, easing me to a seated position.

Vinnie in my peripheral vision, grabbing my hand. "It's me, sweetheart, everything's gonna be okay. We're gonna get you out of here."

I blink hard to clear my vision.

The busted-up screen.

"No!"

Oscar bobbing in the ocean.

"Where'd he go?" I mumble.

"Who?" Vinnie asks.

Arms around me, Manny supports my weight as Vinnie rights the chair.

Tubing tied tight, veins distended like tree roots bursting out of the ground.

"He left me...he...here to die," I rasp, my throat parched.

"You're safe now."

"No. Need to go!"

"We're going, okay? We're taking you to a hospital."

Manny pulling me close. "You're alive. That's all that matters."

The scent of him, woody, calming.

"I didn't," I say as he unties the tubing. "It was him."

Vinnie in my face. "Who? It was who? Who did this to you?"

I gag, a wave of nausea churning in my gut. "Sonny."

"The blond cop?"

I manage a nod.

"We'll get that rat bastard!"

One on each arm, we hobble to the door. "How...How'd you know I was here?"

"When I stopped by last night, Vinnie was in a panic. Said you'd been gone way longer than usual on your run."

"Miranda was going nuts. Wouldn't stop barking. We searched everywhere for you. Called everyone we could think of."

"You came by?" I ask Manny.

"You said I could come over, remember?"

"Thank God he did! He thought he might know where you'd go if—"

"I didn't...relapse."

Manny brushes my hair back. "We know."

"Why'd you need to see me?"

Manny hooks an arm under mine and hauls me up onto my good leg. "Not important right now. We need to get you to a hospital."

"How'd you? I w...wa...was gone. Supposed to di..."

Manny jerks his chin at the empty spray bottle of Narcan. "Had it in my car, from before. Brought it out here. Just in case."

Vinnie leading the way, we shuffle into the blinding sunlight. Limp, suspended like laundry on a clothes line, they maneuver me down the rickety staircase. A Zodiac, like my father's, sits tied up, abandoned.

"I— I didn't..." My vision turns hazy. My eyelids are lead weights.

Manny shakes my shoulder. "Stay awake, Gracie! We need you to stay awake."

Everything spinning. Images swirling above the crystalline water. Sonny crushing pills. Tubing tightening. The needle sliding in...

They prop me up like a mannequin in the back of the boat.

My stump, the gauze filthy and tattered. "He threw it..."

"Hurry, Manny! Hurry! She's fading!"

A stinging slap to the face. "Don't go to sleep. Stay with us!"

Engine revving.

Sea spray stinging my face.

Manny screaming, "Keep her awake! If she loses consciousness again, she'll die!"

Acceleration like a jet-powered roller coaster.

Chapter 35

"That's one hell of a story," Marcus says, squeezing my hand so tightly I wince.

"I wish it were a story," I say, extracting my hand from his death grip. "And where do you fit in?"

"These two called me to notify the authorities, to make sure Sonny Sorenson and Anton Slim never take a breath as free men again." His voice cracks. "I...I wish I hadn't mentioned the Statewide case. I had no idea I was—"

"You were trying to help an old friend."

"Thank God you're okay," Marcus says. "And you're not old, by the way."

I sink back into the pillows. "Yeah? Well, I feel like I'm a hundred."

The bed shifts back to center when Marcus raises his bulk to get me a glass of water from the pitcher on the nightstand. "Don't you worry. We'll get those pieces of garbage."

"Thank God Manny didn't get rid of that damn boat when I told him to," I say, winking at Manny.

Vinnie chimes in from his post in the corner, hands gripping his Marlins cap. "That's one helluva boat."

Manny shoots me a self-satisfied smile over his shoulder. "And she wanted me to get rid of it a while back. Thought it was too *Miami Vice* for a City Commissioner."

"And it still is. Makes you looks like a wise guy."

Vinnie bats his eyelids.

Manny jerks a thumb at Vinnie. "You should have seen this chicken shit. He was pasted to the seat as if he were walking into a hurricane. Never opened his eyes the whole way there and back."

"Hey, I thought I was gonna die out there," Vinnie says, and we all laugh for a second, until what could have been hits us like a brick.

Marcus hands me the plastic glass. "One thing I don't understand is how these guys knew where you were?"

"Educated guess." I flip up the sleeve of the hospital gown. "The coordinates for Stiltsville."

Marcus nods. "Ah, the tattoo."

"Sonny used it as a road map to get rid of me, and the truth right along with me."

"And these two used it to find you."

"Thank God, even if they thought I'd relapsed," I say, gaze shifting to the twinkling Miami skyline out the window, a jagged neon metropolis cut from the onyx sky.

A shadow passes over Vinnie's face. "When I used the master key to get into her apartment, I found her backpack on the table. And a bottle of Jack on top of the fridge."

"The bottle was unopened," I say—I'd chosen Jack Daniel's, my favorite, for my weekly test, to see if I could survive the temptation throughout the stress of Zoe's trial.

Vinnie rushes over and grabs my hand. "I know you don't drink no more, sweetheart. But I know you don't go nowhere without your backpack neither and it was there, and Manny and me, we were besides ourselves and—"

"It's okay, Vin. You guys saved me. And I'm forever in your debt. Maybe you and me, we can call it even."

Vinnie swipes a tear away with the Marlins cap. "Not a chance."

"I knew Stiltsville was the one place she'd go to be alone. To calm her mind," Manny says. "She went out there when she was a kid. When she came back from the war—"

"What he means, Marcus, is that I went out there to drink when we were married."

Manny steps to my bedside. "That's in the past. And what's past is past. Let's leave it there, where it belongs."

I pull the sleeve back over the tattoo. "Stiltsville *used* to be my secret little piece of paradise."

"You're safe, Gracie. That's all that matters." Manny says. "We'll find you another special place."

"Deal, but only after we lock those pieces of you-know-what up for the rest of their miserable lives." I point at Vinnie. "I didn't use the bad word this time."

"All you needed was a near death experience to clean up your language," Vinnie says, smiling.

Marcus rocks back on his heels, arms crossed. "We'll get them all. Sonny and the Slims and anyone else who needs arresting. But, one last thing, how'd Sonny know about Stiltsville?"

Manny retreats to the window, a faraway stare replacing the forgiveness in his eye from a moment ago. "He'd seen the tattoo, hadn't he, Grace?"

To end the awkward silence, Vinnie pounds the fist of his right hand into the palm of the left. "*Testa di cazzo*, let me tell you what I'm gonna do to—"

I give him a time-out sign. "He'll get his. They all will."

A conspiratorial smile brightens Vinnie's face. "If there's anything I can do. I got skills, ya know."

"Speaking of what you can do, what did you do with Miranda? Where is she?"

"She's with Jake. I left the key under the mat when we went

looking for you and called him to come by."

"Who's Miranda?" Manny asks.

"Her dog," Vinnie and Marcus reply in unison.

Manny lowers his head to conceal a smile. "You replaced me with a dog?"

I point at Vinnie, trying not to laugh given the two broken ribs I got from falling off the chair. "Blame your partner in crime over there."

"Can I get you anything before I leave?" Marcus asks.

"Thanks, but no. I'll be getting out of here tonight. Doc says I must have had at least a little tolerance left, otherwise the opioid dose Sonny gave me would have killed me. First time in my life being a pill popper has ever been helpful."

"I see you haven't lost your sense of humor."

"Maybe not, but I seem to have lost my Spidey sense. I thought Reilly was the bad cop."

"People change, Grace."

"I'd like to believe that," I say. I turn to Manny. "Would you two mind giving Manny and me a minute?"

"Let's get out of here, brother," Vinnie says.

"Who you callin' brother?" Marcus asks, moving to the door.

Once they're gone, Manny sits on the side of the bed. "What's this about?"

"Why did you insist on coming over last night? I'm glad you did, but what was so important that it couldn't wait?"

"Britt came by my office yesterday afternoon."

"Britt? Why?"

"He knows about our deal."

I prop myself up on my elbows. "What deal?"

"The one we made to get you on Zoe's case."

My mouth feels as if it's stuffed with cotton balls.

"He said I had to convince you to resign from Zoe's case, or he would leak the details to the press and the Bar which, of course, wouldn't be good for either of us. That's why I needed to see you."

"How could Britt know what we agreed to?" I say, but then remember Britt and Gretchen talking outside the courtroom. I raise a hand. "Gretchen told him."

"That's what he said, but how'd you know?"

I fall back on the pillows. "Dammit! I should have known he was trying to screw me again."

"Why?"

"I saw him after our mediation. He implied there was a story behind how someone like me got on a case like Zoe's. He's one vindictive bastard. He'd love nothing better than to see me fail, preferably in a publicly humiliating way."

"Why does he still have it in for you?"

"He thought I got off too easy. He'd do anything to sink my career a second time and getting me out of the spotlight would be a good start."

"He told Gretchen he'd tell the world her husband is behind the FCP pill mill chain if she didn't tell him why she hired you. Said he'd make Anton look like a drug pusher 'of the lowest order,' is how he put it, and that he'd make sure all his clinics got shut down and the pair of them locked up."

"Well, he's going to get that last part." My stomach turns sour. "Gretchen threw me and you under the bus to protect herself and the lifestyle to which she has become accustomed."

He hangs his head. "I'm so sorry, Grace. For everything."

"Like you said, let's leave the past where it belongs." I sit up and square my shoulders. "And we have to look on the bright side."

Manny raises an eyebrow. "You? Look on the bright side? You must have changed!"

"Scary, isn't it?" I say, landing a playful punch on his arm.

We share a laugh for the first time in ages and the tightness in my chest loosens.

"I mean, Gretchen may be a self-serving piece of work, but we don't have to worry about Britt. He won't follow through on his threat."

"How do you know that?

"As it turns out, my nearly dying saved us both."

"I don't understand."

"He needs me now. Why would Britt let a petty vendetta interfere with burnishing his political credentials? Now he can play the hero by dismissing a case against a wrongfully accused teenager set up by a crooked cop who tried to kill the long-suffering former prosecutor who fought and almost died in search of the truth. And then there's the trials of the Slims and Sonny. Britt's going to need my cooperation for those. I'm his key witness."

"It's a win-win if you both keep your mouths shut about your—"

"Our less than ethical behavior, yes."

Manny shakes his head.

"The business of dispensing justice is a wonderful thing, isn't it. All shades of gray."

"Like the rest of life, I guess," he says, with a faraway look in his eye. "I should let you rest."

"One thing before you go. I don't get why he would come to you and not directly to me?"

"I asked him. He said he wanted what we elected officials call 'plausible deniability.' By using me as the messenger, he keeps his hands clean. He's an asshole."

"And a coward. He knows I'm just crazy enough to tell him to go pound sand."

Chapter 36

"**S**tay out of sight, okay? The chief would fire my fat ass if he knew you were here," Reilly says.

"The chief should have fired your fat ass a long time ago." I point one of my crutches at him. "But then again, I'd like to think people can change."

"Don't go getting all sappy on me now," he says, shooing me behind a concrete pillar in the police parking area adjacent to the courthouse. "You know you got yourself busted, don't you? I just brought the cuffs to your Mardi Gras party."

"Maybe," I mumble. Then, louder, "But thanks for letting me be here, Frank."

"It's the least I can do." He flaps a hand in my direction. "Now get back behind that damn thing."

I'm grateful Reilly's letting me see this nightmare to its conclusion, but I'm of two minds about him still. Right place at the right time? Or did he set me up? He has it in him—he framed Vinnie. If I had to, I could make either argument sound believable—but that's my job, to make the unbelievable sound believable, a task made easier when the unbelievable is, in fact, the truth.

He expels a deep sigh and I peek out from my hiding place. "Everything okay?"

The hairs of his mustache twitching, he speaks in a tight tone freighted with the disappointment of the betrayed. "And to think I showed him the ropes when he got his gold shield, treated him like a son. Shoot, it was me who gave him his nickname."

"Yeah, what's that? I can think of a few choice monikers for that bastard."

"Boy Scout. Can you believe it?"

I stifle a laugh. "Maybe you're not the best judge of character, Detective."

"That makes two of us, Counselor." He flaps his hand at me again. "And get yourself back behind the damn post, why don't ya? He's gonna be here any second."

"Roger that."

"Piece of shit," he mumbles, lighting a cigarette to wait for Sonny. Just like he does before every trial day. Except today isn't any other day. Today they won't be comparing notes, getting their stories straight. Today he'll slap the cuffs on his own partner, the one who betrayed his trust. And mine.

My nerves are on high alert, not only because of what's about to happen, but because I've had no sleep. It was a long day yesterday at the hospital, telling and retelling my story. And Reilly persuading the brass to let him be the one to take Sonny into custody, even pissing off a judge in the wee hours to sign arrest warrants for him and the Slims. We decided to take everyone down at the one place they'd be for sure today—the courthouse. They have to act as if everything were normal.

Reilly crosses himself at the sickly rumble of the engine of Sonny's Jeep.

Sonny pulls into the space beside Reilly's car. The moment his feet touch the ground, a SWAT team swarms in from all directions, weapons drawn. The only words Sonny gets out of his mouth are a strangled "What the fuck," right before they force him onto his belly.

"Soren Sorenson, a.k.a. Sonny Sorenson, I have a warrant for your arrest for the murder of Brandon Sinclair, the attempted murder of Grace Locke, accessory after the fact in the murder of Serena Price, and witness tampering," Reilly says, standing astride Sonny and cuffing his hands behind his back.

A sense of redemption floods my body as Sonny strains against the cuffs, rolling side to side like a roped calf. "I have no idea what you're talking about, Frank," he hisses, head ratcheted to the side, eyes wide, looking around as if he expects someone to say there's been a terrible mistake.

After two SWAT officers the size of mountains manhandle the flailing Sonny to his feet, Reilly gets in his face. "You have the right to remain silent. Anything you say can, and will, be used against you in a court of law."

"Fuck you, Frank."

"You have the right to an attorney. And guess what? As luck would have it, we have one right here for you."

"What the hell are you talking about?

"You can come out now, Counselor."

The moment I step from the shadows, Sonny's face turns whiter than the purest cocaine.

"Bet you didn't expect to see me here, Detective," I say, crutching toward him, my stump purposefully in full view under the hem of my skirt. "That's right, Detective, you have the right to remain silent, but that won't help you. We've got you...What is it you said about Zoe? 'Dead to rights,' wasn't that it?"

As Reilly continues to read the Miranda warnings, Sonny's nostrils flare in and out like the fire-breathing dragons in comic books.

I stand back, content to watch, the sweet sense that justice is being done, an absolution of sorts. "I think we're all even now, Frank."

"Seems as if we are," Reilly says, shoving Sonny into the

back of a waiting police cruiser, using the same motion he had used on me.

***

Inside Twietmeyer's courtroom, cameras click and clack like demented chickens. Reporters from every major local, national, and cable news outlet are here, expecting to witness the trial of Zoe Slim, a twice-accused murderer with a prep-school pedigree.

Reilly's in the last row of the gallery, head held high. I guarantee he's licking his chops. I know I am. He's seated shoulder to shoulder with Detective Chang, Reilly's partner for the day, given his current one is indisposed. Reilly pats his jacket pocket, inside which is the warrant for the arrest of Anton Slim for murder, conspiracy to commit murder, money laundering, and a host of other charges related to the pill mills, some of which will stick, some might not. Regardless, like Sonny, the last thing Slim will see is a needle going into his vein, much like the one Sonny stuck in my arm, the injection a cocktail of the type of drugs Slim peddled.

There had been a few moments, or, more accurately, more than a few, after my abduction when the gauzy euphoria wore off that I thought, *No one would be any the wiser, would they?* I could take the pain meds the docs in the hospital offered to prescribe for my injuries as readily as the quacks at FCP, They look so innocuous, those little pills, like candy the color of the waters swirling around Stiltsville.

But then Manny saw that gleam in my eye, the one he'd learned to detect over time, but not soon enough to save us. The one, he says, that turns my face from an open book into a stone fortress.

And when I saw that look in his eyes, the soul-crushing disappointment that what should have been for us would never be because of me, I asked for a double dose of Tylenol instead.

***

The second arrest warrant is in Chang's pocket. For Gretchen.

It charges her with accessory after the fact in the murders of Sinclair and Serena, and money laundering. A stretch? Perhaps. It comes down to what she knew and when. She can bat her eyelashes all she wants, but the evidence will get her in the end, too. It always does. Unless of course, she gets a persuasive defense lawyer with a talent for conjuring up reasonable doubt, a thought which raises goosebumps on my forearms.

Two deputies lead Zoe in, hands cuffed in front and attached to a waist chain connected to leg irons. She's wearing street clothes instead of a prison jumpsuit, but the baggy blue cotton skirt and wrinkled white blouse make her look more like an escapee from Goodwill than the daughter of a multimillionaire. Like a shriveled weed, she wilts onto the chair beside me. She has no clue what's about to happen.

The moment the clock above the door reads 9:00 a.m., Judge Twietmeyer takes the bench. Never one to shy away from the cameras, Britt's seated at the State's table with Hightower, a self-satisfied smile on his face intended to convey he's solely responsible for exonerating a wrongly-accused teenager and uncovering a conspiracy involving law enforcement and one of the city's most prominent residents. No matter. We're all accomplices in this conspiracy for good, for now. Britt can wait. I have a long memory, too.

The Slims are in their usual spot in the front of the gallery, faces pulled tight, which in Anton's case is due to his feigning the distress of a concerned parent, and, in Gretchen's case, Botox.

"State versus Zoya AKA "Zoe" Slim," Twietmeyer announces, the nasally sound of his voice evidence of a head cold. "Before we commence, I believe we have a preliminary matter to take care of. Is that correct, Counselors?"

Hightower, Britt, and I spring to our feet and reply in unison. "Yes, Your Honor."

Reilly extracts the warrant from his pocket with a flourish and unhooks the cuffs from his belt. Chang does the same, but with minimal theatricality given his role as a bit player in this drama.

Zoe tugs on my sleeve. "What's going on?"

"I'll explain in a minute. Don't say a thing."

Reilly and Chang approach the Slims who are seated directly behind the defense table.

"Anton Frederick Slim, I have a warrant for your arrest for murder and conspiracy to commit murder and money laundering," Reilly says.

Chang follows Reilly's lead with, "And Gretchen Marie Slim, I have a warrant for your arrest for money laundering and accessory to murder after the fact."

A collective gasp rises from the gallery, and the cameras that had been trained on Zoe pivot to her parents.

Reilly grabs Anton by one shoulder and spins him around, cuffing him in a single well-practiced motion. Chang does the same to Gretchen, slapping the cuffs onto her delicate wrists as he would do to any common criminal.

"Excuse me, Detective." Anton says, his face turning purple. "Let me go!"

"Anton Slim and Gretchen Slim, you both have the right to remain silent. You both have the right to an attorney. If you cannot afford one," Reilly pauses, an inordinately wide grin on his face, "if you cannot afford an attorney, one will be appointed for you."

Gretchen cranes her neck around Chang, eyes as big as dinner plates. "Do something, Grace. Do something!"

I cross my arms across my chest and mouth. "Not a chance."

As Reilly walks Anton and Gretchen from the courtroom, the reporters eye each other, uncertain whether to follow what's just happened, or stay and watch what's about to.

The moment the detectives and the Slims are out the door, Twietmeyer bangs his gavel twice to quiet the tsunami of chatter. "Silence, please. Now, Mr. Britt, I believe you have a motion?"

Britt rises. "Yes, Your Honor. The State of Florida moves to dismiss the indictment of Zoya AKA "Zoe" Slim."

"Can I assume that would be a dismissal with prejudice?" he says, alluding to the fact that doing so meant the case can never be refiled.

Britt gives an obsequious dip of his head. "Yes, sir. With extreme prejudice."

Hands on her shoulders, I turn her to face me. "It's over, Zoe."

"For you, maybe." She lowers her head to hide the tears cascading down her cheeks.

I glance back at the door through which the Slims exited the courtroom, the one leading to the holding cells, not the one they entered through with the certainty that wealth and privilege would protect them from their sins. Now it would be their turn to ask for forgiveness.

I tilt her chin up. "Make no mistake about it, the nightmare is over for *you*."

Chapter 37

"**K**iller Cop, Not Killer Kid." The headline on the front page of the *Sun Sentinel* says it all. Case closed.

I toss the newspaper into the trash can under the desk. In addition to a trash can, I now have an ergonomic desk chair from which to dispense my pearls of legal wisdom without getting a backache, all thanks to Vinnie and Jake. They even hung a Welcome Home banner on the wall. Now it's time for some paying clients.

A knock on the window draws my attention and a flurry of barks from Miranda.

"Over here," I say, calling her to sit behind the desk, in case my visitor isn't a dog lover.

Another knock and a hand waving.

"Coming," I say, happy to be walking on two legs again, Oscar 2.0 having been engineered post haste from the original design by my prosthetist who saw my story on TV.

When I unlock the door, I find Zoe, both hands clasped around a gigantic bouquet of pink roses.

She thrusts the bouquet at me. "The man at the florist said pink roses mean 'thank you.' He also said they can mean 'please believe me.'"

I raise the flowers to my nose and breathe in the intense fragrance that transports me back to my mother's rose garden, a reminder that I need to visit Faith soon, even if it means putting up with her fussing over me as she's been doing since I was released from the hospital. She insisted on staying with me. At The Hurricane. On a camp bed. Eating frozen dinners and drinking tap water. All things I thought I'd never see. Perhaps I've underestimated her resilience too, much as I misjudged Zoe. And Vinnie. And Sonny. And Manny. Time will tell, given I promised to visit her in Palm Beach more often than before. It was the only way I could get her to leave. That and a promise to bring Miranda who, after a lifetime of fearing dogs, Faith has come to adore. Just more proof people can change, I suppose.

"Thank you for believing in me, Ms. Locke. You saved my life. But it almost lost you yours. I'm so sorry."

"How many times do I have to tell you it's Grace?" I pull her in for a hug. "And none of this was your fault. *None* of it."

Gretchen sails in, a purse on her arm that cost more than many people make in a year. Fresh out of jail. On bail yes, but fresh as a daisy, as always. I must have missed that lesson in how-to-be-a-good-criminal school. Me, when I got out of jail, I looked like shit and felt worse, unable to look anyone, even Vinnie, in the eye for weeks.

"I can't thank you enough for saving my daughter," she says in a tone so breezy it's as if she's telling me the weather forecast is for sun, no chance for rain. I've resolved to be less judgmental, but she's not making it easy.

I point them to the newly-upholstered client chairs Jake picked up at a second-hand store for my homecoming, along with a similarly upholstered dog bed for Miranda, who is currently cloistered in the back room for fear she might pee on Gretchen's leg—she seems to have a sixth sense for people I dislike and growled as soon as her limo pulled up.

As Gretchen sits, her yellow silk dress settles around her like a wave of liquid gold. Her outward appearance is, indeed, perfect, but a charade intended to further cloak the truth in respectability? I suspect I'll never know. And maybe a charade is all it will take to skate on the charges and back into the high life. Juries have a habit of excusing the well-heeled.

I stand behind Zoe and rest my hands on her shoulders. "My Warrior Princess, Zoya. It's great to see you out of that hideous jail jumpsuit."

Zoe giggles. "Orange never has been my color."

Gretchen runs her hands over her skirt several times. Surely, she can still feel the prickly polyester of the jumpsuit she's just taken off. It's a sensation that doesn't leave you quickly.

"Tell me, how does it feel?"

"How does what feel?" Gretchen says as if she's read my mind.

"How does it feel to be free was the question, but I was talking to your daughter," I say with a dismissive wave. "Zoe, how does it feel to be free?"

Gretchen crosses and uncrosses her legs. "My daughter is adjusting well."

Zoe looks from me to her mother and back again. "Mom, would you mind? I'd like to have a minute alone with Grace."

Gretchen's mouth puckers into an O. "Are you sure, honey?"

"Yes, I'm sure."

I sit down beside Zoe, in the chair Gretchen vacated, the memory of her musky perfume hanging in the air. "Is there something you want to tell me?"

"He came to see me before my trial. In the jail. After trial call on Friday."

"Who came to see you?"

"The cop."

My heart stops. "Which cop? Detective Reilly—the one who arrested you and came to court for your bail hearing? Big man, furry mustache?"

Zoe shakes her head hard from side to side. "No. Detective Sorenson—the cop who was arrested the day they let me go. I recognized his face on TV that night—he was the one who went to the shooting range with Dad and me. I only ever saw the one with the mustache in court." She struggles to catch her breath, swallowing her words. "I'm...so sorry! I couldn't...remember... what he looked like...when I said I handled Dad's guns. I was all...all doped up."

I grab her hands. "It's okay. Take a deep breath and tell me what Detective Sorenson said when he came to see you in the jail."

"He said if I testified I was with Joe when Mr. Sinclair was murdered, he would kill my mom and dad and feed them to the sharks." She squeezes her eyes shut. "I should have told you the truth right away about being with Joe. Maybe none of this—"

"We've been over this already. None of what happened is your fault."

"I'm so stupid! I didn't want Dad to get in trouble. Can you believe that? They're the only family I've ever had. Mom's always lecturing me about drugs. And then it turns out she owns pill mills!" She starts to sob. "I just thought...that you'd be able to prove I didn't do it at my trial. But it almost got you killed. I'm very, very sorry."

Her naive trust in me, in the truth, in the system, takes my breath away.

"There's something I have to tell you, Zoe."

"What?"

"Detective Sorenson threatened Joe, like he threatened you."

"What? Is he okay?"

She reads my silence for what it is—affirmation that Joe is not okay.

She doubles over, clutching her stomach. "What happened to him?"

"He was found out in the Everglades. He'd been beaten to

death."

"Nooooo!" she screams, pounding her fists on her thighs. "He died because of me. They all died because of me!"

I sit on the desk facing her. "He died because of Detective Sorensen. Things seem black now, I understand. But trust me, in time, they'll get better."

"How? How will they get better?"

"Look at me Zoe," I say, and add the only thing I can think of to comfort her, something that should be true, but I can't be sure. "You have your mom, Zoe. Your mom loves you."

She gets up and walks to the window. "Maybe," she says, staring at the idling limo.

"Can I ask you one more thing?"

Her shoulders sag. "What?"

"Did you really want to kill yourself?"

She answers without hesitation, her voice firm. "No. I would never do that."

I bite back my own tears and join her at the window. "So, what now?"

Zoe shrugs. "Move on, I guess. Or, at least, try to."

"It's all any of us can do."

A noncommittal nod. "I'm going into residential treatment, to get things straightened out in my head."

"Good plan."

"I'm going to finish high school there as a correspondence student from St. Paul's."

"Very good plan."

"Then, I'm going to go to college." A smile nudges its way onto her tear-stained face. "And, who knows? Maybe, one day, to law school."

I raised a clench fist. "Now, that's a stellar plan. You are Zoya, remember, and—"

"And I am stronger than I think!"

Gretchen rushes through the door and Zoe pulls back her hand, cutting short our fist bump. She shoves a thick envelope into my hand. "I almost forgot. This is for you, Grace. We owe you more than money can repay."

For a second, we're eye to eye, both holding on to the envelope, before I take it and face Zoe. "Anything you need, you know where to find me. Anything at all."

Zoe hugs me and dashes outside.

Heart pounding like a tom-tom, I rip open the envelope.

Inside is the start of my new life—in cash.

Watching the limo recede into the ghetto twilight, I find myself making a plea to whatever higher power might be willing to intercede, a plea for second chances and happier times—for Zoe, for Joe's and Serena's families, and for all the untold others touched by the greed of evil men. And women. And for me.

Epilogue

"Gracie! Get down here!" Vinnie yells from downstairs.

"What is it? I'm busy," I yell back, stroking fuchsia nail polish onto my five toes. One thing that almost getting killed taught me is not to be ashamed or embarrassed by my leg, but to value it as a sign of my resilience. I've taken to wearing skirts instead of pants, sandals instead of closed-toed shoes, and I've entered myself into a 5K race, my first with Oscar 2.0.

"Get down here! You've got a delivery."

"Coming!"

At the bottom of the stairs, Vinnie grabs me by the shoulders and spins me around.

"I looked out the office window, and there she was," he says, jumping up and down like a kid on Christmas morning.

I blink twice to make sure I'm not hallucinating. But no, it's real. My car. My father's Jaguar, sitting in my parking space, coiled like the feline after which it was named, its green paint resplendent under the noonday sun, its scooped headlights watching me.

"Where? How?"

"I was out for a bit. When I came back to the office, I found her. These were on the desk." Vinnie holds up a set of keys hanging from a Tiffany key chain monogrammed with GL, Esq.

I approach the car, tentative, as if it might disappear any minute, and brush my fingers over the elongated hood. The chrome spokes on the rims have been polished to a brilliant shine. The convertible top is down, the perforated tan leather of the two bucket seats is creased from use, but still soft to the touch. I envision my father in the driver's seat, sporting a tweed flat cap, hands on the polished teak steering wheel, as we glide along narrow country lanes, gold and red leaves swirling in our wake.

"And this was under the keys," Vinnie says, holding out an envelope addressed to me in Manny's handwriting.

I slit the envelope open with one of the keys. Inside, the title to the car in my name and a single sheet of paper embossed with AAM:

Dear Grace:

Congratulations on your one year anniversary! I knew you could do it. You just needed to believe in yourself, and now you do.

I'm sorry things didn't work out as we had dreamed, but the brightest of futures is ahead for you, and that is what you deserve.

Your Friend (I hope),

Manny

P.S. As promised, the keys and title for your car. Maybe you'll take me for a ride sometime.

Lightheaded, I grab the driver's side door.

"You okay? What does it say?"

"In all the ruckus, I forgot. It's today."

"What? What's today?"

"The one year anniversary of my sobriety. I forgot. But he remembered."

Vinnie gives me a high five. "You did it, kid!"

I stare at the note. "And he kept his end of our bargain."

"You know what? Maybe he's not such a bad guy after all."

"Maybe not," I say and poke Vinnie in the ribs. "And neither are you."

"Maybe you should try comedy as your next career," he says, poking me back. "And these are some wheels, sweetheart!" He circles the car but stops when he gets to the rear. "Now, look at that."

I rush to his side to see what he's pointing at.

My new license plate.

It reads: IM BACK.

Acknowledgment

As a long distance runner, I can say with certainty that writing a book is the literary equivalent of running an ultramarathon. Nonetheless, unlike a race, crossing the finish line is not a solitary achievement, but one accomplished only with the support of others.

To the long-suffering members of the Steamboat Springs Writers Group—I am forever in your debt for your patience and expertise in reviewing and commenting on oh so many drafts of States of Grace.

To my editor, Susan Brooks, for seeing potential in Grace and for helping me round out a few of her rough edges without dampening her warrior heart.

To Stacy, your courage and tenacity in the face of adversity inspire me in these pages and every day.

And, while you may be last on this list, you are first in my heart—thank you to my husband and Reader Numero Uno, Andy, both for your attention to the minutiae that always seem to escape me, and for never counting the costs of my chasing rainbows. This book would not have been possible without your love and relentless encouragement.

About the Author

Mandy Miller is an attorney currently living in Steamboat Springs, Colorado, with her husband and Talisker, a rescue mutt. Before moving to Steamboat, she practiced law in Chicago, New York, Latin America, and South Florida.

Mandy is originally from Scotland, but lived in more than a dozen countries with her family before moving to the United States for college. With an undergraduate degree in Spanish and French Literature, she needed to do something to pay the bills, so she did what any good liberal arts student who can write would do, she went to law school. After eighteen years as a corporate lawyer, she planned her escape to another professional life teaching psychology. More school ensued and a Ph.D. in Psychology was granted, but the great escape was not to be. She was dragged back to the law to use her legal and psychological powers for good as a criminal lawyer, specializing in the representation of individuals with mental health and addiction issues in the criminal justice system.

Thankfully, no "good" crime occurs in Steamboat, so she

spends her spare time making up murder and mayhem. In her spare time, she competes in ultramarathons. States of Grace is her first novel.

You can visit her website www.mandymillerbooks.com and read more of her writing on her blog Flash4Words.blogspot. com. Be assured that if you leave your email on either site, it will not be shared with anyone and you can unsubscribe whenever you wish. Subscribers will receive information regarding new books, short fiction and nonfiction, contests, giveaways, and reading recommendations.

—

Author's Royalties from this book will be donated to not for profit organizations devoted to serving veterans.

CPSIA information can be obtained
at www.ICGtesting.com
Printed in the USA
LVHW020317230321
682196LV00006B/79